P9-DEP-313

You SAY IT First

Also by Katie Cotugno

How to Love

Fireworks

Top Ten

9 Days and 9 Nights

With Candace Bushnell

Rules for Being a Girl

You SAY IT First

Katie Cotugno

BALZER + BRAY
An Imprint of HarperCollins*Publishers*

Balzer + Bray is an imprint of HarperCollins Publishers.

You Say It First

 For information address HarperCollins Children's Books, a division of HarperCollins Publishers, 195 Broadway, New York, NY 10007.
www.epicreads.com

Production by Alloy Entertainment
30 Hudson Yards, New York, NY 10001
www.alloyentertainment.com

Library of Congress Control Number: 2019951209
ISBN 978-0-06-267412-8 — ISBN 978-0-06-303248-4 (intl. ed.)

Typography by Jessie Gang
20 21 22 23 24 PC/LSCH 10 9 8 7 6 5 4 3 2 1

❖

First Edition

For all the Collerans

You SAY IT First

ONE

Meg

"In conclusion," Meg said brightly, standing at the podium under the harsh fluorescent lights of the PTA meeting room on Wednesday evening, "it's the position of the student council that our school is already sorely behind in doing its part to combat climate change. Adding solar panels to the roof of the main building is not only the fiscally responsible and environmentally sustainable thing to do, but will help ensure we're living up to the values the Overbrook community has instilled in us all these years." She smiled her most competent smile, sweating a little bit inside her uniform blazer. "Thank you very much for your time."

When the applause had finished and the meeting was adjourned, Meg made her way through the crowd of parents and teachers milling around the room to where her friends were waiting near the table of gluten-free brownies. "That was amazing!" Emily said, blond hair bouncing as she wrapped Meg in a bear hug. Adrienne and Javi saluted her with a pair of black-and-white cookies. "You looked like freakin' AOC up there."

"Nice job, kid," said Mason, ducking his head to peck her briefly on the cheek. Meg grinned and squeezed his hand. They'd been dating more than a year now, though more often they still hung out in a pack just like this—the five of them perpetually clustered around their usual table at the juice place near school, planning a fund raiser or a protest or world domination. By now they'd all heard her solar-panel speech about a thousand times.

"Good work, Meg," added Ms. Clemmey, her AP Government teacher, coming up behind them with a cup of watery-looking coffee, her graying hair frizzing out of its bun. "Now we'll just have to see if they bite."

"They'll bite," Javi declared, all confidence, then stuffed another brownie into his mouth.

Ms. Clemmey quirked an eyebrow. "Anything from Cornell, meanwhile?" she asked quietly.

Meg shook her head, a little bit startled. "Not yet," she said, glancing instinctively over at Emily. Rooming together at Cornell had been their plan for as long as they'd been talking about colleges, but ever since she'd submitted her application, Meg kept finding herself forgetting about it altogether for days at a stretch until somebody, usually Em, said something that reminded her. It wasn't that she wasn't excited—she was, definitely. She just had a lot of other stuff on her plate right now. "We should be hearing soon, though."

Ms. Clemmey nodded. "Well, they'll be lucky to have you."

Meg shook her head, blushing a little. "We'll see."

The five of them went to Cavelli's to celebrate, ordering a large veggie pie so Adrienne could have some and two pitchers of Coke. "To the Green New Deal of Overbrook Day," Emily said, holding up her red plastic cup. They laughed and clinked and ate their pizza, Meg sitting back in her chair and listening as the conversation wandered: from Javi's parents' new labradoodle puppy, to a bunch of idiot sophomores who'd gotten drunk and thrown up all over the skating rink during spring break, to a *New York Times* podcast Emily was obsessed with. It made Meg happy to picture what they must look like from outside the wide front window, their faces lit by the fake Tiffany lamp over the table. Most of all she felt *normal*, like she hadn't for so much of last year.

It was almost ten by the time they paid their bill and headed out, Meg following Mason across the parking lot to where his Subaru was parked right next to her Prius. It was still mostly winter in Pennsylvania, with that damp blue-green whiff of spring on the air if you breathed deep enough. Meg tugged her cashmere beanie down over her ears.

"You were really great tonight," Mason said, turning to face her as he reached his driver's-side door.

"You think so?" she asked, taking a step closer. He looked handsome in the yellow glow of the parking lot light, with his dark eyes and high cheekbones. They'd known each other since kindergarten, back when Meg's mom put her hair in French-braid pigtails every morning and he was still the only Korean kid in their grade. Twelve years later, flush with victory, she wrapped her arms around his neck and pulled him close.

Mason stiffened. "Meg," he said, his hands landing gently on her waist, then letting go again.

"Hm?" she said, tilting her face up so he'd kiss her. Neither of them were into PDA—Meg hated any kind of nonpolitical public spectacle as a general rule—but it was late, and the parking lot was mostly empty. She could make an exception just this once.

"Meg," he said again, and she frowned.

"What?"

Mason hesitated, glancing over her shoulder instead of looking directly at her. In the second before he spoke, Meg had the sudden feeling of realizing too late that she'd stepped in front of a car: "I think we should break up," he said.

She blinked, her arms dropping off his shoulders. "*What?*"

"I just, um." Mason shrugged, visibly embarrassed; he looked eleven instead of seventeen. "I don't really think this is working."

"But like." Meg stared at him for a moment, running a quick, panicky set of diagnostics inside her head. Sure, lately they'd spent more time studying for the SAT Subject Tests and making fliers for the Philly Bail Fund than, like, goofing around or staring soulfully into each other's eyes, but that just meant they were in a mature relationship, right? That just meant their priorities were the same. "We never fight."

Mason looked surprised, and it occurred to Meg a second too late that that had probably been a weird way to respond on her part. "No, I know we don't," he said, tucking his hands into his jacket pockets. The jacket was new, a blue waxed canvas situation his mom had gotten him for his birthday. It made him look, Meg thought snottily, like a postman. "But that doesn't mean—I mean, not fighting isn't a reason to stay together, is it?"

"No, I know that," Meg said quickly, swallowing down the jagged break in her voice. She thought of the gentle, distracted way he'd trace his fingertips over her wrist as they were reading. She thought of the late-night ice cream runs they'd taken while she worked on her solar-panel speech. "Of course I know that." She took a step back, her spine bumping roughly against the passenger-side door of her car. Suddenly, she was cold enough to shiver. "Okay," she said, forcing herself to take a deep, steadying breath. "Well. Okay. I'm going to go, then."

"Meg, wait." Now Mason looked really confused. "Shouldn't we, like—don't you even want to talk about this?"

"What is there to talk about?" she asked, hating how shrill

her voice sounded. "It's fine, Mason. I get it." She didn't get it at all, not really. Actually, she felt blindsided and furious and completely, utterly foolish, but the literal last thing she wanted to do was talk about it, to stand here and fight it out in public like her parents in the last doomed days of their marriage. There was no way she was going to do that. "It's fine, I hear you. Message received."

Mason shook his head. "Meg—"

"Thanks for coming to support the solar panels," she managed. "I'll see you at school, okay?"

She got into her car and slammed the door a little harder than necessary, squeezing the steering wheel as she waited for him to leave, then realizing with a quiet swear that *he* was waiting for *her* to pull out first. Meg did, driving halfway home with her hands at a perfect ten and two, NPR burbling softly away on the radio. It wasn't until Mason turned off the main road toward his neighborhood and the Subaru was safely out of sight that she pulled over onto the shoulder and let herself cry.

Emily was waiting by Meg's locker before homeroom the following morning, her French book in one hand and a massive Frappuccino in the other. "Are you okay?" she asked, holding out the coffee cup. "Here, this is yours. I had them put all the different kinds of drizzles on it. You're probably going to get diabetes, but, desperate times. How are you feeling?"

"I'm good," Meg said cheerfully, sucking a mouthful of

whipped cream through the wide green straw. There was no way she was going to be a drama queen about this—even in front of Emily, who'd basically kept her upright through her ridiculous postdivorce depression fog of junior year. People broke up all the time; that was all there was to it. It was fine. *She* was fine.

"Are you sure?" Emily looked skeptical.

"I am sure," Meg said.

"Okay," Emily said, visibly unconvinced. "Because I'm just saying, nobody's going to blame you if you're not."

"But I am."

"I hear you," Emily said patiently, taking the Frappuccino back for safekeeping as Meg opened her locker, "and that's great. But it sucks when relationships end, you know? Even relationships like—" She broke off.

Meg's eyes narrowed; she closed the locker door again, peering at Em suspiciously. "Even relationships like what?"

"What? Nothing." Emily shook her head, eyes wide. "It sucks when relationships end, full stop."

"Uh-huh," Meg said, smirking a little. "Good try. What?"

Emily wrinkled her nose. "I mean, I don't know," she said, leaning back against the locker beside Meg's and hugging her French book to her chest. "It just always seemed like maybe you weren't actually that into Mason in the first place, that's all."

"What?" Meg blinked. She had so been into Mason. She'd loved Mason. She'd lost her *virginity* to Mason, for Pete's sake.

"We were together for more than a year, Em."

"I know you were!" Emily shrugged. "And in all that time I never heard you say anything like, *Oh man, I love Mason so much, I want to be with him forever and have a hundred million of his babies, he sets my loins on fire like Captain America and Killmonger combined.*"

"Rude!" Meg said, laughing in spite of herself. "First of all, there's more to relationships than your loins constantly being on fire." At least, she'd thought there was. Sure, she and Mason hadn't exactly been generating nuclear power with the sheer force of their physical chemistry, but they'd had fun together. They made a good team. And—most important—they were nothing like her parents, who'd spent what felt like the entire duration of their marriage screaming at each other. Meg had thought that counted for something. "And second of all, who knew belonging to all the same clubs and liking all the same political candidates didn't guarantee a happily ever after?"

Emily grinned. "What does that say about you and me?" she pointed out, helping herself to a sip of the Frappuccino before handing it back. "We belong to all the same clubs and like all the same political candidates."

"We're different," Meg said, zipping up her backpack and looping her arm through Em's. See? Here she was, joking around and everything. She was totally okay. "We like all the same everything. Our happily ever after is fully assured."

"I mean, true," Emily said as they made their way down

the crowded hallway. The two of them had been best friends since second grade, and even back then Meg had been shocked by how much they had in common: They played all the same games at recess. They watched all the same shows on TV. Every year on the first day of class they showed up wearing the exact same pair of shoes, even though they never planned it, and every year they burst out laughing like it hadn't ever happened before. It was the thesis statement of their friendship—that comforting sameness, the knowledge that by the time a thought occurred to her, Emily was already thinking it, too. Sometimes Meg wondered if maybe they were actually the same person, split into two different bodies by some cosmic mistake.

"What are you doing tonight?" Em asked now, stopping outside of Meg's homeroom. "Want to come over and we can watch something stupid?"

Meg did, and badly, but she shook her head. "I have WeCount tonight," she said, though honestly that wasn't the only reason she didn't want to fall back into the easy comfort of a midweek dinner at Emily's house. She'd spent any number of borderline-catatonic nights in front of the Hurds' TV last year when everything was crashing and burning with her parents, Em heaping green beans onto her plate and ghostwriting her Progressive Overbrook agendas and making sure her homework got done. Meg didn't want to be that person anymore. She *wasn't* that person anymore. She was under control.

She was fine.

"I'm sure the Cause will understand if you want to take one night off because you broke up with your boyfriend," Em pressed gently. Then she frowned. "It's me, okay? You can tell me."

But Meg shook her head again. "The Cause waits for no one," she said brightly, then raised her Frappuccino in a goofy salute and headed off to face the day.

TWO

Colby

Colby knew it was a dumb idea to climb the water tower pretty much from the moment Micah said he wanted to do it, but it wasn't like there was anything more exciting going on, so on Wednesday after midnight they all met at Jordan's stepdad's house, zipped their jackets against the skin-splitting rawness of March in Alma, Ohio, and set out for the wide, overgrown field at the edge of town.

"Tell me again why we couldn't just drive?" Colby muttered, balling his chapped, chilly hands into fists in his pockets as he trailed the rest of them through the darkened parking lot of the Liquor Mart, Micah in his army-green surplus coat and Jordan in the Jack Skellington hat he always wore, his ears sticking out like bat wings beneath the brim. Jordan's twin sister, Joanna, had tagged along at the last minute, her blond hair tucked up into a beanie with a furry pom-pom on top of it. Colby had been surprised: Jo, with her key ring full of discount cards and a car that smelled like vanilla cupcakes on the inside, always felt older and less susceptible to half-baked plans than the rest of them, even though Jordan was forever making a big point of telling everyone he'd been born first. But then she'd bumped Colby's shoulder and smiled hello, her straight white teeth like a slice of winter moonlight, and he thought maybe he wasn't actually that surprised after all.

"Stealth, dude," Micah said now, leading them across the service road with the slightly sketchy confidence of one of those guides who brought people down into the Grand Canyon on donkeys. "Car would be too suspicious."

Colby frowned. "More suspicious than the four of us wandering the streets in the middle of the night like a bunch of hobos?"

Micah snorted. "Moran, if you're too much of a pussy to do this, just say so."

"Fuck you," Colby said, glancing instinctively at Joanna before he could quell the impulse. "Let's go."

Alma got a little scruffier as they got closer to the tower, the sidewalk narrowing before it disappeared completely so they had to walk single file along the grassy shoulder, low-slung houses crowding close together like teeth in a mouth that was too small. A broad, stocky pit mix paced the length of a chain link fence, winter-crisped weeds nearly brushing his belly. Colby winced at the casual cruelty of whoever had left him out here, reaching his hand out for the little dude to sniff.

"Come on," Micah said, kicking at Colby's ankle to keep him moving as the dog barked and growled in response, suspicious. "We're almost there."

"I know where we are," Colby muttered, digging the fuzzy end of a package of peanut butter crackers out of his inside pocket and slipping a couple through the chain link. "I grew up here, same as you." Alma wasn't the kind of place people left, as a general rule. Colby didn't have to try real hard to picture them all in ten years, still living with their parents and working jobs that were mostly bullshit, spending every weekend trying to outrun their own boredom just like they had since they were little kids setting stuff on fire in the parking lot outside their Cub Scout meetings at the Knights of Columbus hall. Probably the idea should have bothered him more than it actually did, Colby thought, jogging across the blacktop to catch up. But there were worse things in life than knowing exactly what to expect.

Now they shimmied down into a shallow ravine, Joanna swearing under her breath as she almost lost her footing, then wriggled through a hole in a fence and picked their way through an overgrown lot full of empty beer bottles and shredded tires and, inexplicably, a corduroy armchair set to full recline. Colby was seriously considering telling Micah to screw himself and going home to jerk off in the shower when, finally, there it was: the familiar silhouette of it tall and black and imposing, proud against the purple-black sky. "Shit" seemed like the only appropriate thing to say.

Joanna stopped and gazed at it for a moment, her expression startled in the orange glow of the lone safety light affixed to the rickety-looking catwalk that ringed the water tank. "I didn't realize it was that big," she admitted, shivering once inside her jacket.

Micah shrugged. "It's a water tower, Jo," he said, like that should have been obvious. "Let's go."

Jo cut her eyes to Colby, who held his hands up in the dark. "Don't do it if you don't want to," he told her quietly. He felt protective of her all of a sudden, though he told himself it was just because she was the only girl here. "I don't know why the fuck I'm about to do it, if you want me to be honest with you."

"I always want you to be honest with me," Joanna said, but before Colby could reply one way or the other she was headed across the field, the white pom-pom on top of her hat the only part of her visible in the moonlight. "Come on."

It took them a long time to scale the side of the tower. The ancient iron ladder creaked dangerously, the wind stinging Colby's cheeks as rust on the rungs coated the palms of his hands with a rough orange dust. "Mike," Colby muttered, glancing down and immediately getting dizzy, his fingers beginning to numb. All at once the magnitude of his own stupidity reared up at him—his dad would have skinned him alive for a stunt like this, had his dad still been around to have opinions on things like what Colby did or didn't do. "Shit, dude, this is really high."

"Don't look," Joanna warned from underneath him, her voice surprisingly calm. "If you look it makes it worse."

"I'm not looking," Colby promised, turning his face skyward. If he started thinking about his dad—that day in the garage in the rainstorm, how in May he'd have been gone a full year—he was going to lose the plot for sure, so instead he gritted his teeth and forced himself to think of nothing, hand over cold, clumsy hand on the ladder until finally he swung one leg over the guardrail. He pulled Joanna up after him, the two of them grinning at each other in dumb relief as Micah and Jordan fist-bumped beside them, all of them giggling like a bunch of stoners.

That was when the cops showed up.

Two hours later, Colby sat in a brightly lit holding room, a can of ginger ale going warm on the scarred wooden bench beside him. He had no idea why he'd asked for ginger ale, honestly, like he was flying on a fucking airplane and not sitting here waiting to find out if he was going to jail or not.

He'd never actually been on an airplane, come to think of it. Maybe this was the closest he was going to get.

Colby sighed, leaning his head back against the painted

cinder-block wall behind him. They'd split all of them up into separate rooms; he'd craned his neck for a last worried look at Joanna as a lady guard led her down the pee-smelling hallway and Micah yammered on about his civil rights. Colby's wrists were a little red from the handcuffs, which seemed like overkill. It wasn't exactly like the four of them were a quartet of criminal masterminds here.

This wasn't Colby's first encounter with the Ross County Sheriff's Department, though he'd never been carted down to the station in the back of a squad car until now. He hadn't actually been in this building at all since his second-grade class trip. His dad had been one of the chaperones, Colby remembered suddenly; they'd all gotten plastic sheriff's stars from a gallon-sized Ziploc bag at the reception desk up front.

He should try to stop thinking about his dad.

"Colby," Keith said now, coming into the holding room and shutting the windowed door behind him. He was wearing his mustard-colored deputy uniform with *Olsen* stitched across the pocket, his hair cut short on the sides and slicked back with pomade or gel or something at the top. It was, Colby thought, an extremely try-hard kind of haircut. "How's it going in here?"

"Fine," Colby said, sitting up a little straighter in spite of himself, as if Keith were an actual authority figure and not the same boner he'd been since everyone used to make fun of him for eating his own boogers back in elementary school. "Is Jo okay?"

Keith raised his eyebrows, like he wanted to make it clear that he'd noticed Colby's interest and was filing it away for later consideration. "She's fine, too," he said with a nod. "Her stepdad came and got her."

Colby blew a breath out. Jo wasn't his girlfriend—they'd never even kissed, though Micah never missed a chance to tell him how nutless he was for not having, in Micah's words, *hit that by now*—but that didn't mean he wanted her spending the night at the sheriff's department just because the rest of them were a bag of smashed assholes. "Okay," he said, relaxing a little. "Good."

"He left Jordan here to sweat it out a couple more hours, though," Keith continued, sitting down on the opposite bench and resting his slightly girlish-looking hands on his knees. "Can't say I blame him. The hat alone should be a capital crime."

Colby didn't smile. "Should you be telling me that?" he asked instead, crossing his arms and frowning. Now that he knew Jo was okay, he was back to being pissed—at Keith, at Jordan, at Micah. At himself most of all. "Don't you want to play us all off each other or something? Get us to confess?"

Keith rolled his eyes. "I literally caught you up there, idiot. I don't need confessions." He shrugged. "And anyway, we're not going to charge you."

He said it in a voice like he was doing Colby a favor—which, as much as Colby hated to admit it, he probably was. "Really?" he couldn't keep himself from asking. "Why not?"

Keith scrubbed a hand over his face, a gesture Colby thought he'd probably gotten from *Chicago P.D.* or one of those other shows about weary but good-hearted law enforcement professionals that were basically just delivery mechanisms for Buick commercials. "You're too old for this shit, Colby, you know that? You're what, seventeen?"

"Eighteen," Colby corrected, vaguely insulted. Keith had been in Colby's brother Matt's year in school, which meant he was only twenty-two himself now, maybe twenty-three depending on his birthday. There was a painful-looking spray of decidedly teenage acne along his chin. "How old are you?"

"Old enough not be climbing the water tower like a fucking bonehead," Keith shot back. Then he sighed. "Look," he said, "I know you guys have had a tough year."

Colby felt his whole body stiffen, his bones in their sockets and the teeth in his head. "We're fine," he said immediately. "This isn't—I'm fine."

"Are you?" Keith looked unconvinced. "Dude, I know you. I knew your dad. You're better than this."

Colby looked at him for a long moment, even. "*Dude,*" he said finally—mimicking Keith's expression exactly, leaning his head back one more time. "I'm really not."

In the end, Keith walked him out to the front of the station, handing him a plastic bin that contained his phone and wallet and watching as Colby zipped up his jacket. Outside the smeary Plexiglas windows, rain was coming down in icy-looking sheets. Colby gazed at the downpour for a moment, trying not to let his expression betray him. The walk home would probably take him until dawn.

Keith sighed. “Come on,” was all he said, pulling a set of keys out of his uniform pocket. Colby followed him wordlessly out to the car.

THREE

Meg

As far as Meg was concerned, she and Mason had said everything they needed to say to each other in the parking lot outside Cavelli's last night, but that afternoon she was in the south hallway putting up fliers for a student council sock drive when she turned around and there he was. "Um, hi," she said, with a smile so bright and unwavering she might as well have used the freaking stapler to attach it to her face. "What's up?"

"Hi yourself," he said, this *hey, stranger* look in his eyes like they hadn't just seen each other in AP Lit Comp, and in Spanish 4 before that. Overbrook Day was tiny, only around fifty people per grade; she and Mason had had basically the exact same schedule their entire lives. "Do you need help with those?"

Meg shook her head. "I'm all set." This was going to be a

problem about them being broken up, she realized—Mason was a homeroom rep for student council, just like he was one of the other founding members of Progressive Overbrook and on the steering committee for the spring carnival. It was part of what had made it so easy to date him.

"So, um," he said, shifting his weight in his immaculate white Adidas. He'd loosened his uniform tie and was wearing the new glasses he'd gotten over spring break, which made him look annoyingly cute in a reporter-on-deadline sort of way. "I just wanted to make sure you were doing okay."

"Oh God," Meg said before she could stop herself, then waved her hand, fully aware of how dumb and squeaky her voice sounded. "Yeah. I'm fine. I'm good!"

"Okay," Mason said, his plush mouth turning down at the edges. "But I guess I just mean, if you're ever *not* . . ." He trailed off, the *you can always talk to me* implicit.

"We were friends first, weren't we?"

Meg grimaced. This was true, at least sort of—in a school as small as Overbrook, everyone was friends, or at the very least everyone knew each other. But the two of them had never really talked until the AP American class they'd had with Emily last year, when what had started as a study group for Ms. Lao's notoriously impossible tests turned into their twice-weekly huddle at the juice place with Javi and Adrienne.

Still, she'd been surprised when he wound up at their table at Emily's sweet sixteen, shined up like a new penny in his suit and fancy shoes; Meg had actually gasped when she'd seen him, at the broadness of his shoulders and the sharp cut of his jaw. "You clean up nice, Mason Lee," she'd told him, and he'd grinned. They'd argued gamely about Bernie Sanders for half an hour, then gone for a walk outside the country club, where he'd kissed her in front of a fountain lit up pink and blue and green. Emily had almost murdered them both for missing the dancing.

"Sure," Meg said now, eighteen months later, more to avoid a confrontation than anything else. "We were friends first."

"Okay," Mason said, looking relieved. He hugged her then, the smell of castile soap and the sustainable detergent his mom used. Meg bit her lip hard enough to taste blood.

She waved goodbye and headed out into the chilly parking lot, throwing her backpack onto the passenger seat and zipping across town toward home. Her mom was still at work, and Meg pulled up to the curb in front of the house so she wouldn't be blocked in when she needed to go to WeCount later. It used to be that her mom parked in the garage and her dad parked in the long, skinny driveway, which had led to a lot of shuffling and grumbling about who needed to move whose car when. Sometimes Meg wondered if they'd still be together if both of them had just agreed to park on the street.

Meg's first memory was of her parents arguing, a fact she hadn't realized was unusual until she'd mentioned it offhandedly to Emily at a sleepover in seventh grade and Emily had given her a super weird look, after which point she'd been careful not to mention it to anyone ever again. Still, when she thought of her parents, they were basically always going at it: The time on vacation in California when they'd fought about the rental car all the way down the Pacific Coast Highway, the time her mom had thrown an entire thirteen-by-nine casserole dish of stuffing on the kitchen floor and stormed out of Thanksgiving. The time they'd gotten into a rager at Colonial Williamsburg, screaming bloody murder at each other while Meg read a *Magic Tree House* beside them and a man dressed as Benjamin Franklin pretended not to listen.

Meg knew it should have been a relief when they finally split up last winter—*healthier for everyone*, they'd reassured her, and she was pretty sure they were right—but instead it was like some very important part of her just . . . shut down. She'd sleepwalked through the rest of junior year like a zombie, bouncing between school and Em's and Mason's while her parents outsourced the worst of their fighting to a pair of slick, sharky lawyers. She'd snapped out of it, finally—she was fine, after all—but the truth was that even now, three months from graduation, sometimes it felt like she was still waiting to wake up.

Meg wandered through the big, echoey house and got herself a granola bar from the kitchen, chucking a pair of liquefied bananas into the trash. She was just chasing a couple of fruit flies out of the sink when she heard her mom's key in the door.

"Hey," she called, padding through the dark, cluttered

dining room and out into the hallway. Meg still couldn't get used to seeing her mom in the skirts and blouses she wore to work now, like she was dressed up in some kind of costume. Right when she'd first started interviewing, the two of them had gone to the J.Crew Factory Store and she'd bought the same top in four different prints. "How was your day?"

"Oh, you know," her mom said, dumping her purse on the wooden bench near the doorway and kicking her sensible pumps to the side. A couple of months after Meg's dad moved out, she'd gotten a job through a friend of a friend as a receptionist at one of those big old Colonial-era mansions that hosted weddings and reunions and the occasional Revolutionary War reenactment, answering the phone and handing out informational brochures and adding people's addresses to the mailing list. It sounded totally boring, but Meg knew the truth was that her mom was lucky to get hired at all, since until last year she hadn't worked an outside job since the '90s. Her dad's career was managing Hal Collins, the famous folk singer. Her mom's career was being his wife. "Not as bad as a chicken in my underwear."

Meg smiled. *Not as bad as a chicken in your underwear* was an old joke in their family, though she didn't actually know where it came from. That was one thing she missed about her parents being together—it was like the three of them had had a little civilization with a language all their own, and now there were never enough of them around at once to speak it properly.

They boiled a pot of spaghetti and dumped a jar of tomato sauce on top—neither one of them was going to be winning any cooking competitions any time soon, that was for sure—and carried their bowls past the dust-covered piano in the living room to the sagging couch in the den, her mom stopping by the fridge on the way to pour herself a big glass of white wine. Meg glanced in her direction as she set it down on the coffee table, then looked back at the TV. Both her parents had always been social drinkers, going out to long, boozy dinners in New York with Hal and his band, but lately it felt like her mom was hitting it kind of hard. At least, Meg thought she was. She couldn't tell if her mom was actually doing it more or if it just seemed that way because she was doing it alone.

They settled down in front of a home renovation show, a cheerful husband and wife knocking down walls and installing brand-new cabinets. Meg couldn't help glancing down at the grungy Persian rug in the den. Her dad had always been the more fastidious of her parents, and since he'd moved out a certain amount of chaos had started to creep in around the edges of their big, creaky old house, like vines climbing up over a white picket fence. Tumbleweeds of dust and hair drifted into the upstairs corners. The antique handles on the bathroom faucet had come loose. Water glasses collected on every available surface until they finally ran out altogether and had to wander from room to room rounding them up like wayward cattle. Leaning against the side of the sofa were a bunch of weird abstract paintings her mom had bought at an estate sale right after her dad had moved out, saying she was going to make a gallery wall where their wedding photos had hung, but she'd lost enthusiasm for the project halfway through.

"Maybe we should paint in here this summer," Meg ventured now, licking a smear of tomato sauce off the side of her thumb and squinting at a brownish water stain on the ceiling above the window. There'd been a whole thing with ice dams over the winter, and her parents had gotten into a stalemate over whose job it was to pay for it. In the end, Meg wasn't sure either one of them actually had.

"Oh, definitely," her mom agreed now, holding her hand out for Meg's empty bowl before standing up and heading into the kitchen. "We can go ahead and shiplap the bathroom while we're at it."

Well. So much for that idea, Meg guessed. "Whitewash the fireplace, perhaps."

"Exactly." Meg heard her setting the dishes in the sink, then a long pause and finally the sound of the fridge opening and closing. "Did you know your father and Lisa are in Palm Springs this weekend?" she asked as she came back into the living room, a fresh glass of wine in one hand and her phone in the other.

"He mentioned it, yeah," Meg said cautiously. Lisa was her dad's girlfriend, a lawyer for one of the universities in Philly. She was younger than him—not so young that it was objectively gross, Meg guessed, but young enough that it was her mom's favorite thing to complain about. "Hal was doing some shows in LA."

"Well, good for Hal," her mom said crisply. "And good for Lisa, apparently. She posted all about her luxurious day at the spa on Facebook."

Meg grimaced. "Mom, why are you looking at her Facebook to begin with?"

"I know," her mom said immediately, setting her phone on the arm of the sofa and holding her free hand up. "It's bad of me. It's toxic behavior." She took a sip of her wine. "I'm just saying, it would have been nice of him to see if you wanted to go."

"I have school," Meg reminded her.

"Oh, like he's suddenly so attuned to your academic calendar." Meg's mom rolled her eyes. "And, you know, not for nothing, but if he's got the cash to be tacking romantic spa getaways onto his work trips, you'd think possibly he could also be bothered to—"

"Mom," Meg interrupted quietly. "Come on."

"I'm stopping," her mom said now, holding her hand up again, waving it back and forth. "I'm sorry. I'm stopping."

She was as good as her word, thankfully: her lips were zipped for the rest of the episode, not counting a crack about the ugly mosaic tile the designer picked out for the brand-new backsplash. What she *didn't* stop doing was drinking. Meg bit the inside of her cheek as her mom poured herself another glass of wine, and then another. The next time she got up, just as the clients were oohing and aahing over their brand-new master bathroom, Meg heard the telltale pop of a cork as her mom opened a whole other bottle.

She dropped her head back against the couch cushions and stared up at the splotchy ceiling, swallowing down a weird wave of something like panic and reminding herself that nothing happening right now was actually an emergency. She was safe in the house she'd lived in since she was a baby, even if it did look a little grubbier than usual. Her mom was the same as she'd always been. Everything was fine.

Right?

All at once, Meg stood up, eyes darting around the room like she was looking for the closest available exit. Like if she didn't get out of here soon she might die. "Mom," she called, wiping her suddenly sweaty hands on her jeans and telling herself to stop being so dumb and dramatic. There was no reason to start some huge fight. "I gotta go to work."

"Computers are down again," Lillian reported when Meg turned up for her shift at WeCount, handing her a sheaf of papers held together with a plastic paper clip shaped like a Dalmatian. Lillian was twenty-one and Meg's supervisor; her girlfriend, Maja, worked at a bakery in Philly, and Lillian was forever leaving boxes of palmiers and fruit tarts on the counter of the tiny kitchenette in the office. "So we're working from call sheets tonight."

Meg nodded, taking the list and dropping her backpack on the floor beside her wobbly rolling chair. She'd been hoping that going into work would distract her from thinking about Mason, which was stupid—after all, Mason was the one who'd sent her the link for WeCount to begin with, from a list he'd found online of nonprofits that hired students part-time. Meg had been working here since the previous fall, out of a tiny office suite above a high-end home-goods boutique in Montco. The idea was that people were more likely to register to vote if somebody actively talked them through it—even if that person was a total rando—so three times a week Meg sat in a cubicle for two hours and encouraged people in swing states to fill out forms on the internet.

Tonight, her first call was with an elderly woman named Pearl whose registration had lapsed when she'd moved into her retirement community outside of Cleveland. People in retirement communities, Meg had found over the course of her six months of employment, could usually be counted on to answer the phone. "Perfect," she said once Pearl had successfully navigated to the WeCount home page and clicked the link to register in the state of Ohio. "I can go through the steps with you, if you'd like?"

Meg spent the next ten minutes doodling in the margins of her call sheet while Pearl filled in her information, then another ten listening while she talked about canvassing for Bobby Kennedy back in '68. "You're all set," she concluded finally, once Pearl had completed the registration form. "You should get your confirmation in a few weeks with your polling place. Do you have someone who can bring you to vote on Election Day?"

"Nice work," Lillian said when she was finished, smiling at Meg over the top of the half wall that separated their cubicles. Meg found herself grinning back. She loved working at WeCount; she'd loved politics basically her whole life, since her mom's cool cousin Jodie sent her a picture book about Rebecca Latimer Felton, the first woman in the Senate, for her seventh birthday. She still had that book somewhere, its pages wrinkly and its binding cracked from a million bedtime recitations—just like she still had the program from the benefit concert Hal had done for Obama back when she was in elementary school tacked to the corkboard in her room. She could quote every single episode of *The West Wing*, had convinced Emily to read *The Federalist Papers* in ninth grade, when every girl in their class suddenly had a crush on Alexander Hamilton, and had door-knocked for Larry Krasner when he'd run for DA. She knew it was hugely dorky, but she believed in the system. And she got a not-so-tiny thrill from being a part of what made it work.

She was about to call the next number on her list when her cell dinged quietly on the flimsy desk beside her. Meg opened up her mail app, letting out a gasp when she saw *Cornell*

University Office of Admissions in the sender line. Holy crap—between Mason and her mom, she'd forgotten all about her application again.

Her first instinct, bizarrely, was to close out the window, which was ridiculous considering she had ostensibly been waiting for this exact email for the better part of two full months. Instead, she took a deep breath and clicked.

> Dear Margaret,
>
> Congratulations! We are delighted to inform you that the Committee on Admissions has offered you a place in the freshman class of Cornell University for the upcoming academic year. We look forward to welcoming a student with your outstanding achievements to the Cornell community this fall.

Meg blinked, then blinked again, reading the letter over and over like she expected the words to suddenly rearrange themselves into something other than what they were. She waited for the thrill of victory to hit her, the urge to text Emily and post the email to Snapchat and stand on her chair and announce it to the entire office. After all, this was amazing. This was, and had always been, the plan.

Instead, she just felt sort of numb.

No, she thought, pulling idly on her bottom lip. Not numb, exactly.

It was more like she was . . . disappointed?

Maybe she was depressed again. Meg set her phone down and tilted her head back so far that her dark hair almost brushed the carpet, considering. She guessed it was possible that getting dumped by Mason had ruined her for all other happiness, but for some reason she didn't think that was what was happening here. In fact, the more she thought about it, poking and prodding at her own reaction like running her tongue over a cavity, she was pretty sure what was happening here was that she didn't actually *want* to go to—

Meg hauled herself upright before she could finish the thought, getting a little bit dizzy as the blood rushed out of her head. God, what was wrong with her? This was good news. This was the *best* news, and if the only emotion she could manage to summon up about it in this moment was a vague kind of dread and boredom at the thought of spending the next four years shuffling through ten-foot snowdrifts and taking dutiful notes in giant lecture halls and listening to Emily obsess over whether to pledge a sorority, well, that was her own malfunction. After all, Cornell had a great government program, and it wasn't like she had some other secret dream school in her back pocket. It was college. It was exciting! More to the point, it was what normal people did.

So why wasn't she even a little bit psyched?

Her phone dinged again then, a text this time: *I'M IN!!!*

Emily had written, digital confetti exploding all over the screen. *ARE YOU IN??????*

Shit. For a second, Meg considered acting like she hadn't seen the message; she was at work, after all, which bought her another hour or two of plausible deniability. But, like, what *was* that? What was she even thinking? She'd never ignored a text from Emily in her life.

Ahhh of course you are!!! she typed quickly, plus a row of party hats. *You are such a star.*

Then, her thumb moving seemingly all on its own: *I haven't heard yet!*

WHAT! Em's reply was instant. *HOW IS THAT POSSIBLE.* Then, a second later: *Spam filter???*

Meg looked at the screen for another moment, then down at the next name on her call sheet: David Moran from Alma, Ohio. She dropped her cell into her bag and got back to work.

FOUR

Colby

The sun was just starting to set when Colby got done at the warehouse that afternoon, tossing his orange apron into his locker and sliding his card to clock out. He'd finally been at Home Depot long enough that they'd let him switch over to days, which meant he was back on the same schedule as the rest of the world, though there was a part of him that missed being awake when everyone else was sleeping, driving home as the dawn was seeping up in blues and pinks and reds.

He heard the shower running upstairs when he got inside the house: his mom getting ready for her own night shift at the casino. Matt was in the kitchen, pouring himself a glass of orange juice. The fact that he was a person who drank orange juice at all hours of the day was only one of the many reasons his brother was a douchebag.

"What are you doing here?" Colby asked, dropping his backpack on the floor in the tiny, linoleum-tiled mudroom and bending down to scratch Tris behind her velvety ears. Matt lived by himself in an apartment complex near the Giant Eagle, which made Colby desperately jealous even though he'd never in a million years say it out loud.

"Hello to you, too," Matt said. He was wearing khaki pants and a bright blue golf shirt, like he was a teller at a bank chain on a summer Friday. "I had paperwork for Mom to fill out."

"What kind of paperwork?"

"Insurance stuff," Matt said mysteriously. Colby made a face. The insurance company had refused to pay out after their dad died, and Uncle Rick had convinced their mom to contest the decision, and now almost a full year later it had turned into this incredibly long, drawn-out train wreck involving lawyers and depositions and endless, endless paperwork. Mostly, it just made Colby tired. He would have told them all to forget about it, not that anyone had asked him, except it wasn't like they didn't need the money.

His mom needed it, anyway. His Uncle Rick was doing just fine.

"Heard about your little adventure," Matt said now, finishing his orange juice and rinsing his glass before putting it in the dishwasher. Their mom was fucking maniacal about kitchen cleanliness. "The water tower, dude, seriously? What are you, like, twelve years old?"

"Fuck you," Colby said, though he'd basically been thinking the same exact thing in the moments before Keith showed up. It occurred to him to wonder if maybe there weren't any forms to fill out at all and Matt had just come here to give him a hard time about getting arrested. "Did you tell Mom?"

"No," Matt said, and Colby relaxed again. "But you should, before it gets back to her some other way."

"I'll take that under consideration," Colby said, picking up Tris's metal bowl and heading over to the giant Rubbermaid of kibble by the back door.

"You should." Matt leaned against the counter. "Look," he said, "do you want some advice?"

"Nope," Colby replied pleasantly, dumping a cup of food into the bowl and setting it back down on her place mat, "but that's never stopped you before."

"You should stop hanging around with those dudes. Micah and Jordan and whoever else."

Colby straightened up again, watching as Tris buried her blocky, brindled face in her dinner. "I should, huh?"

"You should. And I know Dad's not here to talk to you about influences or stuff like that—"

"Oh my God."

"Can you just forget whatever sullen teenager routine you're doing for one second and listen to me?" Matt frowned. "Rick keeps asking about you, is the other thing, which—"

Colby snorted. "Good for Rick."

"Is this really how you want to spend the next twenty years?" Matt demanded, tipping his head back against the ancient cabinets with his arms and ankles crossed. "Working the Home Depot stockroom and hanging out with a bunch of burnouts and getting picked up by the county sheriff?"

Colby's face warmed. "Well, I don't want to spend it working for you."

"You wouldn't have to work for me," Matt said—looking almost earnest now, the same way Keith had the other night. *I know you guys have had a tough year,* Jesus Christ. "You could go get your supervisor's license, be running your own construction projects inside a year—"

"I'm not going to work for Rick, either. I don't know how you can, after—"

"Don't." Matt's voice was a warning.

Neither of them said anything for a moment. Tris chomped away at her food. For one traitorous second, Colby let himself think about it: The garage full of tools, old ones from the '90s that his dad had taken perfect care of. A job that was more than just moving boxes all day long. Then he shoved it out of his mind. What was he going to do, help his Uncle Rick put up forty identical town houses with ugly granite countertops and walls so thin you could practically see through them? His dad would roll over in his grave.

"Think about it," Matt said, pushing himself off the counter and heading for the doorway. Colby didn't say anything at all.

"Washing machine is leaking again," his mom reported when she came downstairs in her work uniform a little while later, her cheeks pink with the blush she kept in the top drawer of the upstairs vanity. Colby's mom was a waitress at the buffet in the casino thirty miles away, all black restaurant clogs and the smell of cigarette smoke wafting from her shoulder-length brown hair when she got home in the mornings. She used to do the bookkeeping for his dad's business and a few other clients besides, and she still did some accounting stuff for Uncle Rick, but after everything happened last year, she'd needed something with health insurance. She brought extra pastries from the casino's coffee shop home at the end of her shift. "Do you mind taking a look?"

Colby nodded. He was good at fixing things, usually; one of his earliest memories was watching his dad take apart a broken ceiling fan and put it back together like a jigsaw puzzle. He'd let Colby screw in the last bolt. "I think it just needs a new seal," he told her now. "I can get one at work tomorrow."

"Thanks, baby." Colby's mom smiled. "I didn't have time to make dinner," she said, "but there's potpies in the freezer, or if you're feeling ambitious we've got eggs."

"Eggs sound great," he said, ducking his head to kiss her on one round cheek. "Have a good shift."

Once she was gone, Colby opened his laptop at the kitchen table and scrolled to the apartment he'd been looking at before work this morning. It was a few streets over from the place Matt was renting, and not as nice—just a studio with a sleeping alcove, a kitchen sink the size of a shoebox, and a stall shower so narrow he thought his shoulders would barely fit inside. Still, it got good light for a basement unit, and most important, it was cheap—with a few more weekends of overtime he'd be able to put down first month, last month, and security. And then he could be out on his own.

Colby hadn't been planning to move out, not really—most of his friends still lived at home, so it wasn't like anybody was dying to be his roommate, and the idea of leaving Tris made him feel a little sick—but the closer it got to the anniversary, the more it was starting to feel like he couldn't stay here. The more it felt like the walls were closing in. He kept winding up at the door to the garage without remembering exactly how he'd gotten there; he hadn't slept without a stupid nightmare in weeks. He kind of wanted to tell his mom she should sell the damn house altogether, except that sounded exactly like something Matt would say.

The landline rang as he was heading into the kitchen to see about dinner. They only had a landline to begin with because the bundle made cable cheaper, but his mom still insisted on calling it sometimes if she knew he was home and needed him to do something. He thought maybe she'd forgotten her purse. "Hello?"

"Hi," said a bright, chipper voice on the other end. "Is this David Moran?"

Colby felt that punch to the gut same as he always did when somebody was looking for his dad. It happened less frequently now than it had in the first few months after he'd died, when all kinds of random people—the mailman, the receptionist at the vet's office, the rich people whose gutters his dad cleaned every fall for extra Christmas money—had needed to be told. Colby almost missed it, in a messed-up kind of way. Sometimes it felt like everybody but him had forgotten.

"Uh, sorry," he said now, pulling a scratched-up frying pan out of the cupboard. "He's not available."

"That's okay," the girl said, sounding completely undeterred. "Is there another adult in the home I could speak with?"

He thought one more time of Keith at the station the other night: *you're eighteen, Colby.* "I'm an adult," he heard himself say.

"Great!" the girl exclaimed. "This is Meg with WeCount. Who do I have the pleasure of speaking with this evening?"

Colby made a face at his reflection in the microwave. Who even talked like that? She sounded about eleven years old. "This is Colby," he said, opening the fridge and pulling out the Styrofoam carton of eggs and a stick of butter.

"Are you a registered voter, Colby?"

"Uh," Colby said again, "nope."

"Well, that's okay!" Meg said, in a voice like possibly he'd just told her he didn't know how to read or wasn't toilet-trained. "WeCount is a nonpartisan organization that works to empower Americans through voter registration. Voting is an essential way to defend our democracy and build a nation with liberty and justice for all. I'd love to help you get registered so that you're ready to make your voice heard on Election Day."

Colby dug a couple of bread butts out of the bag on the counter, wondering how many times per night she had to read that little speech, or if possibly she'd committed it to memory. "I'll pass, thanks. Have a good night."

"Are you sure?" Meg asked quickly. "If you've got access to a computer, I can talk you through it right now over the phone. It'll just take a couple of minutes."

If he had access to a computer? Jesus Christ. Colby rolled his eyes. He could just picture this girl in New York or Boston or wherever the hell she was, imagining she was calling him at his one-room shack. "What about the electoral college?" Colby asked.

Meg from WeCount hesitated, just for a moment—surprised, probably, that he'd even had time to learn what the electoral college *was*, considering his busy schedule of chewing tooth-picks and shooting beer cans off fence posts. "I'm sorry?" she asked. "What about it?"

"Well," Colby said, turning the stove on and knocking a spoonful of butter into the pan, not entirely sure why he hadn't already hung up on her. "I mean, tell me if I'm wrong, but hasn't the loser of the popular vote become president twice in the last two decades?"

"I mean, that's technically true," she admitted. "But that's no reason not to—"

"It kind of seems like a great reason not to." Colby cracked two eggs into the pan and tossed the shells into the garbage, starting to enjoy himself a little bit. "And if that doesn't do it for you, there's always government corruption, super PACs, and basically the whole entire history of Congress."

"Well, the system isn't perfect," Meg allowed, a bit of an edge creeping into her voice, "but it's our privilege and responsibility as citizens to engage with it. We need to vote like our rights depend on it, Colby—because they do."

Ooh, a name drop. Colby wondered if that was in her manual or what. "Can I ask you a question, Meg?" he said. "Like, I'm not trying to be rude, and if you get some kind of bonus for me signing up, then you can go ahead and tell your boss I did it, but do you really think you're changing the world here? Like, calling people up one by one and trying to sell them on their civic obligation?"

"Well, I certainly don't think apathy is going to get us anywhere," Meg snapped.

Colby felt his eyes narrow; she'd cut a little close to the bone.

"Is that the problem?" he asked. "My apathy?"

"I'm sorry," Meg said. "I didn't mean—"

"Look," he interrupted. This whole thing was hugely annoying all of a sudden, the idea of some shiny new college grad sitting in a climate-controlled cubicle pestering people at dinnertime. His eggs, he realized, had begun to burn. "If people want to vote, they'll vote. They don't need you calling them up trying to save them from themselves."

"I'm not trying to save anybody," Meg protested, "I just—" She broke off. "Okay," she said, and Colby could hear her taking a deep breath on the other end of the line. "Obviously, we got off on the wrong foot here. But if you could just let David Moran know that I called, then—"

"Dave Moran hung himself in our garage ten months ago," Colby said, the words coming out before he'd even had time to think them. "So I don't think he'll be calling you back. You have a good night, though. Thanks anyway."

He hung up the phone without waiting for her to answer. He dumped the ruined eggs in the trash.

FIVE

Meg

For a moment, Meg stared down at her handset like she'd never seen it before, like it was an artifact from an alien planet dropped unceremoniously from the sky. She set it carefully back in its cradle, her eyes flicking around the office instinctively to see if anyone had been listening. She could taste her own heart at the back of her throat.

"Everything okay?" Lillian asked, her head popping up over the half wall that separated their cubicles. The overhead lights reflected off her glossy black bob.

"Um," Meg said, her whole body stinging, hot and humiliated. Normally, Lillian was exactly the kind of person she'd tell about something like this; Lillian had trained her to begin with and had foolproof strategies for dealing with all kinds of unsavory phone characters, from yellers to bigots to the occasional perv. "Yep." She wasn't sure who she was trying to protect.

Lillian nodded and went back to her call sheet. Meg tugged on her bottom lip. There were strict rules against calling back if someone hung up on you—technically, it counted as harassment, to the point where if you were working off a computer and not a paper call sheet, the system deleted the numbers as they were dialed, just in case—but the urge to defend herself, just to *clarify*, was so strong it was nearly unbearable. It was like trying not to think of a purple elephant. It was like trying to hold back a cough.

She blew out a breath and dialed the next number on her printout, a not-in-service, then left cheery-sounding messages for the following two. She took a bathroom break, staring at herself in the greenish light above the mirror. She ate a churro from the box in the kitchenette.

Then she sat back down at her station and dialed Colby again.

This time the call went to voice mail, which wasn't surprising. Meg didn't know if she was disappointed or relieved. A man's voice—not Colby, but someone older, a person Meg thought she was probably imagining sounded just a little bit sad—explained that the Morans weren't available, but that if she left a message somebody would get back to her as soon as possible.

"Um, hi," she said after the beep, glancing furtively in Lillian's direction. "This message is for Colby?" She cleared her throat. "Colby, this is Meg from WeCount. You and I spoke on the phone a minute ago. I just wanted to apologize for . . ." She trailed off. For *what*, exactly? Pressuring him about the importance of the electoral process? Growing up in a liberal bubble? Not somehow magically intuiting that his dad had died from suicide? "I just wanted to apologize for our conversation earlier. So. Um. I'm sorry." They were not, under any circumstances, supposed to give out their private phone numbers, but hers was out of her mouth before she could stop herself. "Just, like, if you want to call me back or anything." God, she was definitely going to get fired. "Okay. Um. Have a good night."

The rest of her shift seemed to last forever. Half a dozen hang-ups, seventeen calls that went to voice mail, and a woman in Elyria who accused her of being sent by the government to try and read her mind through the phone. "I'll let you go, then," Meg said, staring up at the drop-ceiling tiles and reminding herself that there was no reason to feel like she was about to burst into tears.

When nine o'clock finally rolled around, she basically ran for the staircase, bursting out into the damp spring night and hurrying past the marble-tiled pastry shop and middle-aged-lady caftan boutique until she got to her car. As soon as she was buckled in the driver's seat, she pulled out her phone; she had half a dozen texts from Emily, all Cornell-related. *Ughhhh*, she typed, ignoring all of them, *I had the WORST NIGHT AT WORK.*

Oh nooo what happened?? Em texted back right away. *Did you hear??*

No no, it's not that. Nothing in the spam folder. Meg relayed the highlights of her conversation with Colby, leaving out the part where he'd had a stupidly nice voice. *I feel so gross and guilty*, she finished, stopped at a red light three-quarters of the way home. *Like I was some pushy telemarketer who ruined his entire day because I couldn't take a hint ABOUT HIS DEAD DAD.*

I mean to be fair you are a pushy telemarketer . . . for FREEDOM, Emily reminded her, adding a bald eagle for good measure. *But honestly though, who cares? People make up all kinds of lies on the phone. It was probably some rando bumpkin screwing with you.*

Meg frowned, dropping her phone into the cup holder without answering as the light turned green up above. On one hand, she knew Emily had a point—after all, hadn't her mom said all kinds of weird stuff to people looking for her dad once he moved out last winter? One time she'd convinced some unsuspecting cable guy he'd gone to jail for mail fraud just to see if she could.

Still, it certainly hadn't *sounded* like Colby was messing with her. At the beginning, maybe—all that stuff about the EC and super PACs. But the part about his dad? Meg didn't really think the kind of rawness she'd heard in his voice was something a person could fake.

The lights in the house were all blazing when she finally

pulled into the driveway, like her mom had thrown a party and forgotten to tell her about it, though when she got inside it felt even bigger and emptier than usual. Her mom was asleep on the couch in the den, the same smudgy wineglass from earlier still sitting on the coffee table and the TV blaring *The Bachelor.* Meg hit the power button on the remote and plugged her mom's phone in to charge beside her, then laid a pilling cashmere throw blanket over her and walked through the downstairs, flipping all the switches off one by one.

Up in her room, she changed into her pajamas and pulled her laptop into bed, typing every conceivable variation of *Colby Moran + Ohio* into Google and getting a fat lot of nowhere. He didn't have any social media that she could find. Maybe Emily was right, then, about the whole thing being a con job. Shoot, maybe Colby wasn't even his real name.

Meg stared at the keyboard, wondering exactly how deep she wanted to get in here. *David Moran + Ohio*, she typed. She gasped quietly, though there was no one to hear her—there it was on the first page of search results, a tersely written obituary in the *Ross County Dispatch* from the beginning of last June:

David (Dave) Moran of Alma died suddenly at home on May 25. He is survived by his wife, Jennifer; his two sons, Matthew and Colby; and his dog, Tris, who loved him best of all. Services will be kept private.

So, Meg thought, squeezing her eyes shut, her skin just a little bit too tight, Emily had been wrong.

She tried *Colby Moran + Alma* next, and this time she found an old picture from the paper—a bunch of boys in scout uniforms at a Veteran's Day parade, Colby holding one of those dinky little flags. He wasn't facing the camera, but even from the side Meg could see that he was a nice-looking kid: tall and lean and almost feminine, with long eyelashes and pale cheekbones that caught the light. The caption listed him as twelve, which made him eighteen now—the same age as her, not that it mattered.

He had a serious expression. He had a very nice mouth.

She was still staring at the photo like a creep when her phone vibrated on the nightstand, insistent. *Hellooo*, Emily said. *Did you die?*

Meg slammed her laptop shut, as if Em could somehow see her. *No no*, she typed, *sorry. Home safe. You're totally right though, he was probably a total scammer. I'm over it now.*

Good, Emily said. *The cause of democracy needs you. Meet at Sbux before school? And text me IMMEDIATELY if you hear from admissions!*

Meg hesitated, debating—God, what was *wrong* with her? What was she waiting for, exactly?—before keying in a thumbs-up emoji and setting her phone facedown on the nightstand. She sneaked one more look at Colby's picture before she turned off the light.

SIX

Colby

Colby listened to Meg from WeCount's message standing in the living room while he ate his second attempt at scrambled eggs, plus two pieces of toast with jelly and then a third piece of bread he just ate plain. He stood there for another minute once the machine beeped, then went back and played the voice mail again—he was waiting for that flood of satisfaction to hit him, like when he came up with the perfect comeback to whatever idiotic thing Matt was saying, but to his surprise he just felt like kind of a dick.

He'd been hard on her, he guessed, holding out his crumby plate for Tris to lick clean before he stuck it in the dishwasher.

She'd definitely deserved it. But still.

He rinsed out the sink and wiped the counter, then went back over to the ancient phone mounted on the wall next to the refrigerator, his finger hovering over the button to delete the message. Then, without knowing quite why, he hit the button to save instead. He told himself to stop thinking about it, and he did, mostly. Then he went upstairs to bed and fell asleep.

His mom had stopped asking him to go to church with her, but she did still like for him to show up at Rick and Alicia's for lunch periodically, so on Sunday Colby put on an ugly blue dress shirt his mom had bought for him at Costco and drove over. His Uncle Rick lived in Cedarville, in the nicest McMansion in a development of McMansions he'd built himself. Rick and Colby's dad had been in business together when Colby was small, but they were perpetually fighting about the direction of the company—"Rick wanted to make money, and Dad didn't" was how Matt had explained it to him once—and after everything happened with the Paradise project when Colby was in high school, Rick had bought his dad out and taken Matt with him. Now Rick's face was plastered on billboards all over the county alongside ads for model homes now open. Micah kept saying they should climb up there and draw a giant dick on his face.

"Hi, sweetheart," Alicia said when she opened the door, her thick yellow hair bouncing like something out of a shampoo commercial. Alicia sold essential oils over the internet, lavender and tea tree and something called Thieves that was supposed to keep your house clean of bacteria or evil spirits, Colby wasn't entirely sure. He thought the name probably said it all. Before this, Alicia used to sell leggings, and before *that,* she'd sold some system that involved wrapping yourself in Saran for weight loss, which she'd actually convinced his mother to buy. Colby had come home and caught her doing it once and he could tell she was embarrassed, so he'd wrapped himself in it, too. In the end, they'd had a pretty good laugh about the whole thing, the two of them standing in the kitchen all mummified in plastic, passing a bag of sour cream and onion chips back and forth.

Still, he kind of hated Alicia's guts.

Now he toed off his sneakers per the house rules and headed into the dining room, where his mom and Matt were already sitting at the fake-antique farm table. On the wall was a verse from 1 Corinthians painted in a wedding invitation font on a piece of driftwood, even though they didn't live anywhere near the water, plus a picture of Rick and Alicia and their kids sitting on the front porch of the house all wearing jeans and white T-shirts, their golden retriever, Lucky, at their side. As far as Colby was concerned, Lucky was the only member of the entire family who wasn't an idiot, and even he licked his own butt pretty much constantly.

"So, Colby," Rick said brightly, passing a platter of ham

across the table while the twins, Mykala and Mykenzie, dutifully shoveled green beans into their nine-year-old mouths. "How's big-box life?" He always said it like that when he asked Colby about work, like installing IKEA cabinets was so much better than driving a forklift. Colby was actually the youngest guy in the warehouse trained to handle the thing, which felt like an extremely dumb thing to be proud of but was also the truth.

"Oh, you know," he said now, taking a heaping mound of potatoes, then another for good measure. "The usual. Hanging around with a bunch of losers. Wasting my bright young mind."

"Colby," his mother murmured, taking a sip of her lemonade. Matt snorted an irritated breath. Rick forked some green beans onto his plate, unruffled.

"You know, son," he said conversationally, "if I'd had the week you had, I don't know that I'd be joking quite so cavalierly about the company I kept."

"What?" His mom's gaze snapped up, darting from Rick to Colby and back again. "Why? What does that mean?"

Colby glared across the table at Matt. "It's nothing," he promised, trying to keep his voice even. "Rick's just kidding around."

"I am, I am," Rick said, smiling a megachurch-pastor smile. "And Colby knows I just give him a hard time because I want what's best for him. Which is why he's going to come work for me one of these days, right, Colby?"

"One of these days," Colby lied, feeling a muscle in his jaw twitch.

"Who wants applesauce?" Alicia asked.

They ate in relative peace after that, polite conversation and the sound of forks scraping china. Finally, Lucky whined at the door. "I'll take him," Colby said, shoving his chair out too quickly and heading out into the carefully manicured backyard. He looked out at the spindly crabapple tree and the rosebushes still wrapped in burlap for the winter. Everything in this entire neighborhood, plants especially, looked like something out of a little kid's pop-up book, like it all folded down at night to go to sleep.

He threw a stick down toward the artificial lake, watching as Lucky scooped it up and made absolutely no effort to return it, careening in the opposite direction across the grass. Colby sighed and sat down on the steps of the deck, gazing up at the blue-gray sky and thinking about Meg from WeCount. He hadn't been able to get that stupid phone call out of his head since the other night, which was ridiculous—after all, who got their panties in a wad over being rude to a telemarketer? She'd probably forgotten about the entire conversation the moment she'd hung up the phone. He should do the same instead of playing it over and over in his mind like some kind of creepy weirdo. What the hell was he supposed to do, call her back?

Not that it mattered, but she'd sounded pretty.

"Come on, buddy," he said when Lucky finally came trotting back, drool hanging in strings from his furry mouth and the stick nowhere in sight. "You ready?"

Jordan and Micah wanted to hang out that night, so he met them in the parking lot of a three-story office building plunked all by itself like a spaceship on the side of Route 4. It had been built specifically to house the regional sales office of a medical supply company back when Colby was a kid, but the *OFFICE SPACE FOR LEASE* sign had been there ever since, the lot getting more and more overgrown until someone, Colby didn't know who, periodically came and cut the plants back. One of the plate-glass windows was boarded over. The fountain in front had been drained. Micah said he'd been inside once, that he'd fucked a girl in there back when they were fifteen, but Colby thought he was mostly full of shit—about the breaking in and the fucking both.

Colby sat on the curb with a Bud Light in one hand, shielded from the road by an overgrown thicket of weeds as tall as he was, the rest of them half watching as Micah turned idle backflips in the empty fountain. As a kid, Micah had done gymnastics until way after it was socially acceptable, which meant he'd gotten called gay pretty much constantly until graduation, but it also meant he could do things like that: launch himself into the air and throw his weight around without falling over and bashing his skull open like a cantaloupe. "He only does it because he wants attention," Colby had complained to Joanna once, and Jo had shrugged and said, "Everybody wants attention," in a way Colby had thought about for a long time.

"You okay, Colby Moran?" she called now, from her perch in the open hatchback of her vanilla-smelling station wagon, her hair like a blond halo in the light from the trunk. She'd showed up twenty minutes ago with two of her friends, one of whom was currently trying to execute a headstand of her own for Jordan's benefit. The other one hadn't looked up from her phone the whole time.

"I'm good," Colby promised, heaving himself up off the pavement and heading over to sit beside her. She smelled slightly mysterious, like baby powder and girl. Joanna had dated some dude from Ohio State until this past winter, when somebody had sent her a video of him at a party triple kissing two sorority sisters while a bunch of other people cheered him on like he was doing a keg stand, and that had been the end of that. Colby had not been sorry to see him go.

Now they sat in companionable silence for a moment, drinking their beers and listening to Jordan and Micah argue over whether it was possible to eat seven saltines in a minute. "You want to see me do it right now?" Jordan was asking. "Because we can drive to BP and get a box of them."

Colby sighed. He kept getting this itchy feeling lately, like his clothes were a full size too small—at the house, yeah, but now sometimes outside of it, too. The anniversary was coming, trundling straight at him like a cross-country train, but he didn't think that was the only reason. "I gotta go," he heard himself say.

"Already?" Joanna asked, reaching out and nudging him in the shin with the toe of her ankle boot. "What do you got, a date?"

Colby shook his head, rolling his eyes a little. "Yeah, right," he said with a smile. "Just tired, I guess."

"Well," Joanna said, running one delicate thumb around the mouth of her beer bottle. Colby thought there was a not-insignificant chance he was the stupidest guy ever born. "Rest up, then."

He didn't want to go home, so he drove around for a while, past the Burger King and the post office and the service road that led to Paradise, but he didn't exactly have the money to be cruising around wasting gas, either, so finally he gave up and headed back toward the house, flicking on the lights in the dark, empty living room. His mom was at work tonight, but back when his dad was alive she used to go to exercise once a week and he and his dad used to wait for her to leave so they could eat second dinner, the two of them going through a left-over pan of lasagna or a whole box of frozen waffles while they watched old movies on cable. His dad had liked dad movies—Tom Hanks and Denzel Washington—but he also had a thing for romantic weepers that everybody else in the family was always making fun of. If the movie poster had two white people almost-kissing on it, chances were his dad was a fan.

Now Colby glanced at the calendar hanging on the door of the mudroom, a stupid promotional thing Uncle Rick had given his mom at Christmas. Eight weeks to go until the anniversary.

God, he really did not want to still be living here in eight weeks.

He listened to Meg's message again, her voice echoing out into the empty kitchen. He walked around the house for a while. Finally, he picked up the phone and dialed, biting a cuticle on his thumbnail as it rang and trying to figure out what exactly he was going to say into this girl's voice mail.

"Hello?"

Oh, shit.

SEVEN

Meg

For a long moment, there was silence on the other end of the line, the faint sound of static crackling somewhere out in the ether. "Hello?" Meg said again. Nobody ever called her on the phone—especially not a number that wasn't already in her contacts list—which was why she'd picked up to begin with. She blinked, shifting her weight in her desk chair. She'd been listening to *Pod Save America* and painting her nails, trying with little success not to think about the email from Cornell currently sitting like a stone in her inbox. She still hadn't told a soul she'd gotten in.

"Um." Someone cleared his throat on the other end of the line. "Is this Meg?"

Meg frowned. "Yes?"

"This is Colby Moran," the voice said. "We, uh, talked the other night?"

"Oh my God," Meg said too loud and too quickly, coming embarrassingly close to spilling the bottle of nail polish and falling out of the chair altogether. She swallowed hard, steadying herself on the edge of the desk. "Um. Hi."

"Hi. Um." He cleared his throat again. "I didn't think you'd answer, honestly."

"Then why did you call me?" she blurted. Then, feeling her cheeks warm: "I mean, I'm glad you did, I just—"

"I just thought I'd leave you a voice mail, I guess, or—"

"Do you want to hang up and call back and I won't answer?"

"What?" Colby laughed. "No." There was a pause, like he was gathering his thoughts, but then it lasted so long that she thought maybe he had hung up after all, and she was about to say *hello* one more time when he spoke again. "Anyway," he said, "I'm just calling to say I'm sorry for being such an asshole on the phone the other night. I know you were just doing your job or whatever."

"You weren't an asshole," Meg said automatically.

"Yeah," Colby said, "I definitely was."

Meg tugged on her bottom lip. "I mean, okay," she conceded finally. "A little bit." She screwed the cap back on the bottle of polish before getting up and closing her bedroom door, not entirely sure why she was doing it except that this felt like a conversation that needed to be contained somehow.

She couldn't believe he'd actually called. She'd kind of forgotten about the whole conversation in the bustle of the last few days—a Spanish test and dinner with her dad and her and Emily getting in a weird thing over whether or not to invite Mason out for poke bowls on Saturday. "He's still our friend even if you guys aren't dating anymore, right?" Emily had pointed out gently, which Meg thought was debatable, but she felt so guilty about the whole Cornell situation that she'd just agreed to avoid a fight.

"It was my fault, too, though," she continued now, sitting down on her bed and leaning her back against the wall. "I shouldn't have been so pushy. I was just having a bad day and, like, trying to prove something."

Colby made a quiet sound that wasn't quite a snicker. "By converting me?"

"I'm not trying to convert you to anything," she said, huffing a little. "WeCount is totally nonpartisan. We don't care who you vote for. We just care that you vote."

"I mean, that's literally never true," Colby said.

"It is so!" Meg fired back, crumbs sticking to the bottoms of her feet as she got up again, pacing across the rug. The whole house needed to be vacuumed—and more, probably. She was pretty sure she'd seen mouse poop at the back of the kitchen cabinet the other day. "It's a nonprofit. We can't have political affiliation or we'd lose our tax-exempt status."

Colby made an *I don't know* noise, but then instead of arguing he seemed to think for a moment. "Makes sense, I guess," he finally said.

"I can help you register now if you want," she offered brightly, sensing an opening. "I meant it the other night; it only takes, like, two seconds."

"Oh no." Colby laughed a little, deep and rumbling. "That's okay."

Meg frowned. "Are you sure?"

"Yeah," he said. "I'm all set. I meant what I said the other night, too, you know? I think the whole thing is bullshit."

She sat down hard on the edge of the mattress. "The whole thing, like democracy?"

"I mean, not *democracy*," Colby clarified. "But the way it works in America, yeah, totally. It has nothing to do with actual people or, like, their actual concerns."

"Says who?"

"Says anyone who's paid attention at any point in the last fifty years," Colby shot back. "It's a power grab, that's all. Look, I'm not trying to shit on your job—"

"Aren't you?" Meg asked with a brittle-sounding giggle. God, he was infuriating. She wasn't sure why she hadn't already hung up.

"No!" Colby insisted. "If you like it, if you feel like you're making a difference, then more power to you. I just personally think you're wasting your time."

Meg opened her mouth, then closed it again. "I mean, wow,"

was all she could say. She knew she cared way more about politics than most people, with her job at WeCount and how the bumper of her car was covered in campaign stickers and her dutiful monthly donations to She Should Run, but she'd never encountered anybody—especially not anybody her own age—who just flat-out didn't think it was worth it. "That's really cynical."

"Yeah, well." She could practically hear the shrug in his voice. "I'm cynical."

"Clearly."

Neither of them said anything for a moment, the silence stretching out across the miles and miles between them and the inherent weirdness of this conversation hitting her all at once. She was just about to make an excuse and say goodbye when Colby spoke. "Why did you have a bad day?" he asked.

"Huh?" Meg sat up straighter on the mattress, surprised.

"You said you had a bad day the other day, right? I'm asking why."

"I mean, do you care?"

"I wouldn't ask if I didn't."

Well. She hesitated, trying to decide both how to answer that question and why she felt compelled to in the first place. After all, it wasn't like one specific thing had happened; it was more like the last few weeks had been a creeping accumulation of not-great stuff, the way that dust gathered slowly on the blades of her ceiling fan until all of a sudden she looked up and noticed they were covered with a thick layer of fur. Still, she wasn't about to tell this stranger about the wine bottles clanking in the recycling bin, or her Dad and Lisa going to Palm Springs, or—good Lord—about Mason breaking up with her.

"Just dumb college admissions stuff," she admitted finally, because that seemed like the least personal option. The kind of thing you could tell a stranger on the phone, if you were the type to talk to total strangers on the phone, which apparently she was now. "Which I know you probably think is, like, not a real problem."

Colby snorted. "Why, because my ma has the black lung from mining coal and the roof of my barn is caving in?"

"No!" Meg said immediately. "That's not what I meant at all."

"Isn't it?" he asked, exactly imitating the tone she'd used earlier.

Meg winced. "No!" she insisted. He didn't sound particularly put out, which didn't change how mortified she was. "I just—I mean—"

"Can I ask you a question?" Colby broke in. "Why do you keep doing that? Trying to act like something isn't what it is, I mean."

"What?" She bristled. "I don't. I'm not."

"You kind of are, though," he said. "Like, even at the beginning of this conversation, when I said I was calling to apologize for being an asshole, you were like, *No, no, you weren't.* But it's okay. I *was* an asshole. I don't like being an asshole in general, which is why I called you back."

Meg thought about that for a moment. "I don't know," she said finally. "I was being nice, I guess. I didn't want to have a fight."

"*Nice* is overrated."

She rolled her eyes. "In your world, maybe."

"And what world is that?"

Shit. "I don't know."

"No, I'm serious," Colby said. She thought he might have been smiling, though it was hard to tell over the phone. "When you call us swing state folk to try and persuade us to do our civic duty, what exactly are you picturing?"

"I don't know!" Meg said again. Ugh, he was flustering her, just like he had the other night at work. The truth was she'd barely spent any time in Ohio, even though it was right next door; her vague impression was one of, like, cornfields and a racist baseball mascot, though somehow she didn't think mentioning either of those would win her any points with Colby. "Pennsylvania is a swing state, too, PS."

"Not the part you live in."

"Oh yeah?" she asked, like she was six years old and standing on the playground with her hands on her hips. "And what part is that?"

"The rich part," Colby said immediately.

"Seriously?" Meg bristled, though it wasn't like he was

wrong, exactly. Her parents fought about money all the time, especially now, but Meg had always gotten the sense it was more for sport—or spite—than because either one of them was really afraid of there not being enough to go around. "How would you know?"

"Just a guess."

"Well, I'm just saying, if you don't want me making assumptions about you, then you shouldn't make assumptions about me, either."

"You know," Colby said, "fair enough."

"Okay."

"Okay."

Both of them were quiet for another long minute. Meg looked out the window at the moon. It seemed like a natural place for the conversation to end, though for some reason she was suddenly reluctant to be the one to end it. It was just so unexpected to be talking to him in the first place, she guessed; it was like turning the corner in the upstairs hallway and finding a room she'd never seen before.

"They let you work there in high school?" Colby asked finally, instead of the *okay, have a good night* she'd been expecting. "We All Count, or whatever?"

"WeCount," Meg corrected, faintly relieved and not 100 percent sure why. "And I turned eighteen in September. I'm a little old for my grade." She fussed with the quilt for a moment, dragging the corner of it under her thumbnail. "How old are you?" she asked, even though she already knew.

"Eighteen, too," he said immediately. Meg felt herself exhale. She knew it was an embarrassingly low bar—and more than that, she knew it didn't actually *matter*, considering she was never going to talk to this person again after tonight—but she was glad he hadn't lied. "But I graduated last year."

"Are you in college?" she asked.

"Nope."

"What do you do?"

"What do you think?"

"Uh-uh," Meg said immediately. "No way."

"No way, what?"

"No way, I'm not guessing."

"Why not?"

"Because."

"Well, that's not an answer."

"I don't think you're exactly in a position to be complaining about answers, do you?"

Colby laughed at that. "Fair enough," he said again, but he also didn't volunteer any more information; she wondered if he did something sketchy, or if maybe he didn't work at all. "Sorry about the college thing," he finally said.

"Oh!" For a second, she didn't know what he was talking about; this entire conversation kept distracting her, the whole world narrowing to the sound of his voice. "It's okay. It's *not* actually even a real problem, like I was saying. It's just that I got into Cornell, and, like, obviously I'm going to go, but the more I think about it the less I actually want to."

It was out before she knew she was going to say it, and the sound of it shocked her—she'd never even let herself *consider* it before—but as soon as she heard it out loud, she knew it was true. She didn't want to go to Ithaca in September.

She just had no idea what she *did* want to do.

"Okay," Colby was saying now, his voice slow and curious. "And why do you have to go, exactly?"

Meg hesitated, trying to figure out how to explain it in a way that didn't sound completely spoiled and finally deciding it didn't matter. "Well, it's the best school I applied to," she tried, though it didn't sound particularly convincing even to her own ears. "And my best friend, Emily, and I have always had this plan to go there and room together." Now that she stopped and thought about it, Meg guessed it was mostly Em's plan, concocted last year during the divorce, when their guidance counselor was demanding application lists and Meg could barely comb her own hair, let alone plan her future. Still, Meg had definitely *agreed* to it. "To keep things the same, you know?"

"And you can't keep things the same from the suburbs of Philadelphia?"

Meg's mouth dropped open. "Who says I live in the suburbs of Philadelphia?"

"Don't you?"

She huffed. "Maybe."

"Lucky guess."

Again there was a pause, and again Meg waited for him to tell her he had to go, but instead the conversation meandered: to a family trip to Philly his family had taken when he was in middle school, which they'd spent mostly waiting in line for cheesesteaks and a picture in front of the Liberty Bell; to the Mutter Museum, which was full of medical oddities including a small piece of John Wilkes Booth's thorax and which had an entire room where the walls were covered with mounted human skulls; to Cedar Point, the self-proclaimed roller-coaster capital of the world, which she'd been to on an overnight trip with her debate team freshman year. "I rode, like, eleven different roller coasters," she confessed, lying back on the mattress. She'd turned all the lights off except for the one beside her bed. "And I was doing fine until I got off number twelve, but then I wasn't near a garbage can so I just panicked and barfed into the sleeve of my hoodie."

"You did not," Colby said immediately.

"I know," she said, feeling weirdly pleased with herself. "I can tell by your voice that you think I'm too prissy to have done something so unladylike, but: desperate times."

"Clearly," Colby said. "I think I underestimated you, Meg from WeCount."

"Well," she said, "you shouldn't."

"I'm starting to see that, yeah," he said with a laugh. There was something about that sound, the low, warm grumble of it, that Meg felt in her hands and spine and stomach. A very small voice inside her said: *Oh no.*

"It's late," she said finally, catching sight of the vintage clock on her nightstand. The alarm part didn't work anymore, and Mason had tried to get her to toss it last year when his mom had been on a big Marie Kondo kick, but she wouldn't let him. *It sparks joy,* she'd insisted, setting it back on the nightstand. It occurred to her with a jolt that this conversation was the longest she'd gone without thinking about Mason in days. It made her feel a tiny bit disloyal, even though he was the one who'd broken up with her and anyway it wasn't like this phone call was romantic or anything like that. "I should probably try to sleep."

"Sure thing," Colby said. "I've got work in the morning, too." He cleared his throat. "I work at Home Depot, PS," he said. "In the warehouse."

"Oh!" Meg said, then snapped her jaws shut before she said anything accidentally offensive. The idea of spending your days moving refrigerators and table saws and, like, paint cans from place to place was enormously bleak to her, and she knew it made her an unforgiveable snob. "See?" she said instead. "Was that so hard?"

"No," Colby said after a moment. "I guess not."

Meg wanted to ask if he liked it; she wanted to ask what he did there, and what kinds of people he worked with. She wanted to know if he wanted to do something else or if he was happy, and she wanted to hear him laugh one more time, but she knew she was only postponing the inevitable. "Have a good night, Colby," she said quietly. "It was really nice talking to you."

"Yeah," he said. "It was really nice talking to you, too."

Meg swallowed down a weird surge of panic just then: a feeling like an escape hatch closing in a movie, of being left behind in a dangerous place. *Wait*, she thought, *and take me with you.*

"Good night" was all she said.

Once she'd hung up, she turned off the lamp and stared at the moonlight making patterns on the ceiling. She didn't fall asleep for a long time.

EIGHT

Colby

Colby stopped at Bixby's for coffee the following morning, plunking a dollar in the tip jar and smiling at the barista without letting himself think about why. He was exhausted—it had been damn near impossible to drag his ass out of bed and into the shower this morning—but it felt like a good kind of tired, like when he used to work with his dad on job sites in the summer and came home at the end of the day filthy and sore.

"You hit the lotto or something?" Moira asked when he got to work, coming up behind him with her backpack slung over one shoulder as he punched his employee code into the time clock. Moira was his shift supervisor, a tall skinny black woman in her thirties with long braids down her back.

"Huh?" Colby asked, blinking distractedly. He entered his

number wrong, had to clear it out and start over.

Moira grinned. "You did, didn't you?"

"What?" Colby shook his head, laughing a little bewilderedly. "No."

"I don't know, Colby," Moira said, shaking her head and nudging him aside to get to the time clock. "I think it's the first time since I met you that I've seen you in here without a scowl on your face that could take the bark off a tree."

"That's not—" Colby felt himself blush, though he wasn't sure if it was because apparently he had a reputation for frowning all the time at work or because she'd noticed he wasn't doing it on this particular morning. "I didn't."

"Sure. Sure. Just try not to forget us little people when you're collecting all your money." Moira winked. "Shift assignments in ten, Smiles."

It was a busy morning, thankfully: a shipment of washing machines to unload that meant a full reorg of appliances, plus a long pick list of items to send to the online distribution facility outside Columbus. Colby was real careful to keep his head down. So fine, he'd had a good time talking to Meg from WeCount on the phone last night. Whatever. He was literally never going to hear from her again, so there was no point in getting worked up about it one way or the other.

When he got into the break room for his thirty, Moira and Jerry were staring at a notice on the bulletin board next to the bank of lockers, where people put up shift-switch requests and ads for roommates and the mandatory OSHA posters about unsafe working conditions. “What’s up?” Colby asked, opening his locker and pulling out his lunch.

“They’re cutting overtime,” Jerry reported.

“Wait.” Colby frowned, coming over to look at the flier. “*All* overtime?”

Moira nodded. “That’s what it looks like.”

“I love how they didn’t even talk to us about it,” Jerry said with a rueful smirk, his bald white head gleaming in the overhead lights. “Just stuck it up there for us to find.”

“They did it on purpose,” Moira cracked. “They all know you can’t read.”

“Oh, fuck off,” Jerry said, and the whole thing devolved into a pileup of good-natured insults, but Colby was hardly listening. Well, he guessed, so much for moving out by the beginning of the summer. At this rate, he’d probably be living with his mom until he was forty-five.

He ate the ham-and-cheese sandwich he’d packed that morning and got himself a Dr Pepper from the vending machine. Then he got up and went back to work.

NINE

Meg

Seniors could leave campus during their lunch periods, so Meg met up with Emily in the parking lot and they went to the hipster salad place near school. By the time they got there and waited in line, they usually only had ten minutes to shovel their salads into their mouths, but they went anyway because Emily couldn't get enough of the lime-cilantro dressing and it didn't seem like something worth arguing about, even though Meg was always a tiny bit stressed about getting back before the bell.

"Did you see that new bookstore in Montco is doing Friday open-mic nights?" she asked now. "You want to go this week maybe?"

Emily glanced up from whoever she was texting, raised an

eyebrow. "Why?" she asked. "You hoping to find an audience for your political slam poetry?"

"Rude." Meg pelted her with a cherry tomato, laughing. "I don't write political slam poetry."

"Sure, sure." Emily shook her head. "I can't," she said, setting her phone down and shivering a little inside her Patagonia. It was warm enough to eat outside on the patio, but barely. "I have to help my mom with something."

"Mysterious," Meg teased.

"It's not," Emily said—a little sharply, which was weird. "It was just a computer thing for one of her classes."

"Oh." Meg nodded. "Okay." Emily's mom was getting her master's in social work at Temple, driving into the city two nights a week for seminars and working on research projects at the kitchen table. Meg had asked her own mom if she'd ever thought about going back to school—Mrs. Hurd really liked it, and she'd made all these other middle-aged lady friends and some younger ones besides—but Meg's mom had said she hadn't even liked college the first time, and that had been the end of that. "That's cool."

She poked at her kale Caesar for a moment, pushing the Parmesan crisps to the side for very last and knowing that the only person actually acting strange here was her. It felt like she'd betrayed Emily somehow by telling Colby about Cornell, even though she knew that was silly. She was going to tell Emily about Cornell. She was going to *go* to Cornell.

She just needed a little bit of time to get her head in the game first.

"So, okay," she blurted before she could talk herself out of it, sitting back in her wobbly metal patio chair—wanting to offer Emily *something*, even if it wasn't the thing she knew Em was waiting to hear. "Do you remember the other night when I texted you about that guy who hung up on me at work?"

"Huh?" Emily glanced at her phone one more time before turning it facedown on the table. "Oh. Yeah."

"He called me back."

"He did *what*?" Emily's eyes widened in horror. "Oh my God, how did he get your number? That's so creepy."

"No, no," Meg said, holding her hands up and shaking her head quickly. "I mean, I gave him my number."

"What?" Emily repeated. "*Why*?"

"Because I felt so bad? I don't know." Meg felt her cheeks getting warm. "It just kind of came out. But what I'm trying to tell you is we wound up talking for, like, a million hours."

"Seriously?" Emily raised her eyebrows. "About what?"

Meg shrugged. "All kinds of stuff. I don't know." Suddenly, she felt embarrassed about it, like telling the story out loud had broken some kind of spell. "Our jobs. Vacations. What we watch on TV."

"What does he watch on TV?"

"That's not the point!" Meg blew a breath out. "It was just, like, this super long, intense phone conversation, that's all.

I've definitely never talked that way to a stranger before." She thought about it for a moment, the back of her neck getting dumbly warm as she remembered the sound of his laugh. "I guess it felt like I could talk to him that way *because* he was a stranger, you know? Like: judgment-free zone, or something."

"Yeah, I guess that makes sense." Emily snapped the lid back on her empty salad bowl. "It's just . . . I don't know, man. I mean, I love you, obviously. But that's, like . . . kind of super sketchy, no?"

Meg blinked. "Thanks a lot," she said, holding her hand out for Emily's container and getting up to toss them both in the bin. She knew it was silly to feel protective of a person she'd had two conversations with—to feel protective of the person she'd been on the phone—but she couldn't help it. She wished she hadn't said anything to begin with.

"I'm sorry!" Emily said, rattling the ice in her straw-free cup of raspberry lemonade. "I'm not trying to yuck your yum, I just—who even is this guy? He could be, like, fifty-five."

"He's not fifty-five! He's exactly our age."

"How do you know?"

I Googled him did not sound like an answer that was going to win any points with Emily, so Meg just shrugged again. "I just know." Ugh, this had been a mistake. Best friend or not, there had been plenty of things she hadn't told Emily about over the years—the time she'd gotten her period in line for iced tea at the Short Hills Mall and bled right through her white shorts;

that she'd made out with a girl named Riley the summer she'd been a camp counselor in the Poconos and could see herself doing it again if she met the right person; her parents' divorce until two weeks after her dad moved out and Emily was coming for a sleepover and she couldn't hide it anymore. Sometimes it just felt safer that way. Their sameness was comforting, yes—their sameness had always been comforting—but the flip side of that was that sometimes their friendship felt a little bit like the persuasive essays they'd written last fall in AP Lit Comp, where Meg had purposely left out any evidence that didn't support her argument for fear of the whole thing collapsing entirely.

"Look, you're right," she said finally, digging her car keys out of her backpack. "It was totally random. And it's not like it's going to happen again. I just thought it was a funny story, that's all."

"Wait," Emily said, "are you mad, though?"

"No," Meg promised, and she wasn't. It was more like she felt kind of empty. She felt dumb. It *had* been weird, that phone call with Colby. But it had also made her happier than anything else had in a really long time.

"I'm sorry," Emily said again as they headed out into the parking lot. It was starting to drizzle, a raw trickle slipping into the neck of Meg's denim jacket. "I didn't mean to rain on your parade. You know, your slightly-sketchy-phone-call parade—"

"All right, thank you." Meg laughed. "You've made your point." She bumped Emily's shoulder when she said it in a way she knew would smooth things over, make it into a joke instead of a fight; even as she did it it felt like another betrayal, though this time she wasn't sure of who. "Come on," she said, getting into the car and glancing at the clock on the dashboard. "We're gonna be late."

TEN

Colby

Colby's mom texted to tell him they were out of dog food and milk in order of importance, so he stopped by the Giant Eagle on his way home from work. Colby loved the supermarket, weirdly: the chilly, brightly lit order of it, the dumb '90s Muzak tinkling overhead. His dad used to let him hitch a ride on the back of the cart.

He got the stuff his mom wanted, plus some extra treats for Tris. He was standing in the snack aisle debating garlic Cheez-Its versus Extra Toasty when Keith Olsen appeared beside a cardboard display of Tostitos. "Hey!" he called, sounding genuinely excited by the sight of Colby standing there in his dirty warehouse clothes among the Wheat Thins and barbecue chips. "Colby, dude. I've been looking for you."

"Uh, really?" Colby asked, trying not to sound too outwardly suspicious. *You know where I live and work*, he didn't say. "You have?"

"I mean, not in a professional capacity," Keith clarified, motioning down at his tan sheriff's uniform. A silver wedding ring glinted on his left hand. He was married to a girl who'd broken up with Matt back in high school, which Colby knew drove Matt crazy and therefore kind of appreciated. "Well, kind of in a professional capacity, I guess. But you're not in trouble. I just wanted to see how you were doing, after the other night."

For one demented second, Colby thought Keith was talking about the phone call with Meg from WeCount. Then he blinked and realized he meant the water tower thing. "Oh," he said. "I'm fine, thanks." In fact, he felt a little guilty over how easily he'd gotten off for the whole thing—he knew his dad would have had him make it up somehow, picking up trash or donating to a charity or something—but that sure as shit wasn't the kind of thing he was going to say out loud.

Keith nodded eagerly, either oblivious to Colby's tone or completely undeterred by it. "Good," he said. "That's good." Then, motioning at Colby's dirt-streaked polo shirt: "You just come from work?"

"Yup," Colby said in a way he hoped didn't invite any further questions, tossing the Extra Toasties into his cart.

Keith kept nodding. "You like it over there?" he asked.

"It's fine," Colby said. God, what the fuck did Keith care if he liked it or not? It was like just because he had a badge and a gun he'd decided he was Colby's honorary guidance counselor. "It's a job."

"Yeah, no, I get that." Keith smiled. "You ever think about doing something with a little more room to grow, though? I mean, you're a smart guy. Your uncle would hire you in a second, I bet."

Anger crested inside Colby like a flash flood, sudden and dangerous. "Did my brother ask you to talk to me?" he demanded. "Because I don't actually see how it's any of your business who I work for."

"Dude, easy." Keith held up the hand that wasn't gripping his grocery basket, his jamboree-leader smile falling a little bit. "I haven't seen your brother in months. I'm just asking, that's all." He shook his head. "You know Doug Robard?" he asked.

Colby frowned. He did know Doug Robard, actually; he'd worked as a lead carpenter for his dad and Uncle Rick when Colby was a kid, though he'd gone out on his own and did super complicated, finicky residential shit now. How he made money like that in a place like Alma was beyond Colby, but judging by how many trucks the guy had now, he certainly seemed to. "What about him?"

"He's a friend of mine—"

"Oh yeah?" Colby asked, wiggling his eyebrows pointedly.

"Fuck you, Colby." Keith scowled. "It's not like that. He's got more work than he can handle, and he mentioned he was looking for help. Seems like the kind of thing you'd be good at."

"Why's that?"

"Dude," Keith said, "I remember how you used to help your dad out on jobs all the time when you were younger. And I know how your brother can be, and I get if you don't want to work with him, but something tells me that hauling two-by-fours around at a big-box store isn't exactly the kind of gig that's gonna light your fire forever."

"Oh no?" Colby smirked, even as some small, traitorous voice at the back of his head wondered if Keith might have a point. He wasn't embarrassed about what he did—he'd announced it to Meg from WeCount, hadn't he, basically daring her to say something snotty and prove his point—but the truth was he hadn't *wanted* to tell her, exactly, and eighteen hours later he still wasn't sure what that had been about. "What do you think would light my fire, exactly?"

Keith rolled his eyes. "Just check the guy out on Instagram, okay? If you think what he's doing is cool, shoot me a text and I'll put you in touch."

Colby hesitated. On one hand, he didn't know what Keith's game was here, butting into his business and blowing smoke up his ass. On the other, he couldn't act like some dumb, gullible part of him wasn't the tiniest bit intrigued. "Sure," he said finally, more to get out of here than because he had any intention of actually doing it. He had a job, even if it wasn't a super exciting one. There was no point in tying himself in knots trying to get something better that probably wouldn't even work out. "I'll take a look."

Still, once he'd loaded the groceries into the car and gotten into the driver's seat he found himself pulling his phone out of his pocket, curious in spite of himself. He didn't have Instagram, but Doug's account came up with a minimum of Googling. He *did* do nice work, Colby had to admit that, restoring historic houses all over the county—so that yuppies could buy them, Colby guessed, though he didn't know how many yuppies there were in Ross County. It was super advanced carpentry, huge built-in bookcases with dovetailed corners and antique staircases with complicated trim, the kind of stuff his dad would have totally loved.

He had scrolled almost six months back without entirely meaning to when his phone buzzed in his hand with a text from a number that wasn't in his contacts list—Meg, he realized with a jolt.

Are you also falling asleep standing up? she wanted to know.

Colby smiled; he couldn't help it. *Sitting down. But pretty much.*

What are you up to?

Just headed home from work. Then, before he hit send, he added: *Got accosted in the grocery store though.*

Accosted! The grimace emoji here, its tiny teeth bared. *By who?*

Friend of my brother's, he said, leaving out the part about the water tower. *He wants me to apply for some job.* At the very last minute, he pasted in the link to Doug's Instagram page.

He meant to put the car in drive and head out, but instead he sat where he was with his phone in his hand like a moron, waiting for her to text back. And she did, the phone vibrating in his hand a couple of minutes later: *This is so cool! You know how to do stuff like this?*

A little, Colby typed, hesitating for a moment. The truth was he hadn't done any kind of fancy work like that since his dad had died—or before that, he guessed, since at the end there his dad hadn't been doing much of it, either. *Been a while.*

Are you going to apply?

Colby chewed the inside of his cheek. *Probably not*, he admitted.

Why not?

Well. Colby stared at the screen, debating. He was still trying to figure out how to answer when the phone buzzed again, more insistently this time: holy shit, she was *calling.*

"Um," he said, tapping the button to answer and clearing his throat a little, trying to sound like a person whose heart wasn't doing a tricky acrobatic thing inside his chest. "Hey."

"Hi," she said, casual as anything. "I figured this was easier than texting."

Colby laughed a little. "Makes sense," he said, though it didn't really. Already this was the most he'd ever talked on the phone with someone in his entire life.

Meg seemed unbothered. "Thank you," she said. "I'm very sensible. So who's this guy?"

Colby tilted his head back as he told her, the setting sun making patterns on the insides of his eyelids. He wondered again what she looked like, but as soon as he had that thought, he opened his eyes and reminded himself to stop being such a loser.

"So, okay," she said when he was finished explaining. "What's the problem, exactly?"

"Huh?" Colby frowned, picking idly at a hole in the worn fabric of the driver's seat. This car had been Matt's before it became his, and it had been somebody else's before that. "I mean, there's no *problem*. It just doesn't seem worth it, that's all."

"Why not?"

"I don't know," he said—looking up suddenly, caught a little short. "Like, in a perfect world, sure."

"Well, what's keeping this world from being perfect?" Then she stopped, as if she'd heard herself and realized how absolutely ridiculous she sounded. "Okay, don't answer that. I just mean, what's stopping you in this particular situation?"

Colby wondered what it would be like to live in this girl's universe, where apparently everything followed a logical sequence of events. "This job just probably isn't a real thing, that's all. So there's no point in getting worked up about it, putting all this energy into trying to make it happen when it's probably not going to happen anyway."

"*Energy* being, making a phone call and talking to this guy who might have a cool job for you?"

"Pretty much," Colby said, though he knew she was probably being sarcastic. "Because there's obviously going to be a catch somewhere, right? Either he's going to want somebody with more experience, or the job doesn't actually pay, or the whole thing is a cover-up and they're going to sell me into sex slavery as soon as I walk in the door."

"Oh, *that's* your worry?" Meg asked. He could hear rolling her eyes. "Being sold into sex slavery?"

"Well, it sounds stupid when you say it in that tone of voice," he said, prickling a bit. He'd been kidding, mostly. "But kind of."

"So, like, nobody can pull the rug out from under you if you decide there's no rug to begin with?"

Colby blinked. He didn't think he'd ever heard anyone put it so succinctly before. He didn't actually like it very much. Shit, what was he even doing, sitting here like a chump spilling his guts to a total stranger? He thought about telling her he had to go—he *meant* to tell her he had to go—but in the end he just set the phone on speaker on the dashboard and put the car in reverse. "Uh, yeah," he admitted, pulling out of the parking lot. "Basically."

"Is that your entire life philosophy?"

Jesus Christ, this girl. "Who are you, my therapist?"

"Do you *have* a therapist?"

Colby snorted. "No."

"Why is that funny?" Meg asked, sounding sincerely curious. "Are you one of those guys who's, like, too manly for therapy?"

"I'm not too manly for anything," Colby told her. "I just don't—"

"See the point?" Meg supplied, obviously delighted with herself.

"Very funny." It was almost totally dark out now, the spring trees spindly outlines against the blue-purple sky; he passed the middle school and the Applebee's, the park where he and his dad had taken Tris the last time they'd gone anywhere together. Of course, Colby hadn't known it was the last time when they did it. Hindsight, et cetera. "Do *you* have a therapist?" he heard himself ask.

"I used to," she said easily, like it was nothing out of the ordinary—and it probably wasn't, as far as she was concerned. Where she lived it was probably like getting a brand-new car for your sixteenth birthday or taking a gap year to dick around in Europe. If she were anyone else, Colby would have found her totally fucking annoying, and he didn't know what it meant that he didn't, really. "I went to one after my parents got divorced."

"Why'd you stop?"

"Because I'm perfect, obviously," Meg deadpanned. Then she laughed. "Nah, it was more like my mom stopped caring if

I went or not, and I was feeling less like I was in a weird sad fog all the time, so I stopped going. But it was good while it lasted."

That surprised him a little: she didn't seem like the kind of person who would admit to feeling foggy—or whose mom would stop caring about anything—ever. "I . . . will keep that in mind," was all he said.

"Oh yeah?" Meg asked, the smile still audible in her voice. "Are you lying?"

"Yes."

"Jerk," she said cheerfully. "What are you doing this weekend?"

Getting drunk in Micah's basement and lying in bed staring at the ceiling, probably, but he wasn't about to admit that to her, even if he was enormously relieved by the change of subject. "I don't know," he finally said. "Working, I guess."

"There's a rally in Columbus for Annie Hernandez," Meg reported. "The woman who's running for US Senate in Ohio? You should check it out if you're around."

Colby barked out a laugh. "Holy shit, lady," he said. "Is that the real reason you called me? To try and sell me on some rally?"

"No!" Meg protested. "I'm just mentioning it because—"

"Uh-huh." Colby shook his head at the windshield, still smirking. He couldn't decide if his feelings were hurt or not. "I'll go after my therapy appointment, how about?"

"Rude," Meg said, but she was laughing, too; he wasn't

entirely sure if they were joking around or if they weren't.

Colby stopped at a red light. "How do you even know what political rallies are happening in a city you don't even live in?" he asked. "Do you have, like, some kind of nerdy political bat signal you all send each other?"

"Maybe we do," Meg retorted. "Anyway, Annie Hernandez is amazing, and worth checking out even if you don't go to the rally."

"She is, huh?" Colby asked. Then, even though he knew he was walking right into it: "What's so amazing about her?"

"Well," Meg said brightly, like she'd been waiting for him to ask the question. He wondered if she had note cards on every politician in the whole freaking country, stored in alphabetical order in one of those plastic boxes from Office Depot for easy reference. "She's only thirty-one, first of all. And she has this super inclusive platform. Criminal justice reform, universal pre-K, raising the minimum wage—okay, what?" she asked, breaking off at the low sound Colby hadn't even really meant to make out loud. "Raising the minimum wage? How can you possibly be against raising the minimum *wage*, of all things?"

Colby rolled his eyes at the phone on the dashboard. "Grunt worker that I am, you mean?"

"That is . . . definitely not what I said."

"You didn't have to." He pulled into the driveway of his mom's house, turning off the engine and tipping his head back against the seat. "Raising the minimum wage means it's harder for companies to employ people, right?"

"If you can't afford to pay your workers a living wage, you shouldn't have workers in the first place," Meg countered. "Full stop."

"So it's better that those jobs just don't exist at all, then?"

"I'm saying that if your full-time job doesn't pay you enough to make your rent and buy food and go to the doctor, it's not really doing you that much good to begin with."

"Oh really?" Colby asked, sitting up a little straighter. Now he *was* finding her annoying, same as he had the other night when she'd first called him for WeCount, and for the first time all night he heard the edge in his own voice. "Because it *sounds* like what you're saying is that you've never been in the position of having to work whatever shitty-paying job you can get."

Neither of them said anything for a moment. Colby thought he could hear her breathing on the other end of the phone. He could see Tris's spotted snout pressed against the window in the living room, her head turned quizzically to the side like she wanted to know what exactly was keeping him from coming in with her fucking dinner. He told himself one more time that he should probably hang up. "Look, Meg," he said, unbuckling his seat belt. "I—"

"I didn't call you to try and get you to go to the rally," she interrupted, sounding a little breathless. "Just, like . . . for the record, or whatever."

"Oh no?" he asked, reaching for the phone with one hand

and opening the car door with the other. "Then why did you call?"

"I don't know, Colby." Then, more quietly: "To talk to you, I guess."

That stopped him. Colby looked up at the lights in the windows of his mom's house. He thought of the milk getting warm in the back seat. He imagined what the rest of the night would be like if he said goodbye to her right this second, and then he shut himself inside the car one more time.

"Okay," he said, clearing his throat a little. "Then let's talk."

ELEVEN

Meg

Two weeks passed like that, spring blooming pink and green all over the neighborhood: Meg went to school. She hung out with Emily. And every couple of nights she got in bed and called Colby, staying on the phone for two or three hours at a stretch. They talked about all kinds of stuff: his buddy Micah's fruitless quest to get YouTube famous; Annie Hernandez, who Meg kept trying to convince him to Google; how much he hated orange juice, which was a *lot*. She told him stuff she didn't even know she still remembered until she said it out loud, like the late-term miscarriage her mom had when Meg was in first grade or the time she let Anika Cooper take the fall for breaking a vase at Emily's house even though she'd done it herself.

"Little sociopath," Colby teased, the sound of his laugh like a car on the highway.

"It's not funny!" Meg protested. "I feel enormously guilty about it to this day. At junior leadership retreat last year, we had to write a letter to someone we'd wronged in our lives, and I picked her, but she moved away in middle school and doesn't have social media, so I didn't know where to send it."

"You traumatized her," Colby said gravely. "She'll definitely never be YouTube famous, and it's all because of you."

"Oh my God, stop."

"I'm sorry. I think you can let yourself off the hook now."

"I never let myself off the hook for anything," Meg said immediately.

"Yeah," Colby said. "I kind of got that impression." He paused. "Also. Let's talk about how apparently you went to something called *Junior Leadership Retreat*."

It was strange, talking to Colby. She didn't feel like she needed to explain away the ugly parts of stories, or try to tell them in a more normal way to make them seem less weird, like she did when she was talking to Emily or Mason. One night they talked until the sky got light outside her bedroom window. One night they fell asleep on the phone. One night her mom passed out at, like, six thirty, and Colby taught her how to make Egg in a Frame for dinner—her phone on speaker on the counter, Meg using the last clean water glass to cut a careful hole in a slice of whole-wheat bread. It was almost like he was there.

She liked how his voice got low and raspy when he was tired. She liked how sweetly he talked about his mom. She liked the stories he told about the people he worked with—Janine, who ran the garden department with brutal ferocity, plus Joe and Ali, the guys he played Call of Duty with after his shift sometimes. His boss, Moira, was very into jigsaw puzzles—she called it *puzzling*, which Colby found hilarious—and was always telling him he needed a hobby of his own for maximum life enjoyment, so for three nights in a row they tried to figure out what kinds of recreational activities he could potentially pick up. "Phonebanking," Meg suggested immediately, at which point Colby threatened to hang up on her once and for all. "Oil pastels. Camping, maybe."

To her surprise, Colby didn't laugh at that one: "I could do camping," he said, seeming to consider it.

"I'd go camping with you," Meg said.

"Really?" Colby asked, sounding suddenly interested. "Have you ever been camping?"

"No," Meg admitted, even though it probably confirmed some deeply held suspicion about her on his part. "But I would, maybe."

They were quiet for a moment. Colby cleared his throat. "How was the monster movie?" he asked, and just like that his voice was back to normal again. It was Friday night, late; she'd been getting into her pajamas when he called, and she'd pulled her T-shirt over her head as she answered, wondering weirdly if he could somehow tell she wasn't wearing a bra.

Now she hummed, noncommittal. "We didn't see it, in the end."

"What happened?"

"Emily wanted to see that heist thing instead." She shrugged, even though he couldn't see her. "It's fine, though. I'll see it when it comes on demand."

"Can I ask you something?" Colby said, then didn't wait for her to answer. "Why are you so terrified of your friend Emily?"

"What?" Meg frowned, sitting up and picking at some chipping polish on her toenail. "I'm not terrified of Emily."

"Okay," Colby said.

"I'm not," she insisted, but it sounded a little too whiny to be convincing. "Why do you think I'm terrified of Emily?"

Colby made an *I don't know* sound. "It's just, you seem to know your mind about everything else in the world, but whenever you talk about her it's like, *Emily says we should do this, Emily doesn't like it that way*, or whatever."

That surprised her, and not in a good way. "She's my best friend."

"I know," Colby said easily. "I'm not trying to shit-stir."

"Aren't you?"

"No," he said, and the truth was, it actually didn't seem like he was. It hardly ever felt like Colby was deliberately provoking her, actually. It was more like the most annoying possible thing just came naturally out of his mouth at any given moment.

Meg thought about it. "Her opinion matters to me," she said finally, although even as the words came out it occurred to her that that wasn't the only answer. "And I don't like starting fights, I don't know."

"Oh really, you don't?" Colby snorted. "Could have fooled me."

"Shut up," Meg shot back. "That's different."

"Starting fights with me?"

"Yes."

"And why's that?"

Meg's skin got warm and prickly, like she was wearing itchy wool pajamas instead of boxers and an *I'm With Her* T-shirt. "I don't know," she said again. "Shut up. It just is."

"Okay." To her surprise, Colby actually dropped it. "What are you doing this weekend?" he asked instead.

"Homework, mostly," Meg said, glancing at the pile of books stacked on her desk. "I've got a couple of projects due next week. And tomorrow I'm going to a postcard-writing party at the library."

"I'm sorry," Colby said, the smile audible in his voice. "A what now?"

"A postcard-writing party," Meg said patiently, already knowing where this was headed. "You go and you all write postcards to your representatives encouraging them to take positions on issues that are important to you."

"Ah," Colby said seriously.

Meg rolled her eyes. "Go ahead," she told him. "Say it."

"I'm not saying anything."

"You think it's stupid, I know."

"I don't think it's stupid. A little naïve, maybe."

"Oh, okay," Meg said, stretching her legs out in front of her on the mattress. "So it's not that I'm a moron, objectively. It's just that I don't know any better."

"Easy, tiger," Colby said easily. "Nobody's calling you a moron. Least of all me. I just . . . think the prescription on your rose-colored glasses is very strong to think that's an effective use of your evening, that's all." He hesitated for a moment; she tried to picture him at home in his bedroom, wondered if he was lying down. "I know you're out to change the world here, Meg. But the reality is that most things—and most people, and their lives—stay exactly the same no matter what."

Meg sighed. She hated when Colby got like this. She'd go days at a time thinking he was listening to what she was saying, that maybe she was even starting to change his mind, and then something like this would come out of his mouth and it was like they were right back where they started that very first night she called him from WeCount. "So what, then?" she asked. "You just fully don't believe in, like—"

"The American Dream?" Colby laughed. "No, Meg, I do not believe in the American Dream."

"Not the American *Dream*," Meg protested, huffing a bit. "God, you make me sound like somebody's crusty old grandma who's like, *Pull yourself up by your bootstraps, sonny.* I'm just saying that of course I think it's possible for things to get better—or for people to improve their circumstances, if they have the right resources and help."

"And you're going to help them?"

"I mean, I hope so, yes."

"By writing letters to your congressman and spending the next four years at a college in the middle of nowhere full of people exactly like you because you're too afraid to tell Emily you don't want to go?"

Meg blinked, momentarily stunned into silence. "Wow," she said, all four of her limbs gone hot and prickly. "Been sitting on that one for a while, have you?"

"I'm sorry," Colby said immediately. "That was over the line."

"A little bit." Meg scrubbed a hand through her hair, feeling, stupidly, like she might be about to cry. Colby was still the only person who knew she'd gotten in to begin with—she'd been super vague every time Emily asked about it, which was basically every day, especially since other people had started to hear from schools the last couple of weeks—and she didn't need him of all people throwing the whole thing in her face.

"I'm being an asshole," he said. "I didn't mean it."

"Sure you did," Meg said crisply. "You might as well admit it, Colby. I mean, you basically already did, so."

"It's just . . ." Colby sighed. "I'm sorry. You're so smart, that's all. And, I don't know, you going to some expensive school you're not even excited about just because that's what everybody expects you to do and it's easier than making things awkward is just . . ." He trailed off. "Like, if you actually do want to go change things, if you actually think you *can*, then shouldn't you, like . . . go out there and change them?"

"You're being extremely mansplainy right now, you realize."

"I do, yeah." Colby let out another sigh, deeper this time "I'm going to quit while I'm behind." He was quiet for a moment. "Are you mad at me?"

"A little," Meg said, squeezing her eyes shut and telling herself he had no idea what he was talking about. He was in a crap mood, that was all. He was being obnoxious.

She opened her eyes again, frustrated, her restless gaze skating over the friendly detritus of her cluttered bedroom: the framed photo of her and Emily at last year's student council car wash, the *BUILD BRIDGES NOT WALLS* sign tacked to the bulletin board above her desk. She'd gotten it on her first real date with Mason, the two of them taking SEPTA into the city to go to an immigration protest down at Love Park. It had been a million degrees outside even though it was halfway through October, the midday sun beating down and her shoulders red and blistering. The back of Mason's T-shirt had darkened with sweat. Meg kept waiting for him to complain, or suggest they take off, but he never did, not even when the all-female drum circle played for the better part of forty-five minutes. Instead, he'd gotten her a popsicle from a guy selling them out of a cooler, her hand still sticky with fruit juice when he'd taken it in the delicious air-conditioned chill of the train back home.

Mason would never question her decision to go to Cornell with Emily, she thought sulkily. Mason would never put her through the uncertainty of wondering if possibly he might have a point. She *didn't* want to go to Cornell, not really. It *was* the path of the least resistance. But it wasn't exactly like she had some other brilliant plan.

Finally, Colby cleared his throat. "Hey," he said, "what's your email?"

Meg gave it to him, opening her laptop and clicking over to Gmail; a few moments later, a message from him popped up. "Click the link," Colby instructed.

Meg frowned. "Is this, like, a virus that's going to download a bunch of terrifying porn to my computer?"

"You think I would send you a terrifying porn virus?"

"No, but—"

"Thanks a lot."

"Sorry, sorry. Here I go." She clicked it. It was a link to

a streaming site that did admittedly look a little bit sketchy, featuring the very monster movie she'd wanted to see earlier tonight. He must have searched it while she was talking. Colby was actually really good at computer stuff—he'd taught himself how to use some complicated design software, and he'd just mentioned it like it was no big deal, but when she'd Googled it she'd realized it was what actual architects used. "This is totally against the law, isn't it?"

"Oh my God." Colby snorted. "Do you want to watch it or not?"

"Do you want to watch it with me?" she asked, and held her breath until he answered.

"Sure," Colby said. "Why not?"

"Guess who got into Colgate!" Emily announced when Meg showed up in the senior lounge on Monday morning. She and Mason were sitting on one of the big couches, Adrienne perched on the arm with a giant iced coffee from Wawa in her hand. "Fancy Mason Lee, that's who."

"Mase!" Meg grinned. "Yeah, you did!" She hugged him before she could think better of it, both of them breaking apart a little awkwardly. Still, she was happy for him, she realized, in a way she probably wouldn't have been able to muster up even a couple of weeks ago. "Seriously, that's great."

"You're going to be right down the road from us," Emily said, breaking a KIND bar in half and taking a delicate bite.

"We can all meet up on the weekends, drive home together at Thanksgiving." She leaned back and flicked at Adrienne's coffee cup, the ice rattling. "Ade, you can come up from Skidmore all the time."

"You realize I still haven't heard from Cornell," Meg lied, shifting her weight on the terrazzo. Even as she said it, she felt like a cowardly idiot—after all, she wasn't exactly going to be able to kick this can down the road forever—but still she couldn't make herself tell them the truth. "It's entirely possible I won't get in and you guys will have to go have your western New York state liberal arts adventures without me."

"Are you kidding me?" Emily shook her curly head, all confidence. "You worry too much." She nudged Mason in the shoulder. "Tell her she worries too much."

"You worry too much," Mason parroted obediently.

Meg huffed a laugh. "Thanks." She had assumed it would make things weird in their friend group, her and Mason breaking up, but if anything, Emily and Mason seemed to be getting along better lately. Meg wasn't actually sure if she was okay with that or not.

"So are you definitely going to go?" Adrienne asked Mason, boosting herself up off the arm of the sofa and tossing her cup into the recycling bin in the corner. Adrienne had transferred in from St. Catherine's two years ago after all that creepy stuff had come out about their monsignor. She spoke three languages, wore her white-blond hair in an immaculate French braid every single day, and had the dirtiest sense of humor Meg had ever heard.

"I still have to hear from Fairfield," Mason said, "but yeah, probably. Honestly, I'm just glad to be getting in anywhere. When Colgate first put me on the wait list, I started to get worried I'd get rejected from all the schools I applied to and have to, like, go work as a picker in one of those Amazon facilities where they don't give you any breaks, so you have to pee in a soda bottle and leave it in a corner."

Meg winced. She knew what Mason meant—of course she knew what Mason meant, even if in reality there had never been even the tiniest possibility of him not getting into college, on top of which his parents had the kind of money that pretty much guaranteed he was never going to have to work any job he didn't like—but she couldn't help thinking of Colby. What would he say if he heard that the most horrifying future Meg's friends could imagine didn't look that different from his? Not the peeing-in-a-bottle part—she hoped not, in any case—but still. "There are worse things than working in an Amazon warehouse," she chided gently.

"Working in the Triangle Shirtwaist Factory, for instance," Emily joked. "Now, what are we going to do to celebrate?"

Meg tugged at her lip, wanting to contradict them. She thought she *would* have contradicted them, once upon a time:

back before her parents split up, before fighting—of any kind, but especially the public variety—started to feel so deeply dangerous. She didn't like this version of herself, the one who was too afraid to tell her friends when they were being sort of dickish for fear of starting an argument. The one who held a little bit of herself back all the time.

Except, of course, with Colby.

Who she couldn't even properly defend.

"I've gotta go to my locker," she said, slinging her backpack up over her shoulder and feeling like the worst kind of coward. "Congrats again, Mase."

"Thanks, dude!" he called back, all boy-king smiles. Meg closed her eyes.

Her car was six weeks overdue for its inspection—her dad always used to take care of that stuff, back when her parents were together, and she and her mom weren't great about remembering—and the following week Meg finally got her act together and dropped it off at the mechanic, which meant she had to walk home from school after seventh period. Normally, she would have gotten a ride with Emily, but Emily had a dentist appointment and had taken off early that afternoon, on top of which Meg had gotten an acceptance letter and scholarship offer from Temple the other day, which meant Emily had been on her all week to call Cornell and find out why she hadn't heard from them yet. "How are you not freaking out about this?" she'd asked Meg today, over lunch at the hipster salad place. Meg had shoved a forkful of arugula into her mouth and mumbled something about rolling admissions.

The whole thing was ridiculous; it was beyond ridiculous, really.

But that didn't mean Meg had any idea what to do about it.

She was only about half a block from school when a car pulled up beside her, its driver honking the horn a little obnoxiously. When she turned, she saw it was Mason in his bright orange Forester. "Hey," he said, rolling down the passenger-side window. "You need a ride?"

Meg blinked at him for a second, remembering all at once why she'd fallen for him in the first place, with his messy black hair and his million different podcast subscriptions and his one crooked canine tooth because he hadn't worn his retainer after he got his braces off. Still, as she stood there in the afternoon sunlight she was surprised to realize she could remember the not-so-good things now, too: how annoyingly competitive the two of them got about grades in the classes they shared with each other, and how he could be a little bit of a snob. Maybe Emily was right: maybe it *hadn't* actually been a love connection to begin with. If given the choice, Meg thought for the first time since he'd broken up with her outside Cavelli's, she didn't actually think she'd want Mason back.

Still, it wasn't exactly like she was looking forward to hoofing it all the way home, so she opened the door and settled herself in the passenger seat. "Sure," she said. "Thanks."

"So what's up with you, hm?" Mason asked as he pulled out into traffic. The car smelled the same: like the inside of a Starbucks. On the stereo was Fleet Foxes, who they'd seen last year downtown. A half-eaten PowerBar she'd bought and forgotten about before spring break still nestled in the door niche on the passenger side. It was weird to think that PowerBar had outlasted their relationship. "I feel like we haven't talked in a while."

That's kind of the point of breaking up with someone, right? Meg thought but didn't say. "Just been busy, I guess."

Mason nodded. "Avery keeps asking about you," he confessed. Avery was Mason's little sister, a viola player with a mouth full of braces who, improbably, had become one of the most popular girls in her grade by writing excessively overwrought fanfiction about a series of fantasy books that none of her classmates could get enough of.

"Aww," Meg said. "Tell her I miss her, too."

Outside her house the lawn was still winter scrubby, last fall's dead leaves clogging up the gutters. One shutter on the upstairs window was coming loose. The garbage cans had blown over in the driveway, rolling back and forth a bit like a pair of athletes injured on the field. Meg glanced over at Mason, hoping he hadn't noticed. "Thanks for the ride," she said.

"Yeah, no problem." Mason took a deep breath, long fingers curling around the steering wheel like he was gathering his courage. "Listen, Meg," he said, the words coming out in such a rush they nearly jumbled together. "You're, like . . . good, right?"

Meg laughed a little, not entirely sure what he was getting at. "Yeah, Mase," she promised. "I'm good."

"I mean, you *seem* good," he clarified quickly. "I don't mean to imply—I mean, I didn't think—I guess I just want to make sure you're not, like . . ." He trailed off.

Meg raised her eyebrows. "Crying into my pillow over you every night?" she supplied.

"What? No!" Mason's smooth cheeks turned pink. "Well . . ." He hesitated. "Sort of, I guess."

Meg snorted; she couldn't help it. "No, Mason," she promised patiently. "I am not crying into my pillow over you every night."

"Okay," Mason said, nodding so hard in agreement Meg was surprised his head didn't pop clean off. "I'm glad."

There was no reason for her to think about Colby just then, the bluntness of his questions and the grumble of his voice in her ear. They were friends, that was all—and maybe they weren't even that much. Not to mention the fact that they'd never actually *met*. And if he knew more about her than anyone else in her real life—if he was, possibly, a big part of why her relationship with Mason didn't feel like such a giant loss anymore—well, then that was nobody's business but her own.

"Thanks again, dude," she said now, shaking her head to clear it. "I'll see you around, okay?"

"See you," Mason echoed. Meg tapped the window once with her fingernails before she turned and went inside.

TWELVE

Meg

That night's shift at WeCount was uneventful, mostly. Lillian brought cupcakes Maja had made: a pineapple situation topped with coconut buttercream. Rico's ancient handset inexplicably started emitting a high-pitched, extraterrestrial-sounding squeal. Meg got three voters registered, though, which was a pretty good night, all told, and she was feeling sort of pleased with herself by the time she logged out of the system and headed downstairs.

Her car hadn't been ready at the mechanic's that afternoon, so her mom had dropped her off at work and promised to pick her up later, though she wasn't waiting when Meg and Lillian got down to the quiet, empty street. "I can hang out until she gets here," Lillian said, tucking her hands in the back pockets of the dark-wash men's jeans she always wore. Intricate tattoos of vibrant plants and wildflowers snaked up both of her pale arms.

Meg shook her head. "You don't have to do that," she protested. She remembered this feeling from birthday parties when she was little: that faint anxiety that nobody was going to pick her up at all and she'd be stuck at Funtime Arcade for all eternity, forced to disinfect the ball pits to pay for room and board. "She'll be here in a minute."

"It's cool, Meg," Lillian said with a smile. "I don't mind."

"No, I know, I just don't want you to have to—oh," Meg said, catching sight of her mom's Volvo jerking to a sudden stop at the red light on the corner. "See, there she is. Thanks, though."

"Anytime," Lillian said, holding her ring of keys up in a salute before turning in the direction of the tidy little Volkswagen she and Maja shared. "See you."

Meg waved back, frowning a bit as the light turned green and her mom stepped hard on the gas, speeding halfway down the block before braking close enough to the curb in front of the designer home-goods shop that the front tire of the car scraped against the concrete. "Hey," she said, opening the door and setting her bag on the floor of the passenger seat, then wrinkling her nose: the inside of the car smelled, not faintly, of booze.

"Are you *drunk*?" she blurted before she could stop herself. She'd never said the word out loud in this context before; it landed between them like a dead toad falling out of the sky.

"What?" Her mom whipped around to look at her, squinting across the interior of the car. "No! Of course not."

"Really?" Meg raised her eyebrows, fingers curled tightly around the top of the door. "Are you sure?"

Her mom's eyes narrowed. "You can keep the attitude, thank you. Come on, get in the car."

Meg didn't budge. "Mom, seriously," she said. "How much did you drink before you came here?"

"I'm not—you're not the parent here, Meg," her mom informed her crisply. "I had a glass of wine at home, not that I have to justify it to you."

"You're lying." Meg couldn't believe her. She couldn't believe this was actually happening, here on the street in front of WeCount and not in a movie on the Hallmark channel. "Mom, seriously? Give me the keys."

"Okay, enough now." Her mom waved both hands, like she was trying to swat away a sudden swarm of gnats. "You're being ridiculous. I'm not going to tell you again."

"Hey!" someone called behind them. When Meg turned around, Lillian was standing at her own car across the street in front of the real estate office, her giant key ring still dangling from one hand. "You guys okay?"

"We're great," Meg promised, pasting a wide, *please don't ask any more questions* smile on her face. "Just headed out. See you next week, yeah?"

Lillian gazed at them for a moment longer. "You sure?" she

asked, a little more quietly this time. Something about the way she said it made Meg think she probably could have told her the truth. Still, the specter of a public scene—the idea of her mom losing it in front of Lillian, or worse, *at* her, had Meg nodding frantically.

"Yep!" she insisted, still smiling like a maniac. "Have a good night!" She walked around to the other side of the Volvo, wrenching open the driver's door. Her mom was a person she needed to protect herself from, she realized, and as soon as she had that thought, her eyes filled with tears. "*Mom*," she said, low and urgent. "Come on."

Her mom huffed. "Fine, Meg," she snapped, yanking the keys out of the ignition and thrusting them in Meg's direction before unbuckling her seat belt and shoving past her onto the blacktop. "Move, then, so I can get out." She kept one hand on the car as she made her way to the passenger side—steadying herself?—before flouncing in and slamming the door with enough force that Meg could feel it in her molars. "There," her mom said. "Are you happy?"

"Yeah, Mom." Meg yanked the seat belt so hard it locked before she could get it all the way around herself; she tugged again, twice more, before giving up and letting go. "I'm great."

Back at the house, her mom got out of the car and stalked inside without saying anything. Meg stared after her for a moment, tilting her head back against the seat. Upstairs, she changed into her pajamas and curled up in bed, then picked up her phone and texted Colby. *Are you around?*

He called her back four minutes later. "What about ceramics?" he asked when she answered. "Ceramics is a hobby, right?"

Meg laughed, but then the laugh turned into something else halfway out and suddenly she was terrified she was going to start crying and never, ever stop. She sucked in a quick breath, but it was ragged as torn denim, and Colby heard. "Hey," he said. "You okay?"

"Yeah," she said automatically, but the stupidity of lying to Colby was obvious as soon as she opened her mouth. "No," she amended, and just like that the whole story was spilling out of her like wine from a knocked-over glass. He listened without saying anything, so quiet on the other end of the line that twice Meg interrupted herself to ask if he was still there.

"That sucks," he said, when she was finally finished. "I'm really sorry."

"Yeah," she said, crawling under the covers with her phone jammed between her ear and her shoulder. "It totally sucks."

"Is she an alcoholic, you think?"

"I—*no*," Meg said immediately, startled by the word in the same way she'd been surprised to hear herself say *drunk* earlier tonight. Alcoholics were red-faced and strawberry-nosed, weren't they? They snuck vodka out of plastic bottles they kept hidden in their coat pockets and slumped over stools in dive bars at ten o'clock in the morning.

They show up drunk to get their kids from work, a nasty voice in Meg's head added.

She pushed it away. "She's just still sad about my dad, that's all," she insisted. "And she hates her boring job, and she and my dad never really had a ton of friends. I think she just doesn't know what to do with herself, that's all." Then, in a feeble attempt to muster a joke: "Maybe she needs a hobby, too."

Colby didn't laugh. "Okay," he said. "You'd know better than I would." He didn't sound convinced, really, but the nice thing was how she didn't actually feel like she *needed* to convince him. He wasn't going to judge her either way. "Can you talk to your dad?" he asked.

"I don't know." Meg tucked one arm behind her head, staring up at the ceiling. "I feel so protective of her. I don't want him to find out."

"I mean, sure," Colby said. "But somebody's got to be protective of *you*, right?"

The way he said it made Meg's stomach do a thing, sharp and sudden; just for a second, she let herself wonder what he looked like when he slept. "Yeah," she said finally, gazing out at the dark nothingness of her bedroom. "I guess you're right." Ugh, she didn't want to talk about this anymore. Dealing with her mom lately felt like walking down a long hallway with a door at the end, like a scene from a low-budget horror movie; somewhere in the back of her most secret mind she knew that eventually she was going to have to open it, but whatever was back there was going to be bad and scary and she didn't want to do it just yet. "Tell me about your night," she said instead.

"My night?" Colby yawned a little bit, just quiet; Meg wondered if he was in bed, too. "It was low-key. Hung out with some friends. Gotta work early tomorrow."

Meg glanced at the moon outside the window. Colby's friends were a mystery to her. Most times he talked about them, they sounded like a bunch of boneheads—and like he *thought* they were a bunch of boneheads—but she wasn't entirely sure if he was describing them that way on purpose or not, and she didn't want to say the wrong thing and accidentally sound like a snob. "I was thinking about what you said about them cutting your overtime, actually," she said. "I was listening to this thing on NPR—"

"Something new and different for you," Colby interrupted.

Meg frowned into the dark. She knew he was just joking around—that she was tired, and keyed up, and probably extra sensitive—but something about the way he said it, maybe a little snidely, bothered her. "What does that mean?"

"Nothing," Colby said. "Easy. It's just that most of your news-related anecdotes start that way, that's all. I was kidding."

"So what?" Meg sat up in bed. "What's wrong with NPR?"

"So nothing," Colby said. "It's just . . ." He trailed off.

"If you say *fake news*, I'm going to hang up on you right now."

"I'm not saying fake anything!" Colby laughed, though it

sounded slightly strangled. "Can you let me talk? I'm just saying that NPR has an agenda, just like every other news outlet in America."

"The agenda is reporting the actual news."

"You say that because you agree with what they're saying."

"I say that because it's verifiably true."

"Maybe," Colby said easily, "but when was the last time you actually verified? I'm not saying I disagree with their reporting, even. I'm just saying that if you're accepting whatever you hear on there without checking for yourself, then I don't see how you have more of a leg to stand on than my mom when she talks about something she saw on Fox News."

"Your mom watches Fox News?"

Colby blew a breath out. "What if she does, Meg? Who gives a shit?"

Meg cringed—she couldn't help it—swallowing down a dozen different equally nasty responses. God, sometimes she could go whole conversations without thinking about what ridiculously different universes she and Colby lived in, but every time she remembered, she couldn't help but wonder where either one of them thought this was going. Meg didn't know if that made her silly or realistic. "I mean, *I* give a shit," she said finally. "And if she does, I might encourage her to verify her facts, just like you oh-so-helpfully reminded me to do tonight."

"Don't be mad," Colby said, softening. "I know you had a

sucky night; I'm not trying to fight with you. I'm just playing devil's advocate; you know that."

"Oh, come on." Meg hated that expression. "The devil can advocate for himself, don't you think?"

"Clever," Colby said, in a voice like he didn't think it was, really. He was quiet for a moment; she could hear his getting-ready-for-bed noises in the background, water running and a door clicking shut. "Can I ask you a question?" he asked finally, bedsprings creaking—he definitely was in bed, then. "Like, obviously you don't fight like this with your friend Emily. But do you do it with anybody else besides me?"

"Nope," Meg said, no hesitation.

"Not even Mason?"

It surprised her that he was asking—she'd only mentioned Mason in passing a couple of times—and she tugged at her lip for a moment before she answered, even though she didn't have to think about it. She and Mason had bickered some when they'd first started dating—the kind of good-natured debates that felt natural as breathing back before everything exploded with her parents—but after that the waters had been perfectly, mercifully calm. In fact, the closest they'd ever come was at a party Adrienne had thrown over February break a few weeks before they'd broken up: Mason had been a total grouch for no discernable reason, complaining about everything from the music on Javi's playlist to the burritos they'd picked up at Chipotle on the way over, which had been his idea to begin with.

Meg remembered how uneasy she'd been all night at the prospect of a looming fight, how she'd done her best to ignore the fact that it was happening, and her relief when it had blown over without ever coming to a head. She still had no idea what his problem had been. "No, actually," she said at last. "You're the only one."

Colby laughed at that. "I'm so honored."

"Take it as a compliment," she teased, settling back against the pillows. "I'm totally honest with you."

"Yeah, that's because I'm not impressive enough for you to actually care what I think."

"Wait, what?" She'd thought they were winding down, but just like that, Meg was sitting up again, adrenaline surging through her veins. "That's not true."

"Isn't it?"

"No, Colby. It's not." Her voice was steady, somehow, but even as the words came out she wondered if maybe he had a point. Did she tell him everything, even the bad parts, because she trusted him? Or did she tell him everything—even the bad parts—because the stakes were so low? She didn't want to think about it.

"Can I ask *you* a question?" she said, hating the feeling of being on the defensive and wanting to turn the tables as quick as she could. "Does anybody in your real life even know about me?"

"I—what?" Colby asked. "What does that have to do with anything?"

"I'm just asking." Meg raised her eyebrows even though he couldn't see her. "If we're talking about whose opinion is or isn't important, or whatever."

Colby didn't answer for so long Meg thought he might have fallen asleep right in the middle of their argument. Then he sighed. "I mean," he said, so quietly she almost didn't hear him. "What is there to know?"

"I—" Meg broke off, her whole body getting unpleasantly hot as the utter stupidity of this whole bizarre episode caught up to her all at once: Arguing politics and TV and life philosophies with some lonely, random stranger. Caring so deeply about a relationship that didn't even exist anywhere but in some invisible signal stretching over state lines. "That's a good question, I guess." She felt like she might be about to cry again, which was ridiculous: after all, it was just Colby. He *wasn't* impressive enough to care about, and as soon as she had that thought she felt about two inches tall. "I should go," she said suddenly.

"Meg," he said—and she thought he sounded a little panicky all of a sudden, though she might have been imagining it. Her head was getting fuzzy. She wanted to go to sleep. "I didn't mean—"

"No, it's fine," she said. "It's just late, that's all. I've got school in the morning. And you said yourself you've got to work."

"No, I know, but—"

"I'll talk to you soon," she said, then hung up before he could answer. She shoved the phone underneath her pillow before she started to cry.

THIRTEEN

Colby

Micah's brother had a night game on Thursday, so they all trekked out to the municipal field to see him play. Colby had pitched in high school—he hadn't been particularly good at it, just like he hadn't been particularly good at much in high school—but he'd always kind of liked being out there, the lazy hum of cicadas and the smell of the grass thick in the air. The thing about being done with school was that summer wasn't that different from any other time of the year, but Colby secretly found himself looking forward to it anyway, like Pavlov's dogs conditioned for the sound of the bell.

A month and some change till the anniversary, he remembered suddenly, with a hot rush of shame as he realized he hadn't even really thought about it the last couple of weeks, he'd been so distracted with . . . other stuff. Colby scrubbed a hand through his hair, yanking a little. Jesus Christ, what the fuck did he think he was looking forward to, exactly?

Still, he had to admit it was a pretty night, the spring trees finally getting greenish and the setting sun slipping underneath the clouds in a way that made it look like they were glowing inside like hot coals. He would have taken a picture and sent it to Meg—she liked stuff like that, he'd noticed; was forever sending him snaps of the expensive salads she ate for lunch or a weird-looking dog she saw on her way to get coffee—except for the fact that he was pretty sure whatever he and Meg were doing was officially—or unofficially, he guessed, since they hadn't actually talked about it—finished after last night.

Colby sighed, leaning back on his elbows on the bleachers. It had come out wrong, what he'd said to her, which didn't change the fact that he thought his original question was valid. He wasn't a total idiot. He knew he was some kind of small-town novelty as far as Meg was concerned—her very own redneck whetstone, useful for keeping her ideological knives sharp until she finally got over whatever she was so fucking afraid of and disappeared back to wherever she'd come from. It was a temporary diversion, that was all. What did she want him to do, casually drop it into conversation with Jordan and Micah that he spent three nights a week arguing politics over the phone with some rich girl who'd originally called his house trying to convince his dead father to do his civic duty? What exactly would be the point of trying to explain something like that, especially when there was less than zero chance of it turning into anything real?

Not that Colby *wanted* it to turn into anything real.

He just meant—

Whatever.

Finally, he dug his phone out of his pocket and took the picture anyway, hitting send before he could talk himself out of it. *Thinking about trying out for the minors if my illustrious career in box moving doesn't work out*, he typed, figuring if he acted like things hadn't gone south between them at the end there, maybe she'd forget they kind of had. *How's your night?*

He closed out his messages app, though not before he caught sight of the unanswered text from Joanna from that morning. He'd run into her in the CVS parking lot yesterday afternoon, and they'd wound up standing outside her car talking for the better part of half an hour—about her cousin's bachelorette party and the new Target going in by the middle school, the chilly breeze blowing her cloud of yellow hair in every direction. This morning, his phone had chimed early, while he was getting ready for work: *We should run into each other on purpose sometime, Colby Moran.* He hadn't texted back, and he didn't know why, except for the part where he kind of did know.

A whetstone, he reminded himself, already wishing he hadn't sent that stupid picture. It wasn't going anywhere at all.

Dusk fell, the sky going blue and then a deep, velvety purple, a sliver of moon appearing like a thumbnail behind the trees. "We should go camping this summer," Colby heard himself say.

"What?" Jordan snorted. "Since when do you know anything about camping?"

Colby shrugged. "I could learn."

"Sure you could," Micah put in, pulling a plastic Coke bottle Colby thought was probably mostly rum out of his backpack and offering it around. Then, in a deep newscaster voice: "Locals who have no fucking idea what they're doing torn limb from limb in bear attack."

"There are no bears around here," Jordan said.

"Fuck yeah, there are bears around here!" Micah said. Finding no takers for his backpack cocktail, he shrugged, downing most of it himself in one long swig. "Don't you remember they caught one lumbering around behind the China Star last summer? Deforestation, man."

Colby tuned them out, vaguely sorry he'd said anything to begin with. He dug his phone out of his pocket in spite of himself to see if Meg had texted back, which she hadn't. She had her carnival thing tonight, he remembered suddenly—a fund raiser for something or other, which seemed kind of ridiculous considering how much her fancy private school probably cost. Still, she'd sounded so excited about the whole thing that it was hard not to be a little bit charmed by the idea, even if whenever he tried to picture it all he could think about was the last scene of *Grease*, when they all sing a song and the car flies up into the clouds.

He checked his phone again at the top of the third inning, then again at the bottom of the fifth. "What are you doing?" Jordan asked from the bleacher above him, kicking him gently in the side.

"Buying Bitcoin," Colby said automatically, shoving his phone back into his pocket and telling himself to stop being such a mopey little pissant. So much for her not remembering they'd argued, he guessed.

"They're playing like total bitches out there," Micah complained, turning his cap around backward and scratching his knee through the fray in his jeans. Colby winced, knowing exactly what Meg would say if she heard him talking like that. *Casual sexism denotes a lack of creativity*, probably, plus some statistic about Mo'ne Davis that she kept in her back pocket for occasions exactly like this.

There was no point in thinking about Meg.

He got some sketchy fluorescent nachos from the concession stand. He talked to some stoners he knew from school. He actually sat still and watched the game for a while, but Micah was right—they *were* playing like total bitches, or whatever the nonoffensive version of *total bitches* was, and the longer he sat there with his silent phone heavy in his pocket, the more it felt like some kind of gorge was opening up inside his rib cage, the kind of physical sensation he'd taught himself to stop having after his dad died and didn't fucking appreciate now. He was *lonely*, he realized suddenly, as a direct result of having a stunted, long-distance non-love affair with some spoiled princess from the fucking Main Line that was probably over now before it had even started. The thought of it was so embarrassing Colby actually looked around to make sure nobody had noticed, that it wasn't somehow being broadcast on a neon sign hovering above his head.

"Let's go, Jakey!" Micah yelled as his brother came up to bat, cupping his hands around his mouth and hooting. Colby blew a breath out and nudged him in the arm.

"Hey," he said. "You got any of that Coke left?"

"Sure do," Micah said, offering it to him with a flourish; Colby took a long gulp, wincing at the sweet chemical burn.

"Geez, dude," Jordan said. "Easy."

Colby ignored him, raising his eyebrows at Micah for permission before finishing off the bottle.

By the top of the ninth, he was in a truly terrible fucking mood. What the hell was he thinking to begin with, texting this girl a picture of the fucking sunset like he thought he was some kind of twenty-first-century Walt Whitman? They hardly knew each other. She didn't owe him anything. She was probably out having a life.

Just like he should be.

Colby picked his phone up again, scrolled through his

contacts until he got to Joanna's name. Her text from this morning was still waiting there, calm and familiar as Joanna herself.

*We *should* run into each other on purpose*, he typed, then gnawed his thumbnail for one second longer before nutting up and hitting send. *What are you up to tomorrow night?*

FOURTEEN

Meg

"What can I get you?" Meg asked a gaggle of sophomores, pulling a square of waxed paper from the box on the folding table and trying to sound more enthusiastic than she felt. She was working the doughnut booth tonight, which in reality just meant reselling the two hundred doughnuts Overbrook's student council had gotten donated from the artisan place in town and trying to convince Harrison Lithwick, who was assigned to the booth with her, not to pick all the sprinkles off the chocolate frosted ones like a disgusting monster.

Normally, the carnival was one of Meg's favorite days of the year—the optimism of it, maybe, the smell of cotton candy thick in the air, and the parking lot lit up in pinks and greens and purples. It was an Overbrook tradition, with the seniors all taking shifts at the game and concession booths and all the proceeds going to a rec center in Philly. The teachers took turns in the dunk tank. The dance team and a cappella group both did sets.

Tonight, though, Meg felt as sour as the lemonade Emily was selling on the other side of the parking lot. She'd been in a bad mood since she'd gotten here, wincing at the too-loud music blaring over the sound system, scowling at the over-dressed freshman girls shuffling along the midway even though she knew it made her a bad feminist—and trying, with limited success, not to check her phone every five minutes to see if Colby had texted.

He hadn't.

Not that she expected him to, really.

But she'd hoped.

Meg sighed, setting some more doughnuts out on the table and shooting Harrison a look as he swooped in for a sample. She knew Colby thought she was a ridiculous person, some spoiled duchess who sauntered around in a hermetically sealed bubble and had no idea how the world actually worked. And yeah, he was impossible sometimes—infuriating, even, in ways Meg wasn't entirely sure she'd ever be able to overlook. Still, she'd thought they'd come to some kind of unspoken agreement, all those nights on the telephone. She'd even—God, this was embarrassing—thought maybe they were sort of flirting. It sucked to realize it hadn't meant anything to him at all.

She was making change for a sophomore on the swim team when Emily trotted up to the side of the line. "How's it going?" she asked, ponytail swishing cheerfully. Then, frowning across the booth: "Harrison, dude, seriously. That's so gross."

Meg snorted, wiping her sticky palms on the back of her jeans. "It's been going pretty much like that, actually." Then she grinned, buoyed by the sight of Em in her skinny jeans and student council hoodie, a pair of hearts in Overbrook blue and yellow painted on each of her cheeks. "You're not working?"

Emily shook her head. "Industry downturn in the lemonade business," she said solemnly. "They cut me loose. What about you? Done soon?"

Meg glanced at the clock on her phone, trying to ignore the sinking sensation in her stomach when she saw there still wasn't anything from Colby. God, she needed to get a life. "Another couple of hours," she reported. "Mason was floating around here somewhere, though, if you're looking for company. He doesn't have a shift until tomorrow."

"Yeah, he said something about that." Emily nodded, frowning a little. "Are you okay?" she asked quietly. "Like, besides the inherent personal trauma of being stuck in a confined space with sprinkle-snarfer over there?"

Meg laughed. "I'm okay," she lied.

"Are you sure?" Emily pressed gently. "You look sad."

"I do?" Meg shook her head, weirdly surprised that Em had

noticed, which was dumb—after all, they always knew when stuff was going on with each other. She remembered the weeks after her parents split, when Emily had prowled around her like a lioness protecting a wounded cub, somehow able to magically intuit exactly what Meg needed at any given moment: a cliché and vaguely antifeminist rom-com watched in silence, the gross but admittedly satisfying distraction of a pore strip, a midnight trip to the Sonic drive-thru for cherry limeade and deep-fried mac and cheese balls. Occasionally, she'd needed all three at once. "I'm good," she promised now, pulling a fresh cider doughnut from one of the boxes and handing it to Em on the sly. "I mean, I'll be better when I no longer have to stand here and bear direct witness to Harrison breaking every health and safety code in the Commonwealth of Pennsylvania, but generally fine."

Emily nodded, like *Fair point.* "Listen," she said, breaking the doughnut in two and handing half of it back so they could share, "will you come find me if you've got time to talk later?"

"What, tonight?" Meg felt her eyebrows crawl. "Yeah, why? You sound like Mason." She grinned. "You're not going to break up with me, too, are you?"

Emily's eyes went saucer-wide. "What? No! I just—" She rocked back on her heels a bit, shaking her head. "Of course not. Like—you know you're literally my favorite person in the entire universe, right?"

Meg frowned. "Of course I do. You're mine." She looked at Emily carefully. Did she know somehow? Had she been able to magically intuit that Meg was second-guessing the plan? It was only a matter of time, probably; they knew each other way too well for Meg to have gone on lying to her for this long. "Em," she said, breathing in the sugar-scented air as she peered across the makeshift counter, thinking again of the stupid email burning a hole in her inbox. "What's going on?"

"Nothing!" Emily promised, holding her doughnut half up in a salute and taking a step back toward the fairway. "I'll see you later."

Meg watched her go for a moment, uneasy, before busying herself brushing doughnut crumbs off the bright plastic tablecloth and adjusting their marker-on–poster-board sign. She was wrapping a napkin around a bear claw to hand to a guy on the debate team when her phone buzzed in her pocket. She pulled it out so fast she almost dropped it on the concrete, swallowing hard at the sight of Colby's name on the screen.

Once, when Meg was four or five, she'd wandered off in the supermarket while her mom was ordering salmon for a dinner party, then been completely unable to find her when she came shuffling back down the aisle clutching a package of Halloween-dyed Oreos for which she'd intended to beg. To this day, she shivered a little when she remembered the quietly apocalyptic moments that followed—the crinkle of the cellophane sleeve in her hand as she dashed frantically down aisle after aisle, the sour tang of panic at the back of her mouth.

It felt like hours, though it was probably only a couple of minutes before she finally found her mother, who had moved on to the cheese counter and not yet noticed Meg was gone in the first place. "What's wrong?" she'd demanded, catching sight of Meg's stricken expression. "What happened?"

Meg had shaken her head. The relief was overwhelming and animal, jumbling up any kind of cogent explanation inside her brain: all she'd been able to say was, "I *missed* you," before bursting into inconsolable tears.

Meg didn't know why she was thinking about that right now.

She tucked the phone back into her pocket and did her best to ignore the way her whole chest had loosened, like she'd taken a full breath for the first time all day. Yeah, she was glad he'd texted. Yeah, she'd been worried he might not. But it was also kind of shitty, the way he was totally ignoring the fact that he'd hurt her. And it didn't change the fact that sometimes it felt utterly pointless for them to try and agree on anything at all.

"Harrison," she said now, her voice coming out a little more shrilly than she'd necessarily intended. "Let's get back to work."

By the time Darcy Ramos came to relieve her at the end of her shift, Meg's mood had totally blackened, like one of those gruesome warning posters of calcified cigarette lungs or the pot roast her mom had attempted for dinner a couple of weeks ago. She'd been planning to go find Emily, to see what all the mystery was about, but as she looked out at the buzzing midway, she realized there was absolutely no way she had the courage to get into a fight about their future tonight. She didn't want to get into a fight about anything. She kind of just wanted to go home.

Meg darted past the Fun Slide and the falafel truck, breathing a sigh of relief at the familiar chirp as she unlocked her driver's side door—she'd gotten her car back this morning, her mom having driven her over to the mechanic's in irritable silence. She leaned her head back against the seat for a moment before wriggling around and pulling her phone out of her pocket, staring at Colby's message one more time. *What are you even* after *with me here?* she almost texted. Instead, she dropped her phone in the cup holder and headed home.

The following night, Meg's dad took her to dinner at a steakhouse near UPenn—all dark wood and white tablecloths, votive candles flickering in little glass jars. Since the divorce, the two of them had a standing dinner date every other Friday, and they alternated who got to choose. Meg kind of liked researching new restaurants—reading reviews and scouring menus, deciding exactly what she was going to order ahead of time. Sometimes it was more fun than the actual dinners themselves, although obviously she didn't want her dad to know that.

Tonight she ate her strip steak and scalloped potatoes, chatting gamely about WeCount and the carnival and the paper she was writing for her independent study about Rebecca Latimer Felton. Sometimes as the two of them sat across from each other in a booth or a corner table, both of them casting around a little bit frantically for topics of conversation, it was hard to believe her dad was the same guy who'd changed her diapers and taught her to ride a two-wheeler and carried her screaming bloody murder out of an IMAX movie about dinosaurs when she was seven. They used to sit in easy silence for hours at a time watching Japanese monster movies on Blu-ray. Now she kind of couldn't imagine being comfortably quiet with him for five minutes at a stretch.

"So," he said now, sitting back in his chair as the waiter cleared their plates, "I've got some news."

"Uh-oh," Meg joked. "The last time you said that, you told me you and mom were getting a divorce."

Her dad laughed awkwardly. "Well, hopefully this is happier," he said, then took a deep breath. For a moment, he looked more uncertain than Meg ever thought of him as being—young, somehow. "Lisa and I are getting married."

Meg was hallucinating—she must be. It was like what he was saying didn't make sense in the English language, like he'd suddenly switched to Dutch without warning or recited a bit of poetry in Sanskrit. She only just barely caught herself before she laughed out loud.

"Wait, seriously?" she asked, the words coming out before she could think better of them. Then, schooling her expression into something more acceptable as she realized this wasn't some kind of emphatically un-hilarious joke: "Um. That's great!" Holy *crap*, she really had not thought he and Lisa were that serious. They'd only been officially dating for a year.

"Well, thanks," her dad said, his cheeks pinking up a bit as he fussed with his napkin. "It means a lot to me that you think so, obviously. We're thinking Memorial Day weekend, somewhere here in town."

"Wow," Meg said, blinking about a thousand times. "That's soon."

Her dad nodded. "Lisa's kids leave to be with their dad in Chicago pretty soon after school lets out," he explained. "And then you'll be at college . . ."

Lisa's kids, Meg remembered suddenly. Right. Her future stepsiblings. Lisa's kids were fine; they were young and kind of boring, but not offensive or anything. She'd only met them once.

"Um," she said, realizing abruptly that she was yanking her bottom lip so hard she was starting to hurt herself. She dropped her hands into her lap. "Does Mom know?"

"Not yet," her dad admitted. "I was thinking maybe you

might want to be the one to—"

"What? *No*," Meg interrupted, suddenly panicked. "You have to tell her. And you can't tell her that I knew first."

"I—okay." Her dad looked at her closely. "Meg, honey," he said, and his voice was very quiet. "Is everything okay? With your mom, I mean?"

"Of course," she said too quickly. "Everything's fine."

Her dad frowned. "You could tell me if it wasn't."

Meg shook her head. She knew what the right response was here—she didn't want to be some stereotypical teenager who was an asshole about her dad's remarriage—but there was something about it that felt so profoundly unfair to her, that her dad got this new life while her mom got a huge old house that needed renovating and a recycling bin full of empty wine bottles. And sure, they'd both made their choices, but she couldn't get over the feeling that somehow the options weren't the same for them both.

"Um," she said, pushing her chair back too quickly. Suddenly, she was absolutely, horrifyingly sure that she was going to cry. "Excuse me."

She stared at herself in the mirror in the cavernous, marble-tiled bathroom, her hair frizzing a little around her temples and the beginnings of a pimple on her chin. She sat down on a green velvet couch and dug her phone out of her pocket, scrolling through her messages until she got to Colby's name. She hadn't texted him back last night, trying to teach him some kind of lesson she wasn't entirely sure how to articulate and that felt vaguely embarrassing now, twenty-four hours later, when it turned out he was the only person on Earth she actually had any interest in talking to.

She paused for a moment, thumb hovering, then changed her mind and flicked up to Emily's name instead. She'd said something about going out with Adrienne and Mason and Javi tonight, Meg thought—she hadn't really listened to the details, since she knew she had plans, but suddenly it felt imperative that she get out of this restaurant as soon as she possibly could. *What are you guys doing?* she keyed in.

Emily texted back almost right away: *We're at Cavelli's*, she said. *How's dad dinner?*

Meg texted back a row of upside-down smiley emojis. *I'm going to come meet you, okay?*

A pause, longer this time, the three dots appearing and then disappearing twice before Emily responded. *Yup*, she said. *See you soon!*

Normally, their dorky dad/daughter schtick was to order whatever two desserts were biggest, then split them, but now that she'd located an escape route, even a giant slab of chocolate cake wasn't enough to entice her to stay one minute longer than she had to. "I actually told some friends I'd meet them," she explained when the waiter came by with the menu. "Sorry."

"Oh," her dad said, and she could tell he was a tiny bit hurt; *no other commitments on dad dinner nights* was one of their implicit rules, though she was pretty sure he wouldn't say anything about it, and she was right. "Okay. We'll celebrate another time, then."

"Absolutely," Meg said. "Another time."

She pulled into the parking lot outside of Cavelli's twenty minutes later. There was something reassuring about the sight of it: the neon beer signs glowing in the windows, the rickety benches lined up along the sidewalk for people waiting to pick up takeout orders. Inside it smelled like fry oil and garlic. She took a deep breath and smiled at the surly middle-aged hostess, as glad to see her as if she were Meg's own grandmother. This much, at least, was the same as it had always been.

She hadn't bothered to ask who *we* was, but as she scanned the restaurant she realized it was just Emily and Mason sitting across from each other in a duct-taped booth by the window, a pair of Cokes in red plastic cups and a mostly picked-over plate of toasted ravioli on the table between them. "My dad is getting married again," she announced, flopping herself onto the bench seat beside Emily. "Also, hi."

"What?" Emily's eyes widened, her gaze cutting quickly to Mason and then back again. "Holy crap. To the lawyer?"

Meg nodded miserably, launching into the whole long story as she dragged a toasted ravioli through the little bowl of marinara. "It's not even that I'm not happy for him," she finished, although in fact she wasn't. "It just feels . . . I don't know." She shrugged, glancing from Mason to Emily and back again. It wasn't until then that it even occurred to her to ask, "So, um. Where's everybody else?"

Emily and Mason were both silent for a moment. Something about the look they exchanged then had her sitting up in her seat. Suddenly, everything—Emily at the carnival, Mason in his car the other day, the faint whiff of not-rightness of things among the three of them like a skunk shuffling through the bushes on a summer night—started to make a horrifying kind of sense.

"Oh my God," she said. "Are you guys . . ." She couldn't make herself say it. "Did I just, like, crash your date right now?"

Even as the question came out of her mouth she was fully expecting them to deny it, but Emily only winced. "This definitely isn't how we wanted to tell you," she said quietly. "But then we figured if you were coming here anyway—"

"It's the first time," Mason jumped in. "We don't want you to think—it's not like we've been sneaking around behind your back, or—"

"No, it's fine," Meg said, holding her hands up like an instinct and barely holding back a hysterical giggle; she could feel it lodged behind her breastbone like a bubble of gas. Well, she thought meanly, apparently she and Emily still had more in common than she'd thought. "I just. Huh. Is that why you . . ."

She looked at Mason in his glasses and Yosemite hoodie, the rest of the question dangling between them like a hanged thing. "You know what, don't answer that. It's okay."

"Nothing happened while you guys were together," Emily said urgently. "You know that, right? I would never, ever—"

"Me either," Mason said, solemn as a Boy Scout. Meg could not believe this was happening. They were probably telling the truth, for what it was worth—both of them put too much stock in their own moral codes for them to be lying. But that didn't actually make it any better. If anything, Meg thought it possibly made things worse.

The waitress appeared just then, yanking a pen out of her messy bun and flipping to a fresh page in her notepad. "What can I get you?" she asked Meg.

"Oh!" Meg said, curling her hands around the edge of the laminate table. "I. Um. I think I was just leaving, actually."

"No, no, no," Emily said, "wait." She turned to the waitress. "She isn't leaving."

"Look," Mason chimed in reasonably. "Why don't you stay and hang out, and we can talk about this? We were thinking about ordering a brownie sundae."

Now Meg *did* laugh, a half-insane cackle that echoed even in the crowded restaurant. She clapped a hand over her mouth. "I'm sorry," she said. "No, I'm good. I actually just remembered I said I'd . . ." She broke off, for once in her life totally unable to think of an excuse, a way to make everything normal and fine.

It just always seemed like maybe you weren't actually that into Mason in the first place, Emily had said. "You guys have fun."

"Meggie," Emily said, her lip pushing out like a little kid in pursuit of a later bedtime. "Come on, wait a second."

But Meg was already gone.

FIFTEEN

Colby

Colby picked Joanna up and they went to Highland Burger Bar, which was new and, Colby thought, a little douchey: exposed brick and soldered copper light fixtures, a live band set up on a low stage at the back of the dining room. The menu had thirty-six different kinds of burgers on it. "You know what you're going to get?" Joanna asked, setting her purse on the bench, then on the table, then on the bench again. She was wearing a flowered dress and a pair of ankle boots with little heels on them, her jean jacket rolled up to reveal a delicate gold bracelet on one wrist.

"A salad, definitely," Colby deadpanned, then grinned at her. "I'm kidding."

Joanna smiled. He thought she was nervous, though he had

no idea why anybody would be nervous about a dinner with him at Highland Burger Bar. Especially not Joanna, who'd been one of the prettiest girls in their grade. Now she worked at the front desk of a hair salon, booking appointments and refilling the shampoo bottles and sweeping up huge bags of hair, which she explained with a grimace that was cute instead of actually grimace-y. "What is it about hair that it becomes the grossest thing on the planet the moment it's separated from your head?" she asked as they shared a plate of nachos.

Colby laughed. "I don't know," he admitted. "But you're definitely not wrong." It was easy to talk to her—about their friends and how ridiculous they were, about their mean old math teacher Mrs. Cornish, whose son had gone to jail for cooking meth. It was different from the kind of stuff he talked about with Meg, sure, but the truth was that sometimes when he got off the phone with Meg it was like his brain was on fire, like he needed to take it out and dunk it in a glass of water overnight like a pair of dentures in that old commercial. It was exciting sometimes, but also exhausting. With Jo it just felt normal.

She was halfway through a story about some car Jordan was trying to buy off Craigslist from a guy she thought was probably a drug dealer when Colby's phone buzzed in his pocket. He tried to ignore the instinctive, animal thunk of his heart against his rib cage. Meg hadn't texted back at all last night, or today, either, though he'd spent his entire shift at work sneaking his phone out to double-check like a total chump. It was stupid to get his hopes up now, on top of which Colby didn't even know if he wanted to hear from her at this point. It was probably better in the long run to put an end to things once and for all.

It buzzed again a couple of minutes later, though, then again ten minutes after that. Colby tried to focus on what Joanna was saying, but as soon as she got up to go to the bathroom he pulled it out of his pocket. Sure enough, it was Meg: *Can you talk?* she'd texted. *Tonight sucked.*

Then: *I miss you. Is that weird to say? That's probably weird to say.*

Then: *Ugh, I'm sorry. You're probably out having a life like a normal person. Going to eat my feelings and go to bed.*

Colby set his phone facedown on the table. Took a long gulp of his Dr Pepper. Finally, he swore under his breath and picked it up again: *Give me half an hour,* he typed, then shoved the thing back into his pocket just as Joanna came back from the bathroom.

"Hey," she said, slipping back into the booth across from him. She'd reapplied her lip gloss, the pale pink sheen of it catching the overhead lights. "Everything okay?"

"My mom's not feeling great," he blurted, knowing even as the words came out that he was being an asshole. Joanna's own mom had beaten breast cancer twice already, once when they were in middle school and again the previous fall.

"Oh no," Joanna said, frowning. "Do you need to get home?"

Colby hesitated. They were finished with their burgers by now, though he'd been thinking about asking if she wanted to go for ice cream. "Probably," he said. "I'm sorry."

"No, it's fine," Joanna said, shaking her curly blond head. "Do you want to grab her some soup to go or something?"

Fuck, Colby hated himself. "Nah, it's okay. I should probably just take off."

He paid the check and took her home, the windows cracked to the chilly night air and a Kacey Musgraves album she liked on the stereo. She turned to look at him as they pulled up in front of her house. "I had a good time tonight, Colby," she said.

Colby nodded. "Yeah," he said, feeling like a total dickhead and not sure what to do about it, exactly. "Me too." He knew he could kiss her, if he wanted. He knew from the way she was holding her face that she was probably hoping he would.

"I'll text you" was all he said.

When he got home, instead of going inside he went around the back of the house and climbed the steps to the rickety wooden deck, plunking himself into a lawn chair that Tris had gnawed all the legs on back when she was a puppy. It was still a little too cold to sit out here comfortably at night, the wind stinging the back of his neck and rustling the trees out at the far end of the yard. He tucked his free hand between his thighs and dialed Meg. "Hey," he said when she answered. "Everything okay?"

"I'm sorry," she said, her voice a little thick and unfamiliar. He thought maybe she'd been crying again. "I'm really embarrassed."

"Don't be," he said, leaning his head back. "It's just me."

"No, I know, but I don't want you to think I just expect you to drop everything and talk to me just because I'm having some kind of humiliating existential crisis like you're my therapist or something."

"I don't think I'm your therapist," Colby said, frowning. "Do *you* think I'm your therapist?"

"No," Meg said immediately. "Of course not. That's the point." She took a deep breath. "Are you mad at me?"

Colby hesitated. It didn't feel as simple as a yes-or-no answer. "Are you mad at me?" he finally asked.

"I don't know," she said, which was surprising. He hadn't thought she'd let him get away with not answering first. "I was, a little."

"Yeah." Colby bit his lip. "I'm not mad at you," he said, which was true now, even if it hadn't been twelve hours ago. He didn't know how to tell her *mad* wasn't the right word. "What's going on?"

So Meg sighed and told him: about her dad's wedding and her friend Emily dating her ex-boyfriend, about walking into the pizza place and realizing things were different than she'd thought. Halfway through the story, Tris started scratching at the door to come out, so Colby reached behind him and twisted the knob, watching as the dog trotted across the yard and peed on a fence post before coming back and lying down beside his chair.

"That's totally fucked up," he said when she was finished, though a tiny part of him was weirdly relieved to hear she probably wasn't about to get back together with that guy any time soon. "The two of them sneaking around like that? I'd be pissed, too."

"No, I'm not pissed," Meg protested. "It's fine; they're allowed. It's just—"

"Meg." Colby laughed at her a little; he couldn't help it. "It's fucked up."

Meg sighed loudly. "Okay," she said. "I guess it's a little fucked up."

"There you go," he said, smiling into the darkness. "Does that feel better?"

"Kind of," she admitted. "Maybe. I don't know." He could hear her shifting around on the other end of the phone; he tried to picture her sitting in her frilly bedroom, wondered if she was already in her pajamas. He wanted to ask her what color her hair was, but he didn't know how. "Enough. You tell me something now."

Colby hesitated for a minute, looking out at the scrubby tree line at the far end of the yard and reaching down to scratch Tris on her bristly backbone. I had a date tonight, he thought and didn't say. He wasn't sure *why* he didn't say it, exactly, except that he liked being the person she called when things were shitty. He liked being the person she told things to. And it felt like if he told her about Jo, that might go away.

"I heard a really crappy band tonight," he said finally.

Meg smiled at that; Colby could hear it. "You did?"

"Yeah." He tilted his head back, rubbed a hand over his hair, and told himself he wasn't lying. "I think they were covering mostly Queen songs, but it was hard to tell."

"Did you know that 'We Will Rock You' is an LGBT protest anthem?" Meg asked him, and Colby laughed a little.

"I didn't," he said. "But somehow I'm not surprised that you do."

"I can't tell if that's a compliment or not," Meg said.

Colby considered that. "Yeah," he told her finally. "It's a compliment."

Meg hummed into his ear for a moment, like an engine revving. "Can I ask you something?" she said, the words coming out so fast they were almost entirely strung together. "Would it be totally demented for us to meet?"

"I . . ." Colby blinked. "To meet?" he repeated dumbly. He had literally never let himself think about it before. He'd never let himself consider the terms of their relationship in anything besides what they were.

"So, yes," Meg said. "Okay. Fair enough. Sorry, I didn't

mean to make it weird, I just—"

"I don't think it's weird," Colby blurted, finally finding his words. "Or, I mean, I *do* think it's weird, I guess, but that doesn't mean I don't want to meet you."

"It doesn't?" Meg asked. "I mean, you do?"

Colby hesitated. He did and he didn't, he guessed. He knew it was inevitably going to be a disappointment, that logically none of this was ever going to be whatever he'd been making it in his mind in the weeks since they'd started talking. And yet . . .

"Yeah," he said. "I do."

"Okay." Meg swallowed. "Where?"

"I have no idea."

"Well, what's between where you are and where I am?" she asked. "Like, right in the middle? Actually, hang on. I'll Google it." He could hear her typing away, the determined clatter of her fingers on the keyboard. Colby's heart was slamming away inside his chest. "Literally nothing," she reported after a moment. "Well, there's a truck-stop diner not too far. But I'm not meeting you at a truck-stop diner. What if I just came to you?"

"Wait, seriously?"

"Why not, right?"

"It's far."

"It's not that far," Meg countered. "Google says it's, like, eight hours."

"You want to drive eight hours to see me?" Colby blurted.

"I mean, why not?"

"Have you ever driven eight hours before?"

"Yes," Meg said immediately.

"When?"

"To see Harry Styles last summer, and if you say anything about it, this whole thing is off."

"I'm not saying anything," Colby promised. He couldn't stop smiling. He also felt like he was about to throw up. He couldn't imagine meeting her at all, to be honest, but now that the idea had lodged itself in his mind, he couldn't stop thinking it, couldn't stop wanting it. Already wanted it more than he'd wanted anything in a long time.

He thought for a moment. His mom was working a double this weekend. It was conceivable Meg could be in and out without his mom ever knowing she'd been here. "What about tomorrow?" he asked. It was soon—it was too soon—but he also thought it was possible he'd lose his nerve entirely if they waited any longer than that.

"Oh! Um." Meg sounded surprised, and he wondered for a moment if she'd been counting on him saying it wasn't a good idea, if possibly they were playing some weird game of chicken he hadn't copped onto until it was too late. "Yeah," she said. "Tomorrow could work."

"Are you sure?" he asked.

"Yeah," she said. "I'm sure."

SIXTEEN

Meg

It was barely light the next morning when Meg filled her Kleen Kanteen and tucked a few packets of trail mix and an apple into her backpack, then tossed it into the back seat of the Prius and cracked the windows to the warm spring air. She'd told her mom she was going to Dorney Park with Emily's family. She hadn't told anybody the truth. On one hand, it felt kind of wildly liberating, the idea of not having to answer to anyone but herself for the next thirty-six hours.

On the other, she was extremely worried about getting chainsaw murdered.

Well, Meg reassured herself, she'd packed the portable charger for her cell phone. She had three hundred dollars in cash from her bank account and the Mastercard her dad had cosigned for her when she started her job so she could start building credit. She wasn't an idiot. Not that you had to be an idiot to get chainsaw murdered, obviously, but—

Anyway, this whole line of thinking was irrelevant, because Colby wasn't a chainsaw murderer.

Meg was, like, 99 percent sure.

She headed west on I-76, digging her sunglasses out of the cup holder and turning Janelle Monáe up on the stereo. Her heart thumped with anticipation to the beat of the drums. She peed at a rest stop near Allentown, pulling a bottle of kombucha out of the cooler and smiling at the clerk, a girl about her age who was reading a sci-fi novel at the counter. It occurred to Meg that a rest stop would be a great place to do a voter registration drive, and she made a mental note to mention it to Lillian at work next week.

It was another couple of hours before she crossed into Ohio; she passed power plants and farmland and a giant billboard that just said *HELL IS REAL* in huge black letters on a white background. She wanted to take a picture and text it to Emily, but then Emily would want to know what she was doing all the way out here.

Also, Emily had stolen her boyfriend.

Meg blew a breath out, making a face at herself even though there was no one to see it. God, she wasn't Taylor Swift circa 2009. She knew that nobody could steal a boyfriend who didn't want to be stolen, not to mention the fact that she was literally crossing state lines at this very moment to go see some other guy entirely. Still, the idea of Mason and Emily lying to her—the idea of them strategizing over the best way to let her down easy, like she couldn't be trusted not to fall apart or make some big public scene—made her want to throw up all over the inside of the Prius. She was an adult. She could handle herself. She was fine.

Colby lived in a small town called Alma an hour or so outside Columbus. Meg pulled off the highway and followed the GPS with her bottom lip clamped between her teeth, passing a post office and a Dollar General and a strip mall with a CVS and a hair salon, her nerves getting thicker and more viscous as the landscape outside the window began to thin. Finally, she turned onto a quiet street in a residential neighborhood full of modest houses that looked like they'd all been built around the same time, pulling to a stop in front of a neat brick split-level with a wrought-iron screen over the front door. "You have arrived at your destination," chirped the GPS.

Meg turned off the engine and sat in the driveway for a long moment, hands still curled around the wheel. For all the times she'd imagined meeting Colby in real life—and she *had* imagined it, daydreaming in the middle of calc class and lying alone in her bed late at night—for some reason the idea of marching up the front walk and ringing the bell felt impossible. It occurred to her all at once that there was still enough time to drive away.

Instead, she fished her phone from the cupholder before she could talk herself out of it, scrolling through her recents and pressing her thumb to Colby's name. "Um," she said when he answered, swallowing her heart back down into her chest where it belonged, "I think I'm here?"

"Oh!" Colby said. He sounded surprised, as if he hadn't actually believed she was going to show up. "Okay. Um, hang on."

The screen door screeched open a moment later, and a brown-and-black pit bull darted out, her stocky body trundling down the steps and across the lawn to where Meg was standing by the open driver's-side door. "She's friendly," a deep voice called, even as the dog skidded to a stop in front of her, howling enthusiastically as it jumped.

Meg looked up and there was Colby: broader in the chest and shoulders than she'd been expecting, with shaggy brown hair and a vaguely suspicious expression. She'd spent the better part of last night trying on basically everything she owned before finally deciding on dark jeans and her very favorite T-shirt—another present from her mom's cousin Jodie, a V-neck with a picture of a bespectacled fox and the slogan *I don't care for your misogyny*—but Colby was barefoot in a pair of knee-length basketball shorts, like possibly she'd woken him up from a nap.

"Tris," he said, grabbing the dog by the collar and setting her gently back down on all four paws. "Easy."

"Tris?" Meg repeated, reaching down to scratch behind her

velvety ears. "Like the girl from *Divergent*?"

"Who?" Colby looked at her strangely. "No, um, Tris Speaker. All-time greatest hitter on the Cleveland Indians." He shrugged, something about the gesture weirdly defensive. "My dad named her."

"Oh." Meg nodded, straightening up again. "Right."

Colby nodded back. His face was more delicate than Meg had expected, a jaw as sharp as sandstone and a scattering of tawny freckles across his nose and cheeks. His eyelashes were as long as a girl's.

They stood there for a moment, looking at each other as Meg realized all at once that she had no idea how she was supposed to greet him. Did they hug? Shake hands? She couldn't imagine how she'd somehow failed to think about this. "Hi," she said finally, spreading her fingers in an awkward wave.

"Hi." Colby shoved his own hands in his pockets. So, okay. No touching at all, then. That was fine. There was no reason to feel disappointed about that. "Um. Come on in."

He led her up the front walk, Tris ambling along behind them. The house was small and super neat inside, so different from the expansive, vaguely artsy squalor of her own: Lacy curtains were tied back with gingham bows at the windows. A framed, embroidered Bible verse hung on one wood-paneled wall. A fleece blanket stitched with the logo of the Cleveland Indians was folded tidily over the back of one of those reclining sofas with built-in cup holders in the armrests, the kind her mom always called couch potato skins. Come to think of it, Meg could just imagine her mom's reaction to this whole room, this whole neighborhood: a full-body shudder and a generous slug of wine.

"So," Colby said, setting her backpack down on the seat of a brown corduroy armchair. "How was your drive?"

"Good," she said immediately, her voice coming out loud and a little bit squeaky. Right away, Meg felt herself blush. God, this was *Colby*, who she'd been talking to constantly for nearly a month now. Everything was fine.

Everything . . . did not feel fine.

"Um," she said, trying to think of something to ask him in return and drawing the kind of massive blank Mason always called a brain fart. Oh God, had she just driven eight hours to find they had nothing to say to each other? She looked around, suddenly desperate for someone else to draw into the conversation, someone she might possibly be able to charm. "Is your mom here?" she begged.

Colby shook his head. "She's working a double this weekend," he said, shifting his weight on the carpet. "She won't be back until tomorrow after church."

Meg tugged on her lip, a little bit weirded out. She had figured there would be a female adult in his house, honestly—on top of which something about the way he'd said it had her eyes narrowing in suspicion. "But she's cool with me staying here, yeah?"

"Yeah, yeah," Colby said immediately. Then his face dropped a little bit. "I mean, I didn't mention it to her, exactly. But she wouldn't care."

Meg frowned. "Colby—"

"I'm serious!" he promised. "My friends stay over when she's at work all the time."

"Yeah, but—" She broke off.

"I know," Colby said, sounding for the first time since she'd arrived like the person she was used to talking to on the phone. "I just didn't know how to explain it to her, I guess. I wasn't doing it to be sketchy."

"It feels a little sketchy," Meg said.

"I'm sorry." Colby scrubbed a hand through his hair. "Do you want me to call her now?"

She considered that, watching as he bent down to rub the dog along her backbone. Something about the way he was with Tris made her trust him more, even though she knew that was literally how serial killers lured people into vans. "It's fine," she said eventually, perching on the edge of the sofa. After all, she didn't exactly have a leg to stand on when it came to telling the truth about this particular situation. "If you're sure she's not going to be upset."

"She's not even going to know," Colby said immediately. Then, seeming to sense that wasn't the best way to win Meg over, he plowed ahead. "Are you hungry?" he asked. "We could go out and get something to eat, if you want."

Meg stood up so fast she startled the dog, she was so excited about the idea of an activity. "Sure!" she said, swinging her backpack over her shoulder again. "Let's go."

Colby refilled Tris's water bowl and got his sneakers on, then led Meg outside to the driveway. "Um," she said, hesitating a moment. "I can just follow you in my car." She was reasonably sure he wasn't a murderer at this point, but it felt like the more responsible thing to do, as if she could somehow negate the recklessness of the rest of this whole trip by providing her own transportation.

"Sure," Colby said, looking at her a little oddly. She had no idea whether or not he was glad she was here. For all the times she'd thought about it, asking to come here had been more impulsive than she usually was, the weirdness of everything about her regular life crushing down on her all at once; still, he'd sounded excited about the idea at the time. At least, she'd thought he had. "Whatever you want."

They went to a Subway not far from the Dollar General, Meg ordering the veggie sandwich even though she knew it was probably exactly what he expected her to do. She glanced around the shop. "Do you want to eat outside, maybe?" she asked.

Colby frowned. "There aren't any tables or anything," he pointed out.

"We could go somewhere, though, couldn't we?" she asked. "A park or something?"

"Sure, I guess." He filled his giant cup with Dr Pepper at the soda machine, thinking a minute. "There is one place we could go, actually."

They got back in their respective cars and pulled out into traffic, heading back in the direction they'd come. Meg watched through the windshield as the stores and businesses got farther apart, then almost disappeared altogether, giving way to long stretches of field and the occasional farmhouse, an old-fashioned water tower hulking off in the distance. Finally, Colby pulled off down a narrow, gravel-covered road that twisted and turned before leading to nothing, just an overgrown lot full of weeds and wildflowers. Tall trees made a canopy overhead. The air was thick with pollen, wasps humming noisily. Planted in the ground was a faded, listing wooden sign:

THE PARADISE HOMES

SINGLE-FAMILY ARTISAN RESIDENCES, COMING SOON

"What is this place?" Meg called as she climbed out of the Prius. The grass was already tall even though it was only April, tickling her ankles in the gap between her pants and her sneakers.

"It's mine," Colby said.

Meg's eyes widened. "Really?"

He nodded. "My dad left it to me," he explained. "He bought it when he and my mom were first married, and we always used to come out here for, like, family picnics when me and Matt were real little—the two of us used to run around like wild animals out here, roll down the hill and stuff. We were nuts." He smiled at the memory, his face softening for a moment; Meg could picture exactly what he'd looked like as a little kid. "Anyway, my dad and my uncle Rick used to be in business together—they built houses, you know? And my dad had this idea for putting, like, six of them on this land, all of them totally different styles, and then up there"—he motioned to the hill in the distance—"he always said he was going to build my mom's dream house." He stopped then, like he'd suddenly realized he'd said more than he'd meant to, dropping his sandwich on the hood of the car with a quiet thunk. "He . . . didn't do that, obviously."

"Why don't you do it?" Meg asked immediately.

"What, build my mom's dream house?"

"Build your own dream house."

Colby laughed. "Yeah, Meg, I'm going to just go ahead and build a house by myself with no money. This is real life, not *The Notebook*."

Meg raised her eyebrows, momentarily distracted by the shape of her name in his mouth. "Have you *seen The Notebook*?"

"Maybe," Colby said, with something close to a smile. "My dad liked corny movies."

Meg nodded. She wanted to ask more about his dad—they hadn't talked about him at all since that very first night on the phone—but she could never figure out exactly how to bring it up. "What did he leave to your brother?" she finally asked.

"Nothing," Colby replied, so deadpan that it took her a moment to realize he was serious.

Meg blinked. "Wow."

"Yep," Colby said, in a voice that made it pretty clear that was the end of that.

They climbed up onto the warm hood of his car to eat their sandwiches, sunlight lacing through the trees and a butterfly hovering not far from Colby's elbow. The back of his hand brushed hers as they traded their bags of chips back and forth. "What would you build here, hypothetically?" she asked, pulling her feet up onto the bumper. "If you could build anything?"

"I dunno," Colby said, but she could tell he was lying. "I've never thought about it, really."

Meg rolled her eyes. "Tell me," she said, nudging him with her ankle. "What, do you think I'm going to make fun of you? I don't know how to build anything."

Colby shrugged. "Just a regular house. I don't know."

"You don't have to be embarrassed," she pressed—it felt important, all of a sudden, to get him to tell her. "It's just me, remember?"

"Oh, right, *it's just you*, like you're—" Colby broke off, made a face. "Fine," he said, taking a sip of his giant soda. "Something with a big porch, I guess. And a bunch of fireplaces." He thought. "And a game room."

"See?" Meg said, her skin warming slightly. "There you go. You do have an imagination."

Colby snorted. "Oh, I've got an imagination," he said, almost under his breath. This time when she kicked him he grabbed her ankle and held it, his fingers curling around the jut of bone in a way that set off a string of tiny explosions she felt all over her body. Meg didn't breathe until he finally let it go.

He gazed at her for another long moment, an inscrutable expression in his hazel-brown eyes. "What?" she finally asked.

Colby shrugged, finishing the last of his sandwich in one giant bite. "You look different than I thought you'd look" was all he said.

Meg laughed. "You seriously never Googled me?"

"No," he said once he'd swallowed.

"Really?"

"Why?" He raised his eyebrows. "Did you Google me?"

"Of course I did," Meg admitted immediately, unembarrassed. "Like, the very first night we talked, even. But you're basically impossible to find."

Colby smirked. "That's the idea."

"Well," Meg said, tugging a bit of cucumber out of her sandwich with her thumb and forefinger, "I'm infinitely searchable."

"That is . . . not surprising to me."

"Yeah, yeah." Meg smiled. "Good different or bad different?"

"What?"

"Do I look good different or bad different?"

Colby's mouth twitched then, infinitesimal. "That seems like a trick question," he said.

"How is it a trick question?"

"Meg." He rubbed a hand over his face. "You're pretty, if that's what you're asking. You're, like . . . really, really pretty."

"Oh." Meg felt her whole body prickle—and now she *was* embarrassed, a little, to be caught fishing for a compliment so blatantly. But there was another part of her—the part of her that had asked to come visit to begin with, maybe—that wasn't embarrassed at all. "Yeah," she said, bending down and rubbing her nose against her denim-covered knee, looking at him out of the corner of her eye. "I guess that was kind of what I was asking."

"Uh-huh." Colby gazed back at her for a moment, inscrutable. Then he grinned. "Come on," he said, crumpling up his sandwich wrapper and pushing himself up off the bumper. "Let's get going."

SEVENTEEN

Colby

They were just getting back to the house when Colby's phone dinged with a text from Micah. "Who's that?" Meg asked, reaching down to scratch the dog under her chin.

He watched her for a moment, intrigued; he'd automatically assumed she was one of those people who was going to be weird and stupid about pit bulls, and he was surprised and pleased to find that he'd been wrong. "Just a buddy of mine," he said, tucking the phone back into his hoodie pocket. "They wanted to know what I was doing—well, what we were doing, I guess." That wasn't true, technically, since he hadn't told anyone Meg was coming in the first place. Honestly, he hadn't really thought she was going to show up. Now he kind of wished he had. "They're hanging out."

Meg raised her eyebrows. "You want to go meet them?"

Colby shook his head like a reflex. "That's okay," he said. "We don't have to."

"Why not?" she asked—straightening up again, lifting her chin like a challenge. "You embarrassed of them, or are you embarrassed of me?"

The answer to that question was emphatically *both*, but there was no way to explain that to her. Instead, Colby just shrugged. "Neither," he said, hoping his voice didn't betray him. "We can go if you want. But I'm warning you, they're literally hanging around in front of an abandoned office building. It's not exactly a fun night of culture in the big city."

"I love abandoned office buildings," Meg deadpanned. Colby snorted, fully thinking she was joking, but she shook her head. "No, I seriously do!" she protested. "I love all abandoned places. Have you ever watched, like, those videos of abandoned amusement parks or psych hospitals?"

Colby had, actually, and they scared the shit out of him. He'd never been inside the office building for that exact reason, like at any second some scaly, red-eyed demon was going to dart around a corner and drag him off to Hell. "You're kind of a weird chick, huh?" he said with a grin. He held his breath for a moment after he said it, unsure if she was the kind of girl you could joke around with like that.

"You like it," Meg said, only she was already walking away

from him when she said it, and he couldn't see her face.

But yeah. He liked it.

He changed into a pair of jeans and fed Tris before they headed out, the sun already starting to sink behind the trees at the west side of the house. He tried to think of a way to suggest Meg put on a different shirt before they went—he could already picture the look on Micah's face when he saw the one she was wearing—but couldn't for the life of him figure out a way to do it that wouldn't make things totally awkward, so in the end he just let it be.

He glanced at her across the driveway, watching as she unlocked her prissy little car in the pinkish twilight. She was even more of herself in person somehow, all noisy laugh and strong opinions, the kind of energy he associated with perpetual motion or a nuclear power plant. Colby kept catching himself staring at her like a total chump. He'd meant what he said, back at Paradise—she was *pretty*, with dark hair and skin so pale she reminded him of something out of a storybook, like Snow White or Briar Rose. She looked like somebody who had no business tooling around Alma, Ohio. She looked like somebody who wasn't going to stay for very long.

Jordan and Micah were already in the parking lot when they got there, Jordan digging through his pockets for a lighter while Micah turned idle circles on his hands in the empty fountain.

"Hey," Colby called, getting out of his car as Meg parked the Prius behind him. He had no idea how to introduce her, really, finally settling on, "This is Meg." The miracle of Micah and Jordan was that he knew they wouldn't ask questions, would take what he offered at face value without pressing for more. It was part of why they'd all been friends for so long.

"Hi," Meg said brightly, sticking her hand out like she was running for Congress. "Colby's told me a lot about you guys."

"Really?" Micah asked, his bushy eyebrows crawling.

"Quite the shirt you got there," Jordan said as they shook.

"I could say the same thing about your hat," Meg said, motioning at Jack Skellington's hollow grin even as Colby winced a little. "I love that movie."

"Oh yeah?" Jordan asked, brightening. "It's the best, right?"

Meg nodded eagerly. "My friend Emily and I used to be obsessed with it when we were in middle school. I mean, actually I didn't *go* to middle school—my school is K–12—but anyway, I actually just read this thing on Tumblr about how *The Nightmare Before Christmas* is a great allegory for cultural appropriation, you know? With how they're trying to celebrate somebody else's holiday but messing it all up."

"Uh." Jordan looked at her blankly. "What now?"

"Uh-oh," Micah teased. "Moran brought his librarian to the party."

"She just used, like, four words in a row I've never heard before," Jordan said with a laugh.

"Oh, sorry," Meg said, apparently undeterred. "Cultural appropriation is just when—"

"Did anybody bring food?" Colby interrupted before she could whip out her phone and offer to send them all a clarifying article from BuzzFeed. "I'm starving."

"Did *you* bring food?" Jordan countered, and that was when Joanna's car pulled into the lot.

"Shit, Moran," Micah murmured—quiet enough so that only Colby could hear him, a curly, slightly pervy smile spreading across his face. "You forget to tell your girlfriend your other girlfriend was coming?"

"Neither one of them is my girlfriend," Colby said, which was technically true, though he couldn't help but feel a little bit queasy as Jo got out of the driver's seat, her yellow hair up in a knot at the top of her head. It occurred to him that, in his effort to convince himself that nothing currently going on in his life was a big deal, he might have accidentally been kind of an asshole.

"Hey, Colby," Joanna called, reaching back to take a six-pack of hard lemonade from her friend Maureen in the passenger seat. It seemed like a lot longer ago than just last night that they'd gone to Highland Burger Bar, which didn't keep him from wishing a sinkhole would open in the middle of this parking lot and swallow him. "How's your mom feeling?"

"What's wrong with your mom?" Meg asked, frowning a little. Colby shook his head.

"Um," he said, smiling across the parking lot at Joanna in a way he hoped was friendly but not friendly enough to get himself in trouble. Maureen didn't bother to hide her stink-eye. "She's better."

Joanna nodded, glancing curiously at Meg. "Hi," she said, holding her hand out. "I'm Joanna."

"Meg," Meg said, and they shook.

"How do you guys know each other?" Joanna asked, passing the lemonades off to Micah.

Colby didn't know why the truth felt weirdly embarrassing to him. "We met dressed as furries at Comic-Con," he deadpanned before Meg could answer, which made Jordan laugh his honking donkey laugh. Meg, Colby couldn't help but notice, didn't smile.

A couple of other cars pulled into the lot just then, thankfully; Jordan and Jo's cousin Brady with the painful-looking acne and a couple of the girls Micah worked with at Dollar General, the sound level rising until it felt more like an actual party. Maureen dropped her phone into an empty plastic cup to make a speaker, Jay-Z echoing out into the darkness. Somebody else brought a thirty-rack of Bud Light. Meg sat on the bumper of the Prius with her ankles crossed and chatted with some girl Jo knew from the hair salon, both of them animated. Jordan finally got his joint lit while Micah held court in front of the empty fountain.

"You doing okay?" Colby asked Meg, catching her arm as

she dug in the back seat of the Prius for her water bottle. She wasn't drinking, he'd noticed, though to be fair neither was he. He wasn't exactly dying to add a DUI to his rap sheet, on top of which he had a sneaking suspicion beer actually made his nightmares worse. He'd had another one two nights earlier, blunt and terrifying, his dad screaming his name from inside one of Rick's stupid model homes. It occurred to Colby to wish his subconscious had a little more finesse.

"I'm fine," Meg said now, offering him the bland kind of bullshit smile he imagined she usually reserved for her friend Emily. "Are *you* okay?"

"Uh, yeah," he said, suddenly not sure about her tone. It was weird to have facial expressions to match it with all of a sudden, the delicate arch of her eyebrows and the purse of her heart-shaped mouth. "Why?"

Meg shrugged. "I don't know," she said, picking idly at one of the stickers on her water bottle—the whole thing was covered with them, *Yes We Can* and *HATE* with a red line drawn through it and *This Machine Kills Fascists*, like maybe she was worried the T-shirt wasn't working hard enough to announce her personal brand. "Just wondering." Then, with a raise of her eyebrows so quick he wasn't even sure if she'd really done it: "Joanna seems nice."

Colby almost choked on his tongue. "Uh, yeah," he said, wanting to explain but not knowing how to, wishing briefly for the safety of a telephone line. "Yeah, I mean—"

"Yo, Colby!" Micah called, waving his Bud Light in their general direction. "How many men does it take to open a beer can?"

Oh God, here they went. "How many," Colby asked dutifully, though in truth he wasn't altogether mad about the interruption.

"None," Micah reported. "It should be open when she brings it."

Jordan guffawed. Colby rolled his eyes. "Hilarious," Joanna said, shaking her head indulgently.

Only Meg didn't react. Instead, she got very still for a moment, considering Micah like a prey animal from across the parking lot. "Why is that funny?" she asked, her voice perfectly even. All at once, it occurred to Colby that possibly he'd been wrong about being the only person she was willing to fight with.

Micah looked startled for a moment, like he didn't understand the question. Jordan was still chuckling to himself, though that might have been the weed. "Relax," Micah said. "It was a joke."

"Sure, but why is it funny?"

Micah shook his head. "You know why it's funny."

"I don't, actually." Meg was looking at him with her head cocked just slightly to the side. "I don't understand the conceit of the joke, so I'm asking you to explain it to me."

Colby grimaced. She clearly *did* understand the conceit of

the joke, whatever that meant, but he got what she was doing. It was kind of an epic troll. He might have admired it, except for the part where it was making everything super fucking uncomfortable. Micah could be a boner sometimes, sure, but there was no point in ruining the night every time he said some jackass thing.

"All right, Hillary Clinton," Micah said. "Didn't mean to offend your delicate sensibilities."

"Uh-oh," Colby said. That was all he needed right now, for the two of them to get into some fucking debate about Benghazi or something and then they'd really be off to the races. God, he'd known bringing Meg around his friends was a bad idea from the very beginning, but still it was weird to see it play out, like watching a car wreck in slow motion when he was also somehow the one behind the wheel. "Let's not bring politics into this."

Meg ignored him. "Is that supposed to insult me?" she asked Micah, her voice a click higher than normal. "Calling me that? Like, in your mind, is that something that should make me feel embarrassed or shut me up?"

"It's not supposed to do anything," Micah said, shrugging violently. She was rattling him, Colby could tell. He thought of the first night he'd ever talked to Meg on the phone, that feeling of the ground shifting unexpectedly under his feet. He felt sorry for Micah, a little, thought mostly he just felt annoyed. "I'm just saying, you're kind of a snowfl—"

"Don't even say it," Meg interrupted. "Seriously, buddy, I'm going to just go ahead and save you from yourself right—"

"Moran," Micah said, "control your woman, will you?"

Oh, *shit.*

"I'm not his woman," Meg said immediately, her sharp gaze cutting in Colby's direction for the briefest of seconds. Joanna, who until now had been mostly engaged in a side conversation with her frizzy-haired friend Kylah, whipped around to look at them both. "And he doesn't think you're funny, either."

"He doesn't?" Micah asked. "'Cause you know him so well, right?"

"I know him better than you do, clearly."

"Hey, hey, hey," Colby said weakly—trying, and mostly failing, to make a joke of this whole thing. "Don't get me involved."

"Dude, you brought her here," Micah pointed out.

"I brought myself, actually," Meg told him. "And—"

"Hey, Mike," Joanna jumped in, kicking Micah lightly in the ankle and flapping her hand so he'd help her up off the yellow curb. "Speaking of beers, I need another. Come on, I'll open one for you and everything." And then somehow without even making a show of it she was leading him off across the parking lot like the Mother Teresa of awkward situations, though not before Micah muttered a few choice words under his breath.

Once they were gone, Meg blew a breath out, scooping her

hair off her neck like she'd just run an invigorating relay race and now required a cool beverage and someone to congratulate her on her stamina and perseverance. "Well, that was charming," she said with a shake of her head. "Is he always like that?"

For a moment, Colby just stood there dumbly like a cow you could see from the highway, like flies were going into his mouth. "Is *he* always like that?" he echoed. "Seriously?"

"Wait a second." Meg's eyes flashed. "You're mad at *me* right now?"

"Of course I'm mad at you."

"You are?" Meg looked sincerely baffled. "*Why?*"

"I—because," Colby said, momentarily losing his ability to string a coherent thought together. "Because! You can't just . . . come in here in your ridiculous T-shirt and start shitting all over my friends."

Meg's eyes narrowed. "First of all," she countered immediately, "it's not shitting all over your friends to point out when a joke is sexist. And second of all, what's wrong with my T-shirt?"

Colby blew a breath out. "It's not about your T-shirt."

"Isn't it?" Meg asked. "Because you're, like, the third person to be an asshole to me about it since I got here, so I'm starting to wonder." She rolled her eyes. "Literally all I did was ask him to explain why he thought his joke was funny, Colby. It's not my fault he couldn't do it. And it's not like I told him he was an idiot to his face."

"You kind of did, actually."

"I absolutely did not, which I *actually* thought showed pretty admirable restraint on my part, since—"

"Can you stop?" Colby broke in. "You sound like such a freaking snob right now. You don't even know this kid. You're basing your entire low opinion of him on one harmless joke he didn't even mean—"

Meg's mouth dropped open. "You think a joke like that is *harmless*? Are you kidding me?"

"I don't think it's as big a deal as you're making it out to be, that's for sure."

"Oh my God," Meg said, throwing her hands up and looking around as if she was searching for a studio audience, some like-minded chorus she could look at while she pointed at him, like, *Can you believe this guy?* "Oh my actual God. Okay."

"Can you calm down?" Colby asked, shaking his head a little. "There's no point in—"

"Don't tell me to calm down! What's next, you calling me a hysterical woman?"

"Nobody's calling you hysterical!" Colby said, though he was definitely thinking it. "I'm just saying, the point is, you've been here for all of six hours. This is where I live."

"Yeah, no kidding!" Meg said. "Which is why it's actually your job to educate these guys, not mine, but you obviously weren't about to step up, so—"

"*Educate* these guys?" Colby gaped at her. "Can you even hear yourself right now?"

"You know what I mean!"

"I know you think you're better than me and my friends."

"I *know* jokes about women are backward and unfunny, actually."

"Backward," Colby repeated, shaking his head a little. "That's cute."

"Oh my God." Meg's lips twisted meanly. "Which one of us is too sensitive here, exactly?"

"It was a joke, Meg! What's the big deal?"

"The *big deal* is the wage gap, Colby. The *big deal* is that ninety-five percent of Fortune 500 companies have male CEOs. The *big deal* is one in three women experiencing sexual violence at some point in their lives—"

"Jesus Christ." Colby dug the heels of his hands into his eyes. "Micah isn't a sex predator."

"I'm not saying Micah is a sex predator! I'm saying that jokes about how a woman's main utility is bringing your friend a beer contribute to a culture where stuff like that happens, so why is it such a problem for you to be like, *Dude, just tell a different joke*? Here, I'll give you some. A man walks into a bar. Ouch! What do you call a fish with no eyes? A *fsssh.* Two muffins are in an oven. One of them says, 'Is it hot in here to you?' And the other one says—"

"Enough!" He thought it was possible she would have kept going indefinitely, that they'd be standing here all night while she went through her entire repertoire of ridiculous dad jokes. He would have laughed if he weren't so furious. And that was the problem with Meg to begin with, Colby thought suddenly: he could never manage to feel just one thing about her at a time. "You made your point, okay?"

"Oh, I know I did," Meg said flatly. "You just don't think it matters."

"That's not even—" Colby broke off. "I just don't see how it's worth it to ruin a perfectly good party having theoretical arguments, okay? That's all I'm saying."

"Nothing about this is theoretical to me!"

Colby scrubbed a hand through his hair. "Yeah," he said, "I can see that."

"What does that even mean?" Meg demanded. "Like, where exactly is the line for you for what's worth giving a crap about? Do you laugh when he tells quote-unquote harmless jokes about gay people? Black people? Jewish p—"

"I didn't even laugh at this one, Meg!"

"I don't care! You didn't tell him to shut up—you're mad at *me* for telling him to shut up—and that's the same thing. Worse, maybe."

Colby shook his head again, mutely furious. God, where did she get off? Parachuting into his life out of nowhere with *The Rich Girl's Social Justice Handbook* in one hand and *The Field*

Guide to the Midwestern Hillbilly in the other? She might as well have been wearing a pith helmet. Colby knew exactly what she saw when she looked around this place—the same clueless, small-minded people she'd been expecting to get on the phone the first night she'd called his landline. She had no idea that Jordan had been at the top of their class the first three years of high school—he definitely knew what a fucking allegory was, no matter what he'd said for the sake of giving her a hard time earlier—or that Joanna had started her own side business doing fancy calligraphy on the internet. Meg didn't know that after Colby's dad's funeral, Micah had shown up at his house and they'd played *Warcraft* for seven straight hours without either of them ever saying a word. Part of him wanted to tell her those things, and part of him felt like he didn't owe her any explanation at all.

"This is ridiculous," he said finally. It was getting colder now, a chilly wind rattling the overgrown trees that ringed the parking lot. All at once, Colby wanted to go home. "Obviously, we're not going to agree here, so—"

"How can you not agree with me on this, though?" Meg interrupted, almost pleading. "Like, how can this not be important to you? You're so smart about so many things. I don't—"

"So anyone who disagrees with you is automatically a dumbass?"

"I mean, in general, of course not!"

"But about this."

Meg didn't answer for a moment, which was obviously an answer in itself. "This was a bad idea," she finally said. She looked around for the invisible audience again, hugging herself a little; Colby could see the goose bumps that had sprung up on her pale, bare arms. "God, what am I even doing here?" she asked, more quietly this time. "I'm just—I'm eight hours from my house, and nobody even—" She broke off. "This was a bad idea."

Her voice cracked on the last syllable; she didn't cry, though it looked like possibly she was thinking about it. For a second, Colby almost took a step closer, but that was stupid. She'd said it herself, hadn't she? This had been a bad idea. "Yeah," he agreed, jamming his hands into his pockets to keep from doing something idiotic like reaching for her. Never only just one feeling at a time. "Maybe you should go, then."

Just for a moment, Meg looked at him like he was the most disappointing person she'd ever encountered in her eighteen years on this planet. Then she shrugged. "Yup," she said. "Maybe I should."

EIGHTEEN

Meg

It was too late to start the drive home at this point, so Meg pulled up a map on her phone and drove to the closest hotel that was part of a chain she recognized. The parking lot was the quietest place she'd ever been in her life. "Hi," she said to the clerk inside the empty lobby, clearing her throat and trying to sound as adult as humanly possible. "I'd like a room for tonight?" She hesitated. "Um. And can I pay with cash?"

The clerk gave her a weird look, but in the end all she did was ask for Meg's ID, then hand her a key and direct her to a room on the third floor. Meg glanced over her shoulder as she speed-walked down the hallway, her backpack slung over both shoulders like she was about to hike the PCT.

God, why hadn't she told anyone where she was?

Well, she *knew* why, but—

Ugh.

She couldn't call her mother. She didn't want to talk to Emily. The person she really wanted to talk to, infuriatingly, was Colby himself—but *her* Colby, not the sharp-jawed stranger from tonight, with his hard, hopeless-sounding laugh. It occurred to Meg that even after meeting him in real life—*especially* after meeting him in real life—she had no idea which one of them was actually real.

It didn't matter, she told herself, methodically flicking on every single light in the hotel room. It was done now. He was the kind of person who'd be fine tomorrow, who would probably never think about her again.

So. That was that, she guessed.

The room was small and smelled vaguely of cigarettes, though she was pretty sure smoking wasn't allowed in here. Meg bounced idly on the side of the bed. She was actually *proud* of the way she'd handled herself with stupid Micah, even if it had pissed Colby off: she'd said exactly what she'd wanted to say in the moment she wanted to say it, and she hadn't gotten flustered or clammed up because she was afraid to cause a scene. Honestly, she wished she could be that direct with Emily or her mom.

That's because I'm not impressive enough for you to actually care what I think, she heard Colby say, his voice in her head low and just a little bit hurt.

No, she told herself firmly, ignoring the uneasy part of her that worried maybe he had a point. It was just that some things were too important to let go.

She thought about taking a shower, but there was a hair that definitely did not belong to her stuck to the tile in the bathtub, so in the end she decided against it. Instead, she kicked the duvet cover onto the floor—she thought she remembered something about hotel duvets not getting washed that often—and curled up on the top sheet fully dressed.

Are you okay?

Meg dropped her phone on the mattress, like it had turned to a burning stone in her hand. She turned it over for good measure, facedown so she couldn't see his message.

Flipped it back over again.

She thought about not texting him back, about turning her phone off and going to sleep and driving straight back to Philly in the morning. Nobody knew about him. As far as the rest of the world was concerned, their relationship didn't exist. She could snip him right out of her life and literally nobody would know the difference except her, and the very thought of it made her want to burst into tears.

I'm fine, she typed, then deleted it letter by letter. The whole point of Colby was that she didn't have to lie to him. She wasn't about to start now just because it turned out he was a dick in real life. *I'm safe.*

Are you on the road?

She tugged at her lip again, considering. She watched six minutes of an *Office* rerun on Comedy Central. She tugged at her lip some more.

Meg, come on.

Then, a moment later: *Or I mean, don't text if you're driving I guess.*

Two minutes after that: *Can we talk on the phone?*

The bubble appeared again, then disappeared. Then appeared one more time: *Meg?*

Meg sighed. *Garden Inn*, she typed finally. *324*.

He showed up at her door half an hour later holding three different kinds of chips and a banana. "I didn't know if you ate dinner after you left," he said, shrugging a little bit helplessly. "Gas station was the only thing open. And then I had to go walk Tris, so the banana is from my house."

"Thanks," Meg said, setting the food down on the dresser next to the complimentary eight-ounce bottle of water. She sat on the bed, wrapping her arms around her knees.

Colby nodded. "I'm sorry we fought," he said, leaning against the wall next to an ugly print of an autumn forest and jamming his hands into the pockets of his jeans.

Meg shook her head, gaze flicking up at the popcorn ceiling. "That's not an apology," she said.

"No," Colby agreed evenly. "It's kind of not, I guess."

"Then why are you here?" Meg exploded, flinging her arms out. "Like, if you don't want to apologize to me, then—"

"If *I* don't want to apologize?" Colby's dark eyes flashed. "Why would I apologize when you're the one—"

"What's the deal with you and Joanna?"

Colby didn't answer for a moment, the silence hanging suspended between them. He leaned his head back against the plaster with a quiet thump.

"Seriously," Meg pressed. She hadn't let herself think about it until she got here, not really, but as soon as Joanna had gotten out of the car it had felt like the numbingly obvious conclusion. Jesus Christ, she was going to feel so enormously dumb. "Is she your girlfriend?"

"Do you care?"

"Are you *kidding* me right now?" Meg barked a sharp, mean laugh. "You let me drive all the way to Nowheresville, Ohio, and you think I wouldn't care if—"

"First of all, that's my fucking hometown you're talking about, Meg. And second of all, I didn't tell you to drive to Ohio!"

"Oh my God." Just like that, Meg was up off the mattress, halfway to the door in two quick steps. "Okay. You know what, Colby? You can just go. Thanks for the chips. This was an adventure."

"Wait, wait, wait," Colby said, holding his hands up; for the first time since he'd gotten here, the panic was visible on his face. "No. Stop. I'm sorry. I don't know why I said that. Joanna isn't my girlfriend. She wants to be, maybe. But she isn't."

Well. Meg swallowed hard, crossing her arms. "Why not?" she managed to ask.

Colby dropped his chin and gazed at her, steady. "Why do you think?"

They faced off across the dingy carpet. Meg looked away first. She remembered a thing she'd read online once about liminal spaces, blurry boundary zones between two established areas. This hotel room felt like that. Their whole *relationship* felt like that, actually, now that she was thinking about it; like it only existed, like it only *could* exist, outside normal space and time.

"You're under my skin," Colby said quietly, sitting down on the edge of the mattress. "And I don't know why."

Meg laughed again, a sound like a door slamming. "Because I'm spectacular, obviously."

She was kidding, but Colby didn't smile. "You kind of are," he said.

Something about the way he was looking at her felt like trying to hold her hand against a hot stove. "Your friends didn't think so," she pointed out.

Colby blew a breath out, flopping back onto the mattress. "Yeah, well," he said, "Micah is an idiot."

"I know," Meg said immediately. "Which is why it's so fucked up that you wouldn't just—"

Colby struggled upright. "I don't want to have that argument with you again," he said flatly. "Don't you ever get tired of taking everything so personally?"

"Don't *you* ever get tired of being too cool to care?"

"I'm not too *cool* for anything," Colby countered, making a face like the word was somehow offensive.

"Too scared, then," Meg said immediately. "They can't pull the rug out from under you if you decide there's no rug to begin with, right?"

Colby startled at that, eyes widening almost imperceptibly. Then he set his jaw. They were silent for a minute, just the hum of the AC underneath the window and somebody else's TV down the hall.

"Can I ask you something?" Meg continued finally, perching on the greasy-looking desk and gazing at him across the hotel room. "If I hadn't texted the day after you first called me, you would never have texted me, either, right?"

Colby didn't have to think about it. "No," he admitted. "Probably not."

"Yeah." Meg crossed her arms, feeling meanly satisfied. "That's what I thought."

"Well, congratulations," he said, shrugging a little. "You were right about me, I guess."

Meg looked at him for another long moment. "Do you think we're too different?" she finally asked.

Colby raised his eyebrows, lifted his chin. "Too different for what?" he asked.

Meg shrugged. "Anything, I guess."

"Too different for me to kiss you?"

It was so out of left field she didn't know how to answer; she could tell he'd surprised himself, too, by the expression on his face. Still, he didn't look away from her, his gaze like a weighted blanket. Right away, she wanted it like she'd never wanted anything in her entire life. She'd wanted it for a long time, if she was being honest with herself: since that very first night on the phone, maybe, the low, private sound of his laugh in her ear.

"Well," she said, pushing off the desk and taking a step closer, wiping her suddenly sweaty hands on the seat of her jeans. "Only one way to find out, I guess."

Colby smiled.

It was awkward at first: standing up, he was a lot taller than her, so the angle was funny, and then he came in kind of a lot with his tongue, but she put her hands on his shoulders and pushed him gently back to sitting, and after a moment it got better, their mouths getting used to each other and his palms warm and damp on her waist.

They kissed for a long time, Colby's fingertips creeping up underneath her T-shirt. Meg crawled into his lap on the bed. "Is that okay?" he asked, and she unzipped his hoodie to answer, sliding her palms along his back and stomach and rib cage. The skin on his chest was very warm.

Eventually he nudged her onto her back on the mattress, the weight of his body half-suffocating and half-thrilling and his thigh warm and heavy between hers. Meg could feel her heart scrabbling around inside her chest. Being the kind of person who'd drive to Ohio without telling anyone was one thing, but being the kind of person who'd have sex in a hotel room with someone she'd technically just met felt like something else altogether. As Colby rubbed his thumb over the seam of her jeans, she wondered if it would actually be so bad to be that kind of person, but in the end she pushed him gently away.

"Okay," she said, gasping a little. She wanted to so bad, was the truth. "We can't—"

"No, I know," he said, sitting up right away and shaking his head like he was trying to clear it, breathing through his nose like a bull. "I know, that's—"

"Have you ever?" she asked, before she could lose her courage. It seemed weird that out of all the things they'd talked about, they'd never talked about this. "I mean . . ."

She watched him think about lying to her, but in the end he shook his head. "No, actually. Have you?"

Meg nodded. "With Mason."

She wasn't sure how Colby was going to react to that—not, she reminded herself, that it was any of his business to react to either way—but in the end he just nodded back like he'd figured as much. "Makes sense," he said. "That's what people do, right?"

"Some people," Meg said. It had been fine with Mason; they'd waited until they'd been dating for six months and he'd been extremely respectful, but it hadn't rocked her world or anything. It hadn't, she thought suddenly, felt anything like this. "Not everybody." She looked at him another moment. "Girlfriends?"

"Some, kind of." Then he shook his head again, glancing up at the ceiling. "Not really. I'm stupid with girls. I don't know."

"Not that stupid," Meg teased, slipping a finger into his belt loop and yanking once.

"Pretty stupid." Colby sat back against the headboard, crossing his ankles. Both of them were still wearing their shoes. "I came close a couple times, I guess. This girl Brooklyn I knew in high school, and this other girl who worked the registers at the store for a while."

"Joanna," Meg reminded him pointedly.

"Joanna, maybe. I don't know." Colby shrugged into the pillows. "It's like that whole cost-benefit-analysis thing again, I guess. It just never felt like it was worth it to potentially, like, humiliate myself to try and get over the—the—"

"Hump?" Meg supplied, and Colby laughed.

"Yeah."

She was quiet for a moment, tucking her legs up underneath her. "It feels worth it with me, though, right?" she couldn't help but ask.

Colby smiled crookedly. "I mean, I'm not planning to humiliate myself any more than I already have, if I can help it."

"Well, sure." Meg didn't smile back. "But still."

Colby took a breath. “Yeah,” he said, looking at her across the mattress. “It feels worth it with you.”

Meg didn’t know if she believed him, not entirely; still, she nodded in reply. “Good,” she said, stretching out beside him and resting her cheek against his shoulder. “It feels worth it to me, too.”

Colby reached over and turned off the lamp on the nightstand, leaving the others blazing. The sound of his heartbeat was the last thing she heard before she fell asleep.

NINETEEN

Colby

Colby woke up with a gasp from a nightmare—fisting his hands in the sheets for a moment, not entirely sure where he was. Then he blinked and looked around the hotel room—the lights still on, the dawn dripping up outside the open window, the girl sacked out beside him with her T-shirt rucked up just enough to expose the dimples on either side of her backbone—and remembered.

Meg was sleeping so deeply it felt like a shame to wake her up, but he didn't want her to think he'd bailed without saying goodbye. "Hey," he said, laying a gentle hand on her shoulder. "I gotta go let the dog out before work."

Meg blinked awake, her eyes huge and dark and deep as caverns. "Oh," she said, a moment of her own confusion before she blinked again, sitting up. "Okay." He could see that she was wanting to ask if she was going to see him again. He wanted to ask it, too, and didn't.

Instead, he took a deep breath, reaching out and tucking her hair behind her ear. "Can I kiss you goodbye?" he asked.

"Colby . . ." Meg wrinkled her nose. "I've got morning breath."

Colby smiled; he couldn't help it. "I don't care about your morning breath."

"Well, I do." Meg gamboled upright and darted into the bathroom, returning a minute later smelling like Colgate Total and face wash. He could see where she'd tried to rub the smudges of mascara from under her eyes. She wasn't the prettiest girl he'd ever met—he thought Jo was probably prettier, if you put them side by side—but there was something about Meg that made him feel like his heart was on fire when he looked at her. There was something about her that made him feel like he could build a staircase to the sky.

She scooped his hoodie off the floor and held it out in his direction, but Colby shook his head. "Keep it," he said, aware that he wanted her to have something of his and embarrassed about it in equal amounts.

Meg smiled. "Yeah?"

"Yeah, I don't know. Come here."

Colby put both hands on her face and kissed her, tasting toothpaste and something like hope. She fisted her hands in his

T-shirt, her short nails zipping against the cotton. "Bye," she muttered into his mouth.

"Bye."

He kissed her one more time before he went, the lock clicking softly shut behind him. He spent his whole shift trying not to smile.

She called that night as he was getting ready for bed. "What are you doing?" she wanted to know.

Colby stuck his toothbrush in the holder and wandered down the hall to his room, Tris bumping against his shins before trotting off toward the kitchen. "Just heading to bed."

"Oh yeah?" she asked, a lilt in her voice he'd never heard before. "How about that; me too."

"Oh," he said dumbly, sitting down on the edge of the mattress. They'd talked on the phone when they were both in bed plenty of times, but it felt different now that they'd actually been *in* a bed together, even if nothing had technically happened. *Especially* since nothing technically had. He sat back against the pillows, then scooted down until he was on his back, holding the phone with one hand and resting the other on his stomach. "How was your day?" he finally asked.

"It was okay," she said. "I mean, I spent most of it driving."

"Oh." He nodded. "That makes sense, yeah."

Neither of them said anything for a moment. It felt awkward, suddenly, like it hadn't on the phone before she'd come to visit; then they both spoke at once. "So I was listening to this podcast," Meg started at the same time Colby blurted, "I texted Keith today."

It was true, though he hadn't exactly planned on mentioning it to her. "I told him I'd meet with that guy he wanted to set me up with, the construction dude."

"You *did*?" Meg's voice was eager. "Colby, that's amazing!"

"Relax," he said. "It's just a breakfast."

"Yeah," Meg said, "but still. Look at you, going after what you want. I'm very pleased with myself over here, I'm not going to lie to you. Next thing you know I'll have you knocking on doors for Annie Hernandez."

Colby made a face. "This is all your doing, huh?"

"I'm taking partial credit."

"Uh-huh. You can Venmo me for part of my breakfast, then."

"I will," Meg said immediately. "Seriously, though, I'm proud of you."

"Okay, okay, enough." It made him squirm a little, and not in a good way. He didn't know why she cared so much. "Let's talk about something else."

"Like what?"

Colby considered that for a moment, picturing her back at home in Philadelphia. He wanted to know what her bedroom looked like, but it felt creepy to ask. "What are you wearing?" he blurted instead.

"Seriously?" Meg laughed, and Colby felt like an idiot, only then she actually answered. "A T-shirt."

"With a feminist slogan on it?"

"Shut up," Meg replied. "No. Just plain gray."

"What else?"

Meg didn't answer for a moment. "I mean, underwear," she said finally. "But that's it."

Colby swallowed hard. "That's it, huh?"

"That is it," Meg echoed, a hint of a tease in her voice. "What are you wearing?"

"Just basketball shorts."

"Is that always how you sleep?"

"When I'm not in hotel rooms with random girls, pretty much, yeah."

"Rude," Meg said. Then, more quietly: "I'm not random."

"No," Colby agreed, then cleared his throat a little. He thought of how soft her body was, how warm and smooth the skin of her rib cage had been, and moved his hand off his stomach so he didn't get any ideas. "You're not random at all."

He wanted to tell her other stuff: that he was afraid of how he felt about her, that nothing about this seemed easy or smart. That there was a tiny part of him that hadn't wanted to text her at all today, that had wanted to end things right now so that last night in the hotel room could be hermetically sealed, un-fuck-uppable. *Nobody can pull the rug out from under you if you decide there isn't a rug to begin with.*

But that was ridiculous.

Right?

"I should go to sleep," she said finally, yawning into the receiver; Colby thought of her wet, pink tongue before he could help himself, and balled his free hand into a fist.

"Okay," he managed, and to his credit his voice was only the slightest bit strangled. "Have a good sleep."

"Night, Colby."

Colby hit end and set his phone on the nightstand, then rolled over and groaned once into the pillows before he turned out the light.

Doug Robard was already sitting in a booth at Bob Evans when Colby got there early the next morning, drinking coffee and reading the paper in cargo pants and a polo shirt. Colby didn't know what he'd expected—it wasn't like he thought the guy was going to show up wearing a feather boa—but he still kind of felt like a piece of shit for thinking . . . whatever it was he'd thought. He didn't even know how he knew Doug was gay, other than off-color jokes Rick and Matt had made about him. He cringed to think what Meg would have said if she'd heard.

"Good to see you, Colby," Doug said, once they'd shaken. "Been a long time since you and your brother used to run around on your dad's job sites."

"He hated that," Colby said with a grin.

"Nah, he didn't," Doug said easily. "That guy loved having you two nearby."

The waitress showed up before Colby could answer, a woman a little older than his mom with glasses the size of dinner plates; Colby ordered a stack of pancakes and a side of bacon, then dumped a bunch of cream and sugar into his coffee before taking a sip.

"Keith speaks real highly of you," Doug said, once the waitress was gone.

"He does?" Colby blinked, surprised. Keith was always spouting all kinds of inspirational bullshit, but Colby had always figured it was for his benefit. It was weird to think of him saying it to other people.

Doug smiled. "Yeah, Colby. He says you're a smart kid, that maybe you need some direction." He raised his eyebrows. "Told me about the water tower, too."

Of course he fucking had. "Yeah," Colby said—looking down and picking at his cuticles, trying not to visibly bristle. "That was pretty stupid, I guess."

Doug took a sip of his coffee. "It was," he agreed. "Was stupid back when I did it, too."

Colby's gaze snapped up. "You climbed the water tower?"

Doug nodded. "I was a little younger than you, probably? Scaled it in January of my senior year with a buddy of mine, only once we got up there it started snowing like a mother, and he got the yips and couldn't climb down. Had to scream our asses off until finally some neighbor woman heard and called the fire department to come get us."

"No way," Colby said, unable to hide his smile.

"Way, my friend." Doug nodded his thanks as the waitress topped off his coffee cup. "So," he said, "Keith told you I'm looking for an apprentice carpenter."

"He did," Colby said, then cleared his throat when he heard how dorkily squeaky his voice sounded. "He did."

Doug nodded. "It's not going to be particularly glamorous," he warned. "A lot of grunt work—moving materials, sweeping up, that kind of thing. But in my experience, guys who don't mind grunt work are the same ones you can trust with sophisticated work later on. And if we both feel like it's a good fit, there's room for you to grow."

"I don't mind grunt work," Colby said, trying not to sound too eager.

"Well," Doug said, "that's good to hear."

They talked about the projects Doug had in the pipeline, big restoration jobs up closer to Columbus and a full gut on an old mansion a theater group was converting into a performance space in Chillicothe. When he finally named the salary out loud, Colby had to struggle to keep his face neutral: it was more than twice what he was making at the warehouse.

There was no way this was actually going to happen, he reminded himself, swallowing the last of his pancakes.

Meg's voice whispered: *But what if it does?*

Matt was at the house when Colby got back from work late that afternoon, standing in the yard throwing the tennis ball to Tris. "Mom home?" Colby asked, and Matt shook his head.

"Not yet." He tucked his hands into the pockets of his khakis. "What were you doing on a date with Doug Robard this morning?"

"First of all, fuck you," Colby said, not unpleasantly. He'd known this was coming, though it had happened faster than he thought. "Second of all, who says I was with Doug Robard?"

"Nikki saw you at Bob Evans," Matt said. Nikki was the girl Matt was dating, a snotty redhead who always seemed to be scowling about something. Not that Colby had much of a leg to stand on in that department, he guessed. "Are you working with him?"

"No," Colby said, then shrugged. "What if I am?"

"What if you—" Matt broke off, a muscle in his jaw twitching. "Look," he said in the measured voice he used when he wanted to drive home exactly how much of an idiot he thought Colby was, "if you don't want to come work for Rick, that's your business. But I think it's fucked up to turn around and go take a job with his direct competitor, that's all."

Colby scooped the tennis ball up off the ground and threw

it, watching as Tris took off in pursuit across the muddy grass. "They're not direct competitors," he said.

"Close enough."

"Not really."

Matt rolled his eyes. "Yes, Colby, you think Rick's a hack, we know. You've been very clear." He stepped out of the way as Tris came careening back toward them, overshooting before turning around and trotting over with the ball in her mouth. "If family means nothing to you, then—"

Colby whipped around to look at him. "Are you fucking kidding me right now?"

Matt startled, then held his ground. "Do I look like I'm kidding?"

"You don't, which is why I'm asking." Colby wrenched the ball from Tris's mouth a little more roughly than he meant to, throwing it out toward the woods one more time. "Because that's hilarious coming from you."

"Seriously?" Matt looked momentarily wounded, which was surprising. "Everything I do is for this family. Who do you think helps Mom pay the mortgage? Who do you think kept the lights on all year long? What do you think, because you buy dog food every once in a while you're moving the needle? Do you have any idea how much help Mom needs that she doesn't want to put on you because you're the baby? Ever since Dad's been gone—"

"And whose fault is it that he's gone in the first place, Matt?"

"What the fuck does that mean?"

Colby set his shoulders. "You know what it means."

"I really don't."

"It means you threw him out with the trash, and look what happened." It felt good and gross and painful and satisfying to say it, like ripping a scab that wasn't quite ready. Matt got very, very still.

"Is that what you think?" he asked, half his face lit by the glow of the deck light and the other half in shadow. "What, because I went to work with Rick?"

"See?" Colby asked, vindicated. "You know exactly what I'm talking about. You abandoned him, and two weeks later he—"

"*I* abandoned *him*?" Matt laughed out loud, though it sounded more like he was choking. "By going out and actually making some money? He wasn't fucking working, Colby! Literally, the guy had no jobs lined up and was too depressed to get up and find any. I begged him to get his act together, and so did Mom, and he didn't. Or couldn't, I don't know."

Colby shook his head. "You're lying," he said. He remembered that time, or he thought he did, though all of a sudden he wasn't entirely sure. Work had been slow, that was all. His dad had been working on figuring it out. "He didn't get really bad until after you left him to—"

"He was messed up on and off since before you were born, Colby!" Matt shook his head. "The first time he tried to kill himself I was in middle school. Mom fell all over herself trying to keep you from finding out."

"Wait." It felt like the ground moved suddenly. Colby took a physical step back. "What? Shut the fuck up. You're full of shit."

"Why would I lie about that?" Matt asked, sounding terrifyingly sincere. "You were a little kid still. We stayed with Rick and Alicia, remember?"

Colby shook his head, mulish. "We stayed with them because Dad was doing repairs on the house."

"Repairs." Matt gestured back at the house like a carnival barker—*Step right up.* "What repairs, exactly?" His eyes narrowed. "God, everybody coddled you because you were the baby. And now you're a grown-ass man and you *still* want everybody to coddle you—"

"And *you're* just jealous because Dad left Paradise to me instead of you, so you're—"

"You think I give a shit about Paradise?" Matt demanded. "Paradise is worthless, Colby. Congratulations; Dad liked you better. But Dad's dead, in case you haven't noticed, so if at any point you want to stop using what happened as an excuse for acting like a lazy sack of shit all the time—"

That was when Colby hit him.

It was a sloppy punch, catching Matt at the temple instead of the jaw, where Colby had been aiming; just like that they were a tangle of legs and fists and fingers. There was a ripping sound as Matt grabbed hold of Colby's flannel, Tris barking frantically as she circled around. They used to wrestle all the time when they were kids, even when they were a little too old for it, suplexing one another into piles of dead leaves in the backyard or pile driving one another into the couch. He'd broken Matt's front tooth once by hitting him in the face with the remote control for the DVD player, but they'd never done anything like this.

Colby hit his brother again, then another time, anger erupting out from an inside deeper than he knew he had. He could feel something warm and wet, spit or blood or maybe both, slipping down the side of his chin. His fist caught his brother in the cheekbone. Matt's work boot caught him square in the chest. "You're an asshole," someone said, though Colby wasn't sure which one of them was talking. After that, he didn't hear anything at all.

TWENTY

Colby

"Welp," Meg reported miserably when she called him late that night, Colby's phone vibrating wildly across the nightstand, "turns out Rebecca Latimer Felton was a giant white supremacist."

"Wait, what?" Colby shifted around on the mattress as gingerly as possible. His ribs were bruised, according to the ER doc; every time he breathed it felt like someone was stomping on his lungs. "Who?"

"Rebecca Latimer Felton!" Meg repeated, like if she said it enough times he'd somehow magically know who she was talking about. He could hear her typing angrily away in the background. "The first woman in the Senate! I'm doing my independent study about her, remember? Or I *was*, at least."

“Oh,” Colby said, wincing. “Yeah. Whoops.”

“Yeah, Colby, whoops.” Meg sounded aggrieved. “I read all these scholarly sources about her, I had a freaking *children’s* book, and it wasn’t until I looked at *Wikipedia* of all places that anybody even thought to mention the fact that she owned slaves and was, like, very much in favor of lynching.”

Colby grimaced. “Shit.”

“That’s what I’m saying! My project is due in six days, and it turns out she’s basically the poster woman for the most awful, racist, violent kind of white feminism.”

“I mean, I keep trying to tell you that about politicians,” Colby said, leaning back against the pillows. His head throbbed. They’d only just gotten back from the hospital a little while ago; his mom had gone directly into her bedroom and slammed the door loud enough to rattle the whole house. “They’ll let you down every time.”

Meg made a strangled sound. “It’s not funny, Colby!”

“I’m not joking,” he countered immediately. “This lady sounds like she was hot garbage, which is a good example of why you shouldn’t, like, put all your faith in—”

“Okay, okay,” Meg interrupted. “I get it. But can you just feel bad for me without telling me why it’s stupid to believe in government altogether?”

“I do feel bad for you,” Colby promised, though truthfully he wasn’t super surprised there’d been gaps in her research. Meg meant well—Colby knew that now—but still he got the feeling she only knew what she was talking about, like, half the time. "I mean, I feel a lot worse for all the people she thought she had the right to *own*, but—"

"I mean, yes, obviously. Thank you." Meg sighed. "Are you okay?" she asked a moment later. "Your voice sounds funny tonight."

"I'm surprised you can hear me at all, the way you're pounding on those keys over there," Colby informed her. "Whenever I picture you working, I imagine that gif of Kermit the Frog slamming away on the typewriter. Arms flying all around, clouds of dust everywhere . . ."

Meg laughed at that. "Oh, *that's* how you imagine me?"

"It is," Colby said immediately. "A very sexy Kermit the Frog."

"Perv."

"Prude."

"That's what you think," Meg shot back immediately. Colby smiled, then winced as the butterfly on his cheekbone pulled his skin. His voice sounded weird because there was gauze shoved up into his sinuses: Matt had broken his nose, which Colby guessed was fair enough considering the fact that Matt had needed seven stitches in his lip.

"What are you up to this week?" he asked Meg now, wanting to change the subject. He didn't tell her about his fight with Matt. It felt too complicated to explain, even to her, on top of which he knew it would just underline the stuff she already thought about his family, the idea that they were too dumb or backward to settle their disagreements with SAT words and civilized debate.

To be fair, he didn't know if she actually thought that.

Also, he was a little embarrassed.

After they said good night, Colby lay on his back on the mattress for a long time, trying not to jostle his busted self too badly and also not to think about what Matt had said that afternoon in the backyard. Part of him had meant it when he told his brother he was full of shit—it was fucking absurd to think his dad had just periodically wanted to die for Colby's entire childhood while Colby strolled stupidly around playing PlayStation and eating Little Debbies. He would have known. He would *have* to have known.

Still, the other part of him kept replaying that week at Rick and Alicia's—they'd gone on a hayride, he remembered suddenly, all of them drinking hot apple cider out of Styrofoam cups—and felt like he was going to throw up all over his bed.

It didn't matter, Colby told himself, clicking the light off and trying to put the whole thing out of his head. It ended the same either way, didn't it? All roads led to Rome, or whatever the expression was. He thought Meg would probably know, not that he had any intention of talking to Meg about this. Not that he had any intention of talking to anyone.

After all: What was the point?

...

He had to go to the pharmacy the following morning to fill the prescription for heavy-duty Tylenol the ER doc had given him: "You shouldn't need anything stronger," she'd said as she'd handed it over, like she half expected him to grab her by the lapels of her white coat and demand a year's supply of Oxy. He was heading back to his car when someone called his name from across the parking lot.

"Hey," Joanna said, lifting a delicate hand in greeting. She was wearing a shiny purple blouse and one of those skinny knee-length skirts, her legs long and tan even though it wasn't summer yet. Her hair was a tidy yellow knot on top of her head. "I thought that was you."

"Hey," Colby called back. "I was wondering if you were working today." The hair salon was in the same strip mall as the CVS.

"Could have texted," she pointed out, raising her eyebrows teasingly. "Found out for sure."

Colby knew that, actually. He hadn't on purpose—one, because his face was so fucking busted right now, and two, because he didn't know exactly what to say to her. They hadn't talked since Saturday night when Meg was in town. "Yeah, well," he said, jamming his hands into his pockets. "Didn't want to scare you."

She nodded. "You're pretty ugly," she agreed with a smile that suggested she didn't actually think so. "Jordan told me about you and Matt, but I thought he was exaggerating."

"Yeah, not so much." Colby shrugged. "We went after each other pretty hard, I guess."

Joanna seemed unperturbed. "That's what brothers do, right?" she asked. "Mine used to beat the shit out of each other every day before Pete went to college. Jordan broke his collarbone once throwing him off the side of the deck."

Colby smiled at that, though he guessed it wasn't actually funny. Still, he knew what she was trying to do, and he appreciated it. Talking to Joanna always made him feel like his fuckups weren't that big of a deal. "I remember."

Joanna nodded. "So," she said, rubbing her palms over her bare arms as the breeze rustled through the trees that ringed the parking lot. "Your friend Meg seemed nice."

Colby's eyes widened, at the mention of Meg's name in the first place, and in the second place because he was fairly certain that whatever impression she'd given off that night in the parking lot, *nice* was not it. "She said the same thing about you, actually."

Joanna smiled, a little uncertain. Colby could see she was considering asking him what the hell his deal was. He knew he should take responsibility for the situation—apologize, or at the very least explain what had happened. Jo deserved better, that much was for sure. Still, the truth was he was pretty sure she'd let him off the hook rather than push it, and he was right. "Are you going to this thing at Micah's tomorrow?" she asked, tucking some imaginary hair behind her ears. "The pig roast?"

"What?" He'd known there was a party, though he hadn't really thought about it. He guessed he hadn't thought about much, since Meg's visit. "He's doing a *pig* roast?"

"I mean, I don't know," Joanna amended. "He *says* he is. Where he thinks he's going to get a whole pig is beyond me."

"Hope the security's good at the petting zoo," Colby joked, and Joanna groaned.

"Gross," she said, kicking him lightly in the ankle. "Anyway. I think you should come."

Colby nodded. "Maybe," he hedged. "We'll see what my face is looking like, how about."

"Send me a picture," Joanna instructed, turning on her heel and heading back across the parking lot. "I'll let you know if you're too scary for young audiences!" She was gone before he could think of a reply.

Back in the car, he saw Doug had called while he'd been in the pharmacy. He'd called yesterday after their breakfast, too, to ask a question about Colby's availability, but with everything that had happened with Matt, Colby hadn't gotten around to calling him back. He sat there for a moment now, thumb hovering over Doug's name in his contact list, before dropping the phone in the cup holder and turning the key in the ignition. He'd do it later, he promised himself, then pulled out of the parking lot and headed home to take a nap.

TWENTY-ONE

Meg

That night, Meg was sitting at her desk eating a granola bar and working on her independent study—she'd gotten an extension, and permission to research Maxine Waters instead—when her phone dinged beside her with a text. *I really miss you*, Emily had written. *Can we hang out this week?*

Meg frowned. *We hang out all the time*, she typed, then deleted it letter by careful letter and told herself not to be such a bitch. After all, it wasn't like she didn't know what Emily was getting at: they may have had almost every class together, and they may have shared a bag of Pirate's Booty in the cafeteria every day, but they hadn't seen each other outside school since last Friday with Mason at Cavelli's. Meg had texted both of them when she got back from Colby's to apologize, to promise she'd just been freaked out about her dad's engagement and everything was totally fine, but still there was something weird and chafe-y about their friendship the last few days, like a shoe rubbing a blister on her heel.

Now she sat back in her desk chair, her eyes landing on Colby's gray hoodie slung over the armchair across the room. It still smelled like him: a little like Dial soap and bonfire and a little bit like the hamper. She'd worn it to bed every night since she'd gotten back from Ohio.

I need to get a dress for my dad's wedding, she told Emily finally. Actually, the wedding wasn't until Memorial Day, but it felt like a good low-stakes activity, the kind of thing they could do without talking too much about Mason or Cornell or anything else. *Shopping tomorrow?*

They went to the Short Hills Mall after school, loading themselves down with dresses and cramming themselves into a tiny Nordstrom fitting room just like they had before junior prom last year, both of them trying as hard as they could to act like everything was okay. "Oh my God," Emily said, as Meg pulled a long blue dress off the hanger and over her head. "Did I tell you Andrew walked in on my mom and dad having sex the other night?"

Meg whipped around so fast she almost busted a seam, her eyes wide. Andrew was Emily's brother, a sophomore at Overbrook with big ears and a goofy smile. "No!"

"He showed up in my room looking like he'd just seen the

freaking Babadook," Emily said with a grimace. "I guess he just, like, barged in there looking for clean laundry and got an eyeful of my dad's bare ass? I don't even know."

"I mean," Meg said, trying not to giggle and mostly failing. "I guess it's nice to know that your parents are still, you know, attracted to each other?" She snorted. "You know, like . . . theoretically?"

"Is it, though?" Emily asked, and by now both of them were really starting to lose it. "Is it really?"

They wound up doubled over laughing, the weirdness dissolving between them as they cackled so loudly the saleswoman rapped on the door and demanded to know if everything was okay. They were finally pulling themselves together when Emily frowned. "Wait a second," she said, reaching out and tugging the strap of Meg's dress aside. "Is that a *hickey*?"

"What?" Meg startled. "No." Shit. Meg hadn't even realized hickeys were a real thing until she'd seen it in the mirror when she got home from Colby's three days ago, her whole body lighting up like a pinball machine at the memory of his mouth on her neck. It had faded since then, but not all the way; she'd put a thick layer of her mom's concealer on it in the bathroom this morning, but it must have rubbed off as she was trying on clothes.

Emily frowned, popping up on her tiptoes to get a better look at it. "Are you sure?"

"Who would I have gotten a hickey from?" Meg asked, cringing as her voice echoed through the dressing room, swatting Emily gently away. "I burned myself with the curling iron the other day."

"Ugh, Piper did that," Emily said. Piper was Emily's older sister, who was in a sorority at Penn State. "She got this gnarly scab that filled with pus; it was totally disgusting."

Meg grimaced. "Here," she said, frowning at herself in the mirror and motioning down at the dress, a satiny sleeveless number that made her look like she was going to a seventh-grade formal. "Help me get out of this."

Emily unhooked the tiny clasp in the back, pulling the finicky zipper down and stepping back so that Meg could wriggle out of it. "Hey, have you called Cornell yet to check on your application?" she asked as Meg pulled her jeans back on.

"Um," Meg said, turning away as she reached for her T-shirt. *Just say it*, she ordered herself. *Just tell her you don't want to—*

"I'm just getting really worried now, you know?" Emily continued, clipping the dress back onto its hanger. "It just feels so weird that you wouldn't have—"

"I got in!" Meg blurted, yanking her T-shirt over her head with more force than was really necessary; she blinked in the light of the dressing room, shocking herself.

Emily whipped around to stare at her. "What? Oh my God, you did? When? Why didn't you say anything?"

"I—" Meg broke off. Oh, this was bad. This was not how she had wanted to do this. "Things were a little weird between us, so—"

"Meg! Oh my God!" Emily flung her arms around Meg's shoulders, wrapping her in a Sephora-scented hug. "This is the best news I've ever heard."

"I know," Meg said, squeezing her eyes shut. "Me too."

"You want to come over for dinner?" Emily asked as they headed out to the parking lot a little while later, the sun just starting to sag. "My mom's making stuffed shells."

"Sure," Meg said, cheered by the thought of it. "I have to be at WeCount at seven, but I can just go straight there." Emily's house was nothing like hers—a midcentury ranch in a neighborhood full of midcentury ranches, always bustling, full of various people's winter coats and sheet music and soccer cleats, but never actually messy. Meg loved it there: the lemon-scented hand soap and the detailed dry-erase calendar on the fridge and the fact that there was always some kind of homemade baked good in the big glass canister on the counter. Most of all she loved Emily's mom, who was as sweet and predictable as the raspberry-lime seltzer she drank every night with dinner. You never had to worry about which version of her you were going to get.

They stopped for coffee on the way home, Emily insisting they needed iced campfire mochas to celebrate Meg's acceptance letter. "Let me get it," Emily argued, waving her wallet in protest as they cruised through the drive-thru lane. Meg shook her head and Emily grumbled good-naturedly, clearing a handful of junk out of the cup holder in order to set her coffee inside. "When were you in Ohio?" she asked.

Meg froze, whipping her head around to stare at the passenger seat. Emily was holding the receipt from her lunch with Colby, the address of the Subway franchise stamped in huge letters at the top.

"Meg? What were you doing in Ohio last weekend?" Her eyes narrowed. "Why were you—did you go see that guy? Oh my *God*, is the guy the one who gave you the hickey?"

Even through her panic, there was a part of Meg that was impressed Emily had figured it out so quickly. She hadn't thought their friendship still had the mind-meld quality it used to, like back in middle school when their other friends hadn't let them be on the same team for Celebrity because it wasn't fair to everyone else.

"Em," she began as she pulled out of the parking lot, trying to figure out how she was possibly going to explain this in a way that didn't sound completely demented. "Look, I was going to talk to you about it—"

"Oh my God, are you kidding? That's actually where you were?" Emily looked at the receipt again. "You told me you were at your dad's."

"I know I did," Meg said. "I just—" She broke off.

"You just lied to my face, is all," Emily snapped, her voice surprisingly nasty. "Nice, Meg. What else are you lying about?"

Meg bristled in spite of herself. "Hold on a second," she said, turning onto the leafy green avenue that led to Emily's neighborhood. "Do you of all people seriously want to give me a hard time about lying right now?"

Emily sat up straight in the passenger seat. "What does *that* mean?"

"You know what that means, Em."

"What, because of me and Mason? You said that was okay!"

"It *is* okay!"

"I mean, clearly not."

"It's fine," Meg insisted. "But it just doesn't feel fair for you to be holding yourself up as some gold standard of transparency when—"

"We're not talking about me!" Emily exploded. "Did you tell anybody where you were going?"

Meg blew a breath out. "Not exactly," she admitted.

"I don't believe this," Emily said. "What did you do, you just got in your car and drove to his house? Do you have any idea how stupid that was? You're lucky you're not trapped in some terrifying rape dungeon where nobody knows where the hell to find you. You're lucky you aren't *dead*."

"Can you stop being so apocalyptic?" Meg asked. "It wasn't like that."

"Then what was it like?" Emily countered. "However it

was, you obviously felt like you had to lie about it."

"I felt like I had to lie about it because you were totally judgmental from the very beginning!"

"It's not being judgmental to say it's sketchy to drive across state lines to meet some rando from your telemarketing job!"

They were pulling into Emily's driveway now, Mrs. Hurd standing in the front yard in a hoodie from the resort in the Poconos Emily's family went to every summer, pulling damp winter leaves out of the flower beds. She waved at Meg, her hand encased in a dirt-covered gardening glove; Meg smiled at her reflexively, then frowned. "Emily . . ." she tried again, but Emily was already unclicking her seat belt, scooping her purse up off the floor of the car.

"Forget it," she said, snatching her iced coffee out of the cup holder. "I can't talk to you about this right now. I'll text you later, okay?" She slammed the passenger door before Meg could reply.

Meg knew something was wrong before she even got her key in the door. Bonnie Raitt was turned up so loud on the stereo it was audible even with the windows shut. When she got inside, her mom was sitting at the kitchen island, a mostly empty bottle of sauvignon blanc open beside her. "Hey," Meg said, picking her mom's phone up off the counter and using it to turn the music down. "I'm home."

"I see that," her mom said without quite making eye contact, pouring the last of the wine into her glass. "How was the mall?"

"It was fine," Meg said cautiously, gaze flicking around the kitchen in a way she hoped wasn't too obvious. The garbage was piled over the top of the can in the corner, the edges of the bag pulled up to halfheartedly contain the overflow. There was something sticky—honey, maybe?—glistening on the counter. Meg had been trying to do a better job keeping up with stuff around the house lately, but it felt like there was always something left to do: a mountain of laundry in the bathroom hamper or a bunch of moldy leftovers to throw out in the fridge. She wanted to say something about it to her mom, to suggest they get a cleaning lady or something, but she felt like doing it would start an argument about her dad not paying enough alimony and also puncture some kind of illusion both of them were still holding on to. "How are you?"

Meg's mom didn't answer. "I heard from your father today," she said instead, and all of a sudden Meg knew exactly what the music—and the wine—were about. "He had some news."

"Oh yeah?" Meg said, hedging. "What about?"

Her mom made a face. "Why don't you tell me?" she said. "Since apparently you already know all about it."

Meg dropped her bag on the counter. "Okay, Mom, listen—"

"How long have you been sitting on that?" her mom interrupted. "How long did you know he was *engaged* and—"

"He wanted to be the one to tell you," Meg interrupted, aware even as she was saying it that she was lying all over the place lately. "He asked me not to say anything."

"So your loyalty is to *him* and what *he* wants?"

"No, Mom." Meg shook her head. "It's not—"

"That's good to know, since I'm the one feeding and housing and clothing you."

Meg gaped at her for a moment. "That's not fair," she said, a feeling like tears rising dangerously in her throat. It was a *lot*, all of a sudden, her mom being mad and her dad getting married and her fight with Emily and everything that had happened with Colby; she felt like an overfull glass. "You can't just stick me between the two of you guys like that. It isn't fair."

"Life isn't fair, Meg." Her mom stood up unsteadily, her elegant hands gripping the side of the island for balance. "If I can impart one life lesson to you, as your mother, let that be it."

"*Mom.*" Now she really did start crying, one ragged sob that slipped out before she could stop it. It broke the spell, and suddenly her mom was herself again: the same person who'd managed to explain sex in a way that wasn't embarrassing and knew if Meg had a fever by feeling her cheek with the back of her hand, who always poured potato chips into a bowl and ate the broken shards because she knew Meg liked the big ones best. "God."

"I'm sorry," her mom said immediately, scrubbing her free hand over her face. "You're right, that was shitty. I'm sorry."

"We can't keep this up," Meg said, not sure which one of them she was talking to, exactly. Suddenly, she felt like some low-budget actress performing to a totally empty house.

"Keep what up?" her mom asked, sitting back down again. Meg wondered with some horror if possibly she was too drunk to walk. "Come on, Meg, my girl."

Meg shook her head. "It's fine," she said, grabbing her backpack and heading for the doorway. "I have to go to work."

By the time she picked up a burrito for dinner and made it to the WeCount offices, she felt like a cartoon character who'd been in a fistfight, like she ought to have a missing tooth and an old-fashioned bandage wrapped around her head. "You good?" Lillian asked, raising her eyebrows over the partition.

"I'm good," Meg promised.

Lillian nodded, eyes just slightly narrowed. "There are chocolate chip cookies in the kitchen" was all she said.

Meg spent the next hour talking to a sweet old man in Toledo and a grouchy old lady in New Hope, then left four voice mails in a row before finally leaning back in her chair, staring up at the fluorescent lights in the drop ceiling overhead. Em would forgive her, she told herself firmly. She'd forgive her, and they'd room together at Cornell just like they'd always planned, and if the thought of it made Meg feel like the walls of this office were closing in on her by the second, she'd just have to be a damn adult and get over it.

After all, what else was she going to do?

She tugged on her lip for a moment, remembering the

conversation she'd had with Colby way back when: *If you actually do want to go change things, if you actually think you* can, *then shouldn't you, like . . . go out there and change them?*

She glanced over the partition at Lillian, who was talking animatedly into her headset, then opened her internet browser and put in the address for Annie Hernandez's website. She scrolled all the way down until she found it, there at the very bottom: a blue rectangular button that said *Work with Annie.*

It wasn't a real plan, she chided herself firmly.

She didn't know anyone who'd ever done anything like it.

Still, she took a deep breath and clicked.

TWENTY-TWO

Colby

"I'll tell you the worst part," Meg said on the phone late that night, her voice bright and brittle like it always got when she was putting on a little bit of a song-and-dance number. "I didn't even get a dress for the stupid wedding."

Colby laughed. He was lying faceup on the scrubby grass in the backyard, Tris farting periodically beside him. It had been warm out today, or almost. "Is that really the worst part?" he asked.

Meg sighed theatrically. "I mean, no, of course not, but try to find me charming, will you? I'm doing a whole bit here."

"I hear that," Colby murmured, sifting a rock out of the soil and twirling it between the fingers of his free hand. "That's kind of my point, though."

"What is?" Meg sounded suspicious.

Colby shrugged into the grass even though she couldn't see him. "That you don't have to do a bit with me. I don't know."

"Oh really?" Meg huffed. "I thought me *not* doing a bit with you meant I didn't think you were fancy enough to try to impress."

"Easy," Colby said mildly, pushing himself up on one elbow in the weedy grass. "That's not what I said."

"Isn't it?"

"No, actually." At least, he didn't think so; talking to Meg tied his brain into knots sometimes, until he wasn't sure what his point had been to start with. "Or if it was, then it's not what I meant."

"Fine," Meg said in a slightly snotty voice, like she didn't agree with him but wasn't about to waste time and energy arguing about it. "Anyway, my point is, doing a bit isn't always a bad thing. I don't actually think there's anything wrong with not wanting to be full of doom and gloom all the time."

"It's not being full of doom and gloom to say you fought with your friend and your mom was drunk in the middle of the afternoon on a weekday," Colby said, though when he said it like that, even he had to admit it did sound kind of bleak. "Do you think *I'm* full of doom and gloom all the time?"

"Yes," Meg said immediately, but then she laughed, so he wasn't entirely sure if she was serious or not and wasn't sure how to ask her without sounding like a weenie.

"You've got time, right?" he said instead. "To get a dress, I mean."

"Yeah," Meg said, sounding resigned. "The wedding's not till Memorial Day weekend. And the dress is the least of my problems, honestly." She was quiet then, like she was weighing something. "You could come, you know."

Colby opened his mouth so fast his scabby lip split all over again, the iron tang of blood in his mouth. He reached up and wiped it away with the back of his hand. "To your dad's wedding?" he asked. "Like, as your date?"

She blew a breath out on the other end of the phone. "Yeah, Colby, like, as my date."

"I—oh." Colby thought about that for a moment. It was a truly terrible idea for all kinds of reasons, obviously: First of all, he had no idea where he was going to get gas money to drive to Philly. Second of all, his left eye was currently a charming shade of plum. He tried to imagine it: her fancy house and her fancy friends and her dad's fancy wedding. It would probably be a fucking disaster. The smart thing to do would be to stay far, far away.

"Yeah," he said, almost before he had decided. "I'll come be your date."

Meg smiled; he could hear it. It sounded like someone handing you a chocolate chip cookie, or coming inside after being out in the snow. "Really?"

"I mean, yeah." Colby squeezed his good eye shut, already

wondering what he'd just gotten himself into. Already wondering if there was a way to bail out. "If you want me to be."

"I wouldn't have asked you if I didn't."

"Okay," he said—reaching out and running his palm along the silky ridge of Tris's backbone, reassuring. Memorial Day weekend was the anniversary, was the other thing. He didn't know if that made it better or worse. He glanced down at his still-scabby knuckles, *not the first time* like a drumbeat at the back of his head. "Well, then. It's a date."

They talked a little while longer, about her Maxine Waters project and a news story he'd seen about a skunk running around a Cleveland suburb with a yogurt cup stuck on its head and the Senate race she was forever trying to get him to be interested in. Annie Hernandez was behind in the polls, which seemed unsurprising to Colby, though Meg was relentlessly optimistic about her chances. "I looked on her website about maybe doing an internship," she confessed, sounding shyer than he thought of her as being. "Tonight when I was at work."

That got Colby's attention. "What, like, for the fall?" he asked, propping himself up on elbow. "Like, instead of Cornell?"

"I mean, no, I'm totally going to Cornell," she said quickly. "I guess I just . . . I don't know. I was curious." She cleared her throat. "Hey, speaking of job stuff: Have you called that guy Doug back yet?"

"Nah," he said, yawning a little; it was getting colder, and he had to be at work at seven a.m. "Not yet."

"You probably need to get back to him, right? If you're going to do it?"

Colby frowned. This wasn't the first time she'd asked, actually—always like the thought had just occurred to her, her tone always just a little too casual. He almost wished he hadn't told her about it in the first place. "Who says I'm going to do it?" he asked.

Meg paused at that, infinitesimally. "I mean, you did, didn't you?"

"I didn't, actually."

"I—okay," she said, her voice hardening. "Whatever. You don't have to get defensive about it. I'm just asking."

"Are you, though?"

"What's *that* mean?"

"I mean, I'm just saying." Colby sat up in the grass and pulled his knees up, rocking forward a little and raking his free hand through his hair. "Do you want me to get this job for me, or do you want me to get this job because you don't want me to come visit and have to tell your friends you're messing around with a guy who works at Home Depot?"

Another pause, this one just long enough for Colby to realize that was more or less 100 percent the wrong way to put it. Sure enough: "Is that what we're doing?" Meg asked—her consonants getting crisp like they always did when her hackles were raised, like she wanted to remind him just how educated she actually was. "Messing around?"

Colby exhaled. "Don't do that," he said, sliding a hand down over his face.

"Do what?"

"Try to make this conversation about something other than what it's about. I just meant—"

"I know what you meant, Colby. I'm just trying to clarify the terms, that's all."

"Meg," Colby said, though it came out more like he was sighing at her. "Come on."

"*You* come on," Meg snapped. "Is that what you think of me, seriously? That's how shallow I seem to you?"

"It's not about being shallow," he tried. "I'm just saying that kind of stuff matters to—"

"You're making me sound like this huge monster who's obsessed with appearances."

"You *are* obsessed with appearances!"

"Wow." Her voice was flat. "Okay. Screw you, Colby."

Shit. "Meg," he said again. "Wait. I'm sorry. That came out wrong."

Meg blew a breath out. "Why are you picking a fight with me right now?"

Colby felt himself bristle. "I'm not picking a fight with you," he protested. "I'm just—"

"You are, though," she interrupted. "Which sucks, because I literally just invited you to this wedding, and now I'm actually kind of thinking maybe it's *about* the wedding, which, like—"

"It's not," he said, though suddenly he wasn't totally sure if that was the truth. Hadn't he just been wondering if there was a way to get out of it, in the back of his secret brain? "It's not."

"Then what's it about?" Meg asked, sounding wounded. "I don't care what you do, Colby. Take the job or don't take the job; I won't bring it up again. I just want you to be happy. Like, actually, honestly, sincerely happy. Whatever you might think."

Colby was silent for a moment, staring out at the darkened tree line. He wanted to believe her, but he didn't know if he did. Even if she thought she meant it, what exactly was going to happen when her bossy friend Emily found out he'd barely graduated high school? What was going to happen when this whole thing inevitably crashed and burned?

Still, though. Still.

Colby flopped back onto the grass so hard he winced, his ribs protesting. Just for a moment, he'd forgotten his whole body was bruised. "I don't think we're messing around," he admitted finally, his voice barely more than a mumble. Tris, sleeping fitfully now, grumbled quietly at his side. "At least, I don't think that's *all* we're doing."

Meg cackled a sound that wasn't a laugh, not really. "Oh no?"

"No," he said, swallowing the fear down. "I don't."

"Then what are we doing?"

"You tell me."

"Absolutely not."

"Why?"

"Because that's not how this works, Colby."

"Why?"

"Because it's not!"

"That doesn't sound very feminist of you."

"Oh my God. I'm hanging up."

"Meg—"

"No, *I* am, because—"

"Meg—"

"I don't know what your problem is tonight, but—"

"Meg!"

"What?"

"You want to be my girlfriend?" he heard himself blurt.

Meg didn't answer for a moment. Colby could picture her, the way she pulled at her bottom lip when she was thinking about something. "Do you *want* me to be your girlfriend?" she finally asked.

"I wouldn't be asking you if I didn't."

Another pause. Then, more quietly: "Okay."

Something turned over in Colby's chest, surprised, though honestly he wouldn't have asked her to begin with unless he'd been reasonably sure she'd say yes. Still, the feeling pressed at the inside of his rib cage, buoyant: his *girlfriend*. Jesus Christ on a cracker. Colby smiled dumbly into the dark.

TWENTY-THREE

Meg

It was her dad's turn to plan their next dinner, but instead of sending her a restaurant link like usual, he suggested dinner at Lisa's house in Penn Wynne. "I think it would be nice for us all to spend some time together," he said, which Meg felt kind of violated the spirit of their tradition, though it didn't feel worth it to argue. "Um, sure," she said. "Sounds great."

Lisa lived in a tidy Cape Cod at the top of a hill with a swing set in the yard and a *We Are All Welcome Here* sign staked into the tulip bed. All the furniture was made of pale blond wood. Literally everything, from the glass canister of whole-wheat flour on the kitchen counter to the wire bins of art supplies on the bookshelves in the living room, had been labeled with a white paint pen in Lisa's immaculate hand.

"So, Meg," Lisa said, heaping more barley salad onto Meg's dad's plate. Lisa was a strict pescatarian, and her kids had a million different food allergies Meg could never keep track of. They all ate a lot of grilled mahi. "Your dad told me about Cornell! Did you send them your acceptance yet?"

Meg nodded. She'd done it the night before, in fact, at basically the absolute last second before the deadline, waiting to feel anything other than numb. "I did," she said, the words tasting a little bit like sand in her mouth. She glanced at her dad across the table, and then she just blurted it out. "What do you think about me maybe taking a gap year?"

Her dad looked surprised. "A gap year?" he asked. "To do what?"

"I mean, I don't know, exactly," Meg lied, already kind of wishing she hadn't said it out loud. She thought of the thrill that had built in her belly the other night as she'd filled out her application on the Annie Hernandez website, how she'd bumped up against the character limit as she frantically typed out her answer to the question *Why do you want to work with Annie?* In the end, though, she'd been too chicken to click submit. "An internship, maybe? Or I could probably pick up more hours at WeCount—"

"Don't they have internships at Cornell?"

Meg hesitated. "No, of course they do, but—"

"Is this about your mother?" Her dad frowned, shooting a glance in Lisa's direction. "Because if she's giving you grief about money—"

"No, no, it isn't that." Meg shook her head, feeling something inside her deflate a little. Probably she was just being dumb. "Forget it," she said, mustering a smile. "I'm just being silly. Cold feet about leaving for college, that's all."

"I want to look at colleges when we go to New Orleans," Brent piped up from across the table.

"It's a little soon for you to be looking at colleges," Lisa said, even as Meg felt her eyebrows shoot up. It was the first she had heard of a trip to New Orleans, and she glanced across the table at her dad before she could quell the impulse. He looked like he wished the earth would open and swallow him whole.

"Their school year ends a couple of weeks before yours does," he explained, looking embarrassed. "And Hal's got a gig in Baton Rouge a couple of days later, so . . ." He trailed off.

"No, it's fine," Meg assured him. A trip to New Orleans with Lisa and her kids wasn't even something she'd want to do. It was just strange to think about, she guessed, the four of them taking family pictures and getting beignets at Café du Monde and trooping through airport security together. She thought of all the vacations they'd taken with her mom, all the nights she'd fallen asleep against her dad's shoulder in booths at restaurants. Lisa's kids had extremely strict bedtimes.

After dinner, they all headed into the TV room to watch a

movie. Lisa's kids were eight and ten, and so the four of them had been working their way through every superhero franchise ever made. Meg thought there was something totally bizarre about her dad getting excited about Batman: he and her mom used to be total movie snobs, with a membership to the fine arts theater in Philly, which they talked about more than they actually used. It occurred to her to wonder if this was what her dad had wished he'd been watching the whole entire time.

"You want ice cream?" Lisa asked as Meg's dad settled onto the couch and scrolled through the Netflix menu with the casual comfort of someone who'd obviously spent a lot of time in this exact position. Miley, the little one, curled up beside him. "I've got vanilla and mango."

Meg shook her head, knowing that by *ice cream*, Lisa meant some kind of hippie coconut concoction that cost twelve dollars a pint and would have been deeply appalling to Colby. Still, she smiled. "No thanks." She liked Lisa fine, actually—she could tell Lisa was trying from the way she asked questions and saved magazine articles about voter registration and emailed links so Meg could pick out a new sheet set and comforter for the guest room in her house. *I want you to feel at home here*, she'd said the first time Meg had come over. Meg didn't know how to tell her she hadn't felt totally at home anywhere in a long, long time.

Now she wriggled around in the armchair she was perching in and dug her phone out of her pocket. *What are you up to?* she texted Emily. They'd hardly spoken at all since their fight the week before, though Meg had apologized about a hundred times. She didn't actually regret not telling her about Colby, was the secret truth of it. Mostly what she regretted was getting caught.

Emily didn't answer, predictably. Meg was trying to figure out if she should text again when her phone buzzed in her hand. *Hey!* Lillian had written. *What are you doing right now?*

Meg raised her eyebrows, surprised: Lillian had never texted about something that wasn't WeCount-related. *Watching Ben Affleck being emo in tights and wishing I could bail out of my future stepmom's house*, she typed. *What about you?*

Oh noooo, Lillian said. *Is she awful?*

Not at all, Meg reported. *Which kind of makes it worse.*

Lillian texted back an emoji with her hand over her face. *Maja's sister was supposed to come with us to a show at Union Transfer, but she has period cramps and doesn't want to go. Any interest?*

Meg looked across the room at her dad and Lisa holding hands on the sofa, at the kids and their coconut dessert. *Give me twenty minutes.*

She made it downtown in half an hour, parking her car in a spot she hoped was legal and hurrying around the corner to where Lillian and Maja were waiting outside the theater. "You made it!" Lillian said, looking sincerely happy Meg had shown. "What'd you tell your dad?"

Meg grinned guiltily. "Period cramps."

"Nice." Maja laughed, her bleached-white hair swishing. "I think my sister was probably faking, too."

Meg had never heard of the band that was playing—she hadn't even asked who it was before she'd agreed to come—but they turned out to be an all-female bluegrass ensemble, with fiddles and a standing bass and a tiny redhead wailing away on a washboard. Meg couldn't wipe the grin off her face. It wasn't the kind of thing she and Emily would have ever done—Emily hated city driving; she got stressed out by big crowds—but for the first time it occurred to her that she didn't actually care what Emily would have thought.

"Can I ask you something?" she said to Lillian, filling a cup at the water station as Maja fought the crowd at the bar. "Where did you go to college?"

Lillian shook her head, looking surprised by the question. "I didn't."

"I—really?" Meg couldn't quite keep the alarm out of her voice.

Lillian laughed. "Really," she said, reaching out to take the can of craft cider Maja was proffering. "Thanks, babe." She turned back to Meg. "I had a partial scholarship to Penn, actually. But even with the help, my loans would have been insane, and then I met this organizer at a rally in Rittenhouse Square, and it all just kind of . . ." She waved a hand. "I still might go at some point," she finished, with the unconcerned smile of a person who really liked her life. "Or maybe not. Who knows?"

Meg took a deep breath, suddenly anxious, like even saying the words out loud was somehow disloyal to Emily, or to the future she'd assumed she would have. "Do you think it would be totally bonkers for me to take a year off and try to get a job on a campaign?"

"What?" Lillian shook her head, smiling curiously. "Why would that be bonkers?"

"I don't know." Meg shrugged. "I guess it's just not what I'd planned, that's all. And not something any of my friends would ever do."

"I mean, we're friends, aren't we?" Lillian raised her eyebrows, mischievous.

"No, of course we are," Meg amended hurriedly. "But you're, like . . . brave."

"You're brave," Lillian countered. "And you're smart, and you're capable." She took a sip of her cider. "Who do you want to work for? Hernandez?"

Meg's eyes widened. "How did you know?"

"Well, your endless parade of campaign swag gave me a clue," Lillian said with a grin. "You wear your heart on your sleeve, Meg—literally. And not for nothing, but it's not like you've spent the last six months prancing around in a Cornell hoodie."

Meg glanced down at her *Anne with a Plan* T-shirt. "Yeah," she admitted, her response barely audible over the chorus of *nos* and *wrong*s and *stupid*s clanging deep inside her head. Still, it was like saying the words out loud had broken some kind of invisible seal: it was out there now, a possibility. A different kind of life. "I guess you're not wrong."

When the show was over, Maja and Lillian walked her to her car and hugged her goodbye, Maja promising to send something delicious to WeCount on Tuesday. "I'm really glad you came out tonight," Lillian said. She paused a moment, like she was debating saying anything. Then she took a deep breath. "Look," she said, "I know we don't know each other that well outside of work or whatever. But if you ever need anything, you can call me, okay? I stay up late."

Meg thought of that night with her mom outside the WeCount office, wondering again how much Lillian had overheard. Normally, her instinct would have been to play dumb and cheerful, to promise them both that everything was fine, but something about the way Lillian was looking at her had Meg nodding.

"Thanks," she said, waving good night before climbing into the Prius. She tapped the horn twice as she went.

Meg had texted to say she was coming home early, but still she was a little nervous about what might be waiting for her when she went inside the house. To her surprise, though, her mom was sitting on the couch in front of the classic movie channel in the den, a mug of Diet Coke on the coffee table in front of her. "Whatcha watching?" Meg asked, dropping her purse on the chair.

"Some dopey old thing," her mom reported. "And extremely sexist, actually. But not as bad as a chicken in my underwear, et cetera."

Meg smiled, perching on the edge of the sofa. "Where does that even come from?" she asked. "That expression, I mean."

"You don't know?" Her mom's eyes widened. "It came from you."

Meg blinked. "Really?"

Her mom nodded. "You were like four, and we were at Nanny Warren's funeral out on Long Island. And I was crying—I really loved your father's mother; it's a shame you didn't get to know her better—and you petted my arm and said, in this very small, serious voice: *Don't worry, Mommy, it's not as bad as a chicken in your underwear.* Your dad and I were dying. To this day I have no idea where you got it."

Meg grinned; she couldn't help it. "Me either," she admitted. "It's a mystery."

"It's a mystery," her mom echoed, tilting her head back against the sofa. Finally, she took a deep breath. "I'm sorry about the little performance I put on the other day," she said quietly. "It was out of line on my part."

Meg didn't know how to reply to that, not really. "It's okay," she finally said. "I appreciate it."

Her mom nodded, straightening up and clearing her throat a little. "How was dinner?" she asked.

Meg hesitated. As much fun as she'd had at the concert, the truth was she felt hugely guilty for the way she'd skipped out on her dad. So much of having divorced parents felt like a balancing act, trying not to hurt anybody's feelings. Trying to keep everybody fine. "I kind of bailed," she admitted.

She was expecting her mom to wave it off as something her dad deserved, but instead she tilted her head to side thoughtfully. "He's trying, you know," her mom said finally, which was the most generous thing she'd said about him in a long time. "I know it's got to be hard, and strange for you to be over there. And I know I probably haven't made it any easier on you. But I don't want things between him and me to poison your relationship with him. He's still your father."

Meg nodded. "I know," she said. "You're right."

Neither of them said anything, the TV screen flickering quietly. Meg looked at the paintings leaning against the wall. "We should hang those this week," she blurted out before she knew she was going to say it.

Her mom looked surprised for a moment, then nodded. "Okay," she said without sarcasm or argument. "You're right."

Meg got up and headed to bed not long after that. "Night," she said, bending down to press her cheek against her mom's.

She smelled like the same perfume she'd worn since Meg was a little kid.

"You know," her mom said when Meg was almost to the doorway, hitting mute on the remote and looking thoughtfully around the room, "maybe we should give this whole place a bit of spring cleaning."

Meg raised her eyebrows, her heart doing a tricky, hopeful thing inside her chest. "Really?" she couldn't help but ask.

"Why not?" her mom said, smiling a little bit crookedly. "It's starting to look like Grey Gardens in here. Next thing you know, both of us will be wearing head scarves and speaking in fake British accents."

Meg laughed at that. Her mom was funny, she remembered suddenly; she'd forgotten that at some point in the last couple of months. "That's a brilliant idea, dahling," she said with a grin.

Upstairs, she plugged her phone in and got into bed, then pulled it off the charger again and scrolled down to Emily's name. *I really am sorry,* she typed. *I should have been honest with you. I knew you thought it was weird, that's all.*

She was about to set the phone back down when three dots showed up on Emily's end. Meg breathed in, holding the air in her lungs until the reply came through: *It IS weird,* Emily had written. *But I still wish you'd told me.*

I know. I'll tell you everything, I promise.

Hipster salad place on Monday?

Relief seeped through her. *Of course,* she texted back.

We have to be able to talk about these things, you know? Emily wrote. Then, along with the twin girls emoji: *Roomie.*

Meg squeezed her eyes shut, opened them again. *You and me*, she promised, then hit send and turned out the light.

She lay there for a long time, staring at the familiar shadows on her ceiling—thinking of Emily and Lillian and Mason and Colby, of the life she'd always assumed she had ahead of her and the one she was terrified—and exhilarated—to realize she wanted instead. *If you want to change the world, go out and change it*, Colby had told her. She just didn't know if it was possible to do that without causing a little bit of a scene.

Finally, Meg turned the light back on and got out of bed, padding barefoot over to her laptop and pulling up Annie Hernandez's website one more time. It didn't take her long to pull up the text she'd written about herself and why she wanted to work on the campaign. She took a deep breath and clicked submit.

TWENTY-FOUR

Colby

"Do you know anything about headlamps?" Meg asked when Colby called her on Saturday. She was in the Flashlights and Lanterns aisle at REI, she'd reported when she picked up, sounding pleased with herself. "I need one for next weekend, but there are, like, a surprising variety of them here."

"You need one why, exactly?" Colby asked with a laugh. It was his lunch break at the warehouse, so he was sitting in the driver's seat of his car with the door open, eating his usual ham-and-cheese sandwich. A couple of sparrows fought over the remains of a bag of chips across the concrete. "What, is your prom, like, a wilderness survival theme or something?"

"Overbrook doesn't do a prom," Meg replied primly. Her year was winding down, with final projects and senior class open-mic night and all her friends planning their various backpacking trips. Why you'd drop all that money just to spend a perfectly good summer humping all your shit around a place where you didn't speak the language and probably getting pickpocketed was beyond Colby, but he guessed that's why it was good he hadn't been born rich. "Like five years ago, the senior class decided it wasn't inclusive enough, so now we do a lock-in at the Franklin Institute instead and nobody brings a date."

"Of course you do," Colby said.

"I think you're making fun of me right now," Meg chided, "but I don't even care because it's going to be super fun. They bring in cheesesteaks from Geno's and there's an ice cream sundae bar and everybody plays Sardines in the dark in the middle of the night. Thus, the headlamp."

"Sounds fun," Colby said, and he had to admit it kind of did, in an extremely dorky way. He'd skipped his own prom, the theme of which had been *A Night in Monte Carlo,* and gotten drunk in Micah's yard instead. He thought maybe he would have gone, though, if he'd known Meg back then.

He thought maybe he would have done a lot of things differently.

It was weird, having a girlfriend. Every time Colby thought about it, he couldn't help rolling his eyes at himself, like he was performing in some dumb high school play. Still, he thought about it a *lot.* On one hand, his day-to-day life was exactly the same as it had always been: He went to work at the warehouse.

He played video games with Jordan and Micah. He ignored his brother at all costs. But Meg did things like tell him she missed him and add the kiss emoji to the end of her texts and send him senior skip day pictures of her long bare legs on a picnic blanket, her toenails painted a bright screaming pink.

So. His life wasn't *exactly* the same as it had always been.

"I have no opinions about headlamps," he told her now, crumpling up his tinfoil into a ball and squeezing. "Probably you should take pictures of yourself in all of them, though, and send them to me so I can tell you which one looks most durable."

Meg snorted. "Jerk," she said, but two minutes after they hung up, his phone dinged with a text and there she was, all ponytail and goofy smile, the stupid headlamp glowing like a beacon calling him home.

The sun was just setting when Colby got home from baseball practice that night, the sky gone orange and juicy-looking and an electric crackle in the air. His mom was at exercise class, so he made himself a roast beef sandwich and ate it standing up at the counter, flipping idly through the Best Buy circular and scratching the back of his knee with the toe of his opposite sneaker. He was just finishing up when Tris gamboled in, whining for a bite of his dinner. Colby glanced in her direction, then did a double take, freezing with the end of the sandwich halfway to his mouth.

She was tracking bloody pawprints across the linoleum.

"What happened?" he demanded, his heart like a missile as he sank to his knees and grabbed her by the collar, running his hands over her bristly fur. "Where are you hurt?"

Tris whined, distracted, still after the sandwich. The blood wasn't coming from her, Colby realized dumbly, his eyes catching the rusty trail and following it backward: it was seeping out from the mudroom, trickling out from underneath the door that led to the garage.

"Dad?" he yelled, a sick kind of knowing rolling through him.

That was when he woke up.

Colby lay flat on his back in the dark for a moment, his heart slamming away inside his chest and his breath coming in ragged gasps like somebody was smothering him with a wet towel. His sheets were soaked clean through. "Fuck," he muttered, sitting up and scrubbing his hands through his sweat-damp hair so it stood up in all directions. His head was throbbing wildly. His mouth was totally dry.

He flicked on the bedside light, blinking around at his bedroom: the old wooden dresser and the kid-sized desk he hadn't been able to comfortably sit at since middle school, the Indians pennant on the wall. Everything was fine, he reminded himself. The worst thing had already happened.

Colby flopped back down onto the mattress, willing his chest to stop feeling like it was going to explode. He thought about calling Meg, but what the fuck was he going to tell her? *My dad killed himself and I found him and now I have grisly dreams like some kind of Shakespearean sad sack?* Great idea, Moran. What college-bound suburban princess wouldn't want to hear that from her brand-new boyfriend? Totally sexy. Not pathetic at all.

He thought about changing the sheets, but that seemed like a lot of work for nothing. Instead, he got up and padded downstairs to the mudroom, where Tris was sleeping curled up like a doughnut in her fleecy purple bed.

"Hey," he said, nudging her gently with one bare foot until she woke up, cracking one heavy eyelid and looking at him with benign annoyance. Colby kept his back turned to the door to the garage. "Come with me."

Tris sighed noisily and went through an elaborate stretching routine, but in the end she followed him just like he'd known she would, trotting up the stairs and burrowing herself under his covers before immediately passing out again. Colby listened to her snore all night long.

TWENTY-FIVE

Meg

The lock-in at the Franklin Institute was the following weekend, all forty-eight members of the Overbrook Day senior class peering through the giant telescope in the observatory and giving themselves crazy hair with the Van de Graaff generator, making out with each other in the darkened corners of the Viking exhibit. "Remember when your mom took us here when we were little?" Emily asked as they wandered down a carpeted hallway lined with photographs of the human brain.

Meg blinked. She did, actually, though it was hard to imagine her mom had ever been the kind of parent who voluntarily organized educational field trips to science centers over February vacation. "You got the barfs in the planetarium," she said with a laugh. "She had to buy you a constellations T-shirt to change into, and then I threw a fit, so she bought me a matching one."

"That was a great T-shirt," Emily recalled a little wistfully. "Maybe I should work to incorporate more Day-Glo into my wardrobe at college."

Meg laughed. Things seemed better between them lately; she thought Emily had mostly gotten over the whole Ohio thing, though Em hadn't exactly made a secret of the fact that she still thought it was totally sketchy. She'd shown up to their lunch at the hipster salad place with a pair of matching Cornell baseball caps she'd ordered off the internet and overnighted to her house, presenting them to Meg with a dorky flourish. "Peace offering," she'd announced grandly, then made them take a selfie right there in front of the organic lemonade dispenser. If Meg's smile looked a tiny bit hollow when she looked at the picture on Snapchat later, maybe a little panicky, she didn't think anyone could tell.

Still, things felt almost normal now as they spent way too long goofing off in the Isaac Newton exhibit with Adrienne and Mason, then wandered around taking selfies inside a two-story replica of the human heart. The four of them puzzled their way out of an intergalactic-themed escape room with seven minutes left to spare, laughing almost too hard to stand upright by the time the door finally opened. It was almost like it had been before she and Mason had broken up, Meg thought—or earlier than that, even. Before her mom and dad had split, back when she was sure of the world and of her place in it.

"Nicely done," Mason said when they were finished, holding up his hand for Meg to high-five. Meg grinned.

"So, okay," Emily said a little while later, after Mason and Adrienne went off to watch an IMAX movie with Javi and some of his track team friends and the two of them had snaked their way through the make-your-own-sundae line. Technically, all food was supposed to stay in the huge lunchroom reserved for the sticky almond-butter fingers of elementary school kids, but Em led Meg out the door toward a floating staircase overlooking a bank of enormous plateglass windows, the lights of the city glittering outside. "Can we talk about your fifty-five-year-old Ohio boyfriend for a second?"

"Oh my God!" Meg protested, setting her sundae down so hard she nearly lost her compostable spoon. "He's not fifty-five!"

Emily wiggled her eyebrows. "Sure he's not."

Meg blew a breath out. "I'm serious," she insisted. She wanted to explain that things with Colby felt different than they ever had with Mason, more important maybe, but she didn't know exactly how. "I like him, okay? Like . . . a lot."

That seemed to get Emily's attention. "Oookay," she said slowly, plucking a maraschino cherry out of her sundae. "Care to be a little more specific?"

"I don't know!" Meg said, squirming a little, self-conscious. "He's funny. He really loves his ugly dog. He makes me think about stuff differently. When I'm talking to him, it feels like I can kind of imagine the future, you know? And not even a future with him, necessarily—but, like, a future for *myself.* Does that make sense?"

Emily looked unconvinced. "I mean, sure," she said, "as long as you don't forget there's nothing wrong with the future you already have picked out."

The future you *already have picked out*, Meg amended silently, then immediately felt like a jerk. After all, Em was just being sweet.

"Anyway, you'll get to judge for yourself," she said finally, picking at her own rapidly melting sundae. "He's coming here for my dad's wedding."

Emily's eyes widened. "Seriously?"

"Yeah," Meg said, digging a trench in her chocolate ice cream. "Don't be weird about it."

"I'm not!" Emily protested. "I'm not. Did you ever get a dress, by the way?"

"I ordered two of them," Meg said, "but I don't know if either of them are actually winners."

Emily nodded. "I was thinking you could borrow the one I wore to junior formal, if you wanted. That one of Piper's with the twisty straps."

"That would be perfect, actually." Meg grinned.

Em smiled back. "You're sure it's okay that Mason comes?"

"It's fine," Meg assured her, though she kind of couldn't

imagine him and Colby meeting each other. Then again, she couldn't imagine Colby and Em meeting each other, either. "It would be weird if he wasn't there, honestly."

"Okay," Emily said. "Thank you. And also, I know I haven't really said it, but, like, thank you for being so cool about me dating him. I mean, not that I would have expected you *not* to be, but I know it's awkward and probably super weird for you, even if you do like somebody else now." She bumped Meg's knee with hers, gently. "I'm happy for you, PS. I know I give you a hard time about Colby, but I'm glad you found somebody you feel that way about. I was worried about you for a little while there."

Meg felt the back of her neck get warm, chafing a little at the idea that she'd ever been the kind of person anyone—even Emily—had to worry about. "I was okay," she promised, "but I'm glad I found him, too. And I'm happy for you and Mason, honestly. You guys are a good fit."

"I'm so glad he's going to be at Colgate in the fall," Emily said, licking the back of her spoon thoughtfully. "He was making all that noise about Berkeley, but I just want us all to stick together, you know? I don't want us to be one of those friend groups where everything gets weird and fractured after graduation."

Well, there were probably better ways to go about that than dating my ex-boyfriend, Meg thought, unable to stop herself. Still, she pushed the thought aside and set her sundae down on the step beside her, knowing in her gut that this was the moment to talk to Emily about next year. "Em," she started.

"Yeah?"

Meg hesitated, the words heavy as pennies at the back of her mouth: *I don't want to go to Cornell in September. I don't know if I want to go to college at all. I have a phone interview with the Annie Hernandez campaign on Tuesday. I've been lying to you for a really long time.*

"Nothing," she said finally—hating herself a little, wishing this were half as easy as delivering a passionate endorsement of the electoral process or telling some stranger that his joke made him sound like an ass. Meg knew politics weren't 100 percent straightforward—she wasn't that naïve, no matter what Colby might think—but they were easier to talk about than a lot of other things in her life, that was for sure. "I'm glad we're friends again, that's all."

"Of course we're friends, dummy," Emily promised. "We'll always be friends."

TWENTY-SIX

Colby

The following week, Colby dug the one suit he owned out of the back of the closet, tried it on over his T-shirt, then stood in front of the mirror on the back of his closet door, staring at himself in consternation. The sleeves were too short. The pants showed his pale, hairy ankles. And every time he breathed, it felt like the seam on the back of the jacket was straining, like he was going to Hulk out of the whole thing altogether if he made one false move.

He guessed he shouldn't have been surprised: he hadn't even taken it out of the closet since Brooklyn Greer's sweet sixteen, which had been a ridiculously fancy affair at a banquet hall involving a chocolate fountain and a mashed potato bar. He'd worn jeans and a hoodie to his dad's funeral, because he'd been in the mood to be an asshole, and nobody had dared to give him a hard time either way. His mom had wanted him to try it on before graduation, only then Jordan and Micah had thought it would be hilarious if they all went naked under their graduation robes. And you know what? It *had* been hilarious. Jordan and Micah had been correct.

None of which changed the fact that there was no way he could wear this fucking getup to Meg's dad's wedding.

He was sitting on the side of his bed trying to figure out how much a new one would cost when his mom knocked on his bedroom door, easing it open before waiting for Colby to tell her to come in—one of his least favorite habits of hers, and another reason he wanted to move out as quickly as humanly possible. "I'm headed out," she announced, then looked at him with great alarm. "Colby," she said, like she was possibly concerned he hadn't noticed, "that suit does not fit you."

Colby flopped backward onto the mattress. "I know that," he said to the ceiling. "Thanks." Still, when he sat up again, something about the way she was gazing at him had him confessing: "I'm invited to a wedding."

He watched half a dozen questions flicker across her lined, serious face—*where? Who with? Do you have a girlfriend I don't know about?*—and if she'd asked any of them he probably would have shut down entirely, but in the end all she said was "Follow me."

Colby got up and trailed her down the narrow hallway into

the room she'd shared with his dad, his bare feet sinking into the carpet. He didn't come in here a lot lately, but mostly it looked the same as it always had: the pink flowered wallpaper border along the ceiling, the heavy oak furniture they'd inherited from Grandma Moran. Photos of him and his brother as babies sat in silver frames on top of doilies on the dresser, along with a picture of his parents smushing cake into each other's faces at their own wedding. Colby glanced away from that one, jamming his hands into his pockets.

Glanced back.

His mom dropped her purse on the neatly made bed, then opened the closet that had been his dad's. "There's a couple of them in here," she explained, rummaging through the hangers. "They probably aren't hip or anything, but they should get the job done."

Colby nodded wordlessly. With the closet door open, the whole room smelled like his dad all of a sudden: bar soap and orange Tic Tacs and overstock cologne from Odd Lot, so strong that Colby felt a lump form immediately in his throat. In the year since his dad had died, the rest of the house had shifted to accommodate his absence, his slippers disappearing from the mudroom and his favorite mug migrating to the back of the cupboard and their subscription to *Newsweek* lapsing, like scar tissue thickening over an open wound. In here, though, it was like he was still alive. Just for a second, Colby would have sworn he was going to walk in any minute to change his clothes after work, to put on his Indians hoodie and get himself a Coors Light from the fridge. Colby didn't know what had happened to that Indians hoodie, actually; suddenly, he was seized with a physical urge to rip through every drawer in the house until he found it.

"Here," his mom said, the sound of her voice startling in the quiet room. When Colby turned to look at her, she was holding out a sober-looking gray suit. "Try this one."

"Um." Colby cleared his throat, blinked twice. "Sure."

His mom turned her back to give him privacy while he changed into it, then turned around and looked at him skeptically. "I'd need to hem the pants," she decided, reaching out to pluck at the waistband. "Maybe take it in a little, too, but that's not hard. When do you need it?"

"This weekend," he admitted with a grimace. "Saturday night."

His mom nodded, those same unasked questions written all over her face. "You look like him, you know that?"

That surprised him; people always said that Matt looked like their father, but never Colby. "I do?"

"You do," she said, sitting down on the edge of the bed and pulling her purse into her lap like a cat she was thinking of petting. "You remind me of him, too. Not in a sad way; I don't want you to think that. But sometimes when you're fixing something around the house or I see you out in the yard with Tris in the morning. The way you hold your fork. I don't know." She shrugged. "I'm being maudlin."

I miss him, Colby wanted to tell her. "It's okay," he said instead. Then, before he even registered thinking it: "Can I ask you something kind of important?"

His mom's pale eyes widened. "Of course, Colby," she said, in this sort of overly confident voice like he should know he could—like they had the kind of relationship where they talked about personal or important things all the time, which they definitely didn't. It would have made him laugh on a different day. "Anything."

"When Matt and I got in that fight, he said . . ." He broke off then, losing his nerve, reminding himself once and for all that there was no point in actually knowing. Still, though: "Dad hadn't tried it before, had he? Like, before he actually did it?"

For a long time, Colby's mom didn't say anything, wrapping the strap of her purse around her fingers until the rough skin of her knuckles turned bone white, then unwinding it and repeating the process. "Matt said that?" she asked quietly.

"Uh, yeah," Colby said, his voice cracking a little bit like he was going through puberty all over again. "I told him he didn't know what he was talking about, but . . ." He cleared his throat. "He doesn't know what he's talking about, right?"

Another pause, even longer this time. Finally, she set the purse back down on the bed. "Colby," she said.

Colby sat down on the edge of the mattress, all the air going out of him at once. "Oh."

"I didn't want you to find out," she said, shrugging almost girlishly. "I wanted to protect you—gosh, your *dad* wanted to protect you. But now that you know, I don't want you to think that if somehow . . ." She shook her head. "There was no saving him, Colby."

"How can you say that?" Colby demanded, standing up so fast he almost tripped on the too-long hem of his dead dad's suit pants. "You have no idea. I could have talked to him. I could have—"

"Colby . . ." His mom reached out like she was planning on touching him, then thought better of it. Both of them stared silently at the carpet for a moment before she spoke again. "He was the best man I ever knew, your father. But somewhere in there, when I wasn't paying attention, he stopped being able to see the possibilities in life. Do you know what I mean? He couldn't see anything but what was in front of his face at that particular moment. And then at the very end, he couldn't even see that."

Colby thought he knew what Meg would say right now, about depression being a medical illness the same as diabetes or cancer. But he also thought he understood the point his mom was trying to make. There was a part of him that wanted to keep talking, to tell her about the nightmares—to tell her about Meg, maybe—but in the end he shrugged off the suit coat and draped it carefully over the footboard of the bed. "Thank you for doing this," he said. "I mean, thank you for doing everything, but—yeah. Thank you for doing this."

His mom lifted her head and looked at him then, smiling a little. "My pleasure, honey. Leave it on the bed here, and I'll do the sewing when I'm home on Thursday." She stood up, slinging her purse over her shoulder. "I'm happy for you."

"Thanks," he repeated, reaching out and brushing her arm with the tips of his fingers. "I'm kind of happy for me, too."

The week passed, the air getting warmer; sweat soaked through his T-shirt twenty minutes into his shifts at work. He took Tris to get her heartworm test. He mowed the backyard for his mom. Friday morning, he hung his freshly hemmed suit on the hook in the back of the car and threw his duffel bag on the floor beside it, then climbed into the driver's seat and dialed Doug's number.

It rang three times before it went to voice mail. Colby took a deep breath before he spoke. "Hey, Doug," he said. "It's Colby Moran. I just wanted to follow up with you on that job offer. I'm out of town this weekend"—he liked how that sounded: *out of town*, like he was an actual adult—"but I'll be back on Sunday, and I'm available to start any time next week. Just let me know. Thanks. Uh. Take care."

He hit the button to end the call, feeling his shoulders drop and his chest fill up with something like anticipation. He rolled down his windows and headed for Meg.

...

When he pulled up eight hours later, she was sitting on the steps in front of her house, dressed in denim shorts and sunglasses and a pair of hippie sandals. She launched herself up off the brick and booked it across the grass, dark hair streaming behind her like a flag. "Hi," she said when she reached him, her voice breathless. She flung her arms tightly around his neck.

"Oof," Colby said, his own hands hovering awkwardly in midair for a minute before they got the message to hug her back. Nobody had ever greeted him that way in his entire life, and it was kind of overwhelming for a second—the smell of her neck, the softness of her body underneath her T-shirt. He really did not want to be popping a boner in the middle of her front yard first thing. "Uh," he said, his head clanging a little as he set her down. "Hi."

"Hi," Meg said again, pushing her sunglasses up into her hair, her cheeks going a little bit pink. He'd embarrassed her, he could tell, but he didn't know how to explain that it wasn't that he didn't want her to touch him. That actually he wanted her to touch him all the time.

She tucked her hands into the back pockets of her shorts, tilting her head toward the front door. "Come on in."

Colby slung his duffel over his shoulder and followed her up the mossy front walk. The house was big, which he'd expected; an old brick colonial situation with a red door and shutters decorated with cutouts in the shape of old-fashioned candles. Inside, a grand staircase filled the front hallway, antique Persian rugs on the floors and a baby grand piano visible through a set of French doors that led to a formal living room. It looked like a set for a movie about rich, neurotic liberal people.

It was also—there was no other way to put this—a fucking *pigsty*. The whole place smelled like it needed an airing. Every flat surface was covered with a layer of dust. The giant dining room table was heaped with what looked like a year's worth of junk mail, and the plaster on the ceiling was flaking in pieces the size of Colby's fist, speckling the fancy rugs like so much snow. He thought, randomly, of the conversation they'd had back in Alma about abandoned places, then told himself to stop being so dramatic: obviously Meg didn't live in a deserted amusement park or a decommissioned mental hospital. Still, something about this house kind of gave Colby the same vibe—of something that used to be, maybe, but wasn't anymore.

He glanced around half-furtively, clearing his throat. His mom wouldn't have been able to keep herself from immediately asking where the nearest mop was, from wiping the grimy windows and hauling out the trash. The whole tableau left Colby off center and a little bit ashamed, like he was seeing something he shouldn't, but Meg seemed totally oblivious to the mess—or, if she wasn't, she was doing a bang-up job of pretending it wasn't there. "Mom!" she called. Then, more quietly, "I told her you were a friend of a friend of Emily's and we met at a party over spring break."

Colby raised his eyebrows. "Seriously?"

"What?" She frowned.

"I mean, nothing. I'm just saying, for a person who gave me such a hard time about whether my mom knew you were coming or not—"

"My mom knows you're here, obviously," Meg interrupted. "I just wasn't about to start a fight with her over the details."

"It would cause a fight if she knew you met me through your job?"

"It would cause a fight if she knew I drove eight hours to go visit you without telling her."

Colby considered that for a moment. "Fair enough."

"Thank you," Meg said primly, and Colby nodded. Still, he couldn't get over the sense that sometimes she required more from him than she was willing to give herself.

He followed her into the kitchen, which he knew his dad would have loved—original oak cabinets and wide-plank wooden floors, a pair of six-paned windows over the sink looking out onto an overgrown backyard. Sitting at the table peering at her phone was a woman with aggressively highlighted blond hair; she had that slightly stringy look that middle-aged ladies got when they drank more than they ate, but her blue eyes were sharp and canny. "This is my mom," Meg announced. "Mom, this is my boyfriend, Colby."

Colby blinked. It was strange to hear himself introduced that way; he had to admit he'd thought there was a chance she'd try to fudge it, which made him feel kind of like a turd. "Nice to meet you," he managed to say.

"Nice to meet you, Colby." Meg's mom offered a manicured hand for him to shake. She didn't *look* like an unpredictable alcoholic, with her can of Caffeine-Free Diet Coke and an off-white short-sleeved sweater he thought was probably made of something expensive. Then again, he guessed his dad hadn't looked like . . . someone who would do what he did, and everyone knew how that had turned out.

They made small talk for a while, about his drive and the summer weather and the fact that she'd once dated a guy who'd gone to law school at Ohio State. "Where are you headed in the fall, Colby?" she asked.

Meg winced. "Mom," she said, before he could answer, "Colby works, remember?"

"Oh," her mom said vaguely, "that's right." She hesitated, a pause that lasted a second too long. "What time is your father's thing?" she asked, glancing at the clock above the window—which, Colby couldn't help notice, didn't actually seem to be running. "Can't be late for a rehearsal dinner."

"It's soon," Meg said, ignoring her mom's acrid tone. "We should go get ready."

Colby smiled politely and held a hand up before following Meg back the way they'd come and up the creaking stairs to the second floor. "Sorry," she muttered as they rounded the corner.

"I told her you weren't in school, but I guess she was a little bit more in the bag than I thought."

"It's cool," Colby said, though in truth he was already dreading having that identical exchange with her dad, and her friends, and probably her freaking mailman. *This is Colby! He hauls appliances off trucks for a living but still manages to bathe himself and use tools, like a gorilla who knows sign language!* "No worries."

Meg nodded. "Watch the runner," she said absently, pointing to the place at the top of the stairs where the fraying carpet was peeling up. "I don't want you to break your neck if you get up to pee in the night."

She brought him into a guest room at the end of the long hallway, which held a double bed and an antique dresser along with about a million unopened boxes from Amazon and an expensive-looking exercise bike with dry-cleaning bags draped over the handlebars. "Sorry there's so much crap in here," Meg said as Colby looked around for a clear surface to set his bag on; finding none, he dropped it at the foot of the bed with a quiet thump.

"Don't worry about it," Colby said, wanting to reassure her and not sure exactly how to do it. "I'm getting the full experience, that's all."

"That . . . does not sound great," Meg said with a grimace. For a moment, she looked like she was going to add something else, then decided against it. "Okay." She tucked her hands back into her pockets. "Um, I'll let you get settled, I guess."

"Okay." Colby nodded, watching as she turned to leave. "Meg," he blurted, grabbing her wrist and tugging her hand out of her pocket, pulling her back and pressing his mouth against hers. It wasn't particularly artful, which didn't keep all the blood in Colby's body from immediately rushing straight to his dick. "There," he said finally, pulling back and gazing at her, her eyes gone a full shade darker than he thought of them as being. "Now I'm settled."

Meg laughed, loud and ringing. "Welcome to Philly," she said, and kissed him again.

TWENTY-SEVEN

Meg

Her dad and Lisa's rehearsal dinner was that night, at an Italian place downtown with a view of the river and a gluten-free pasta option for Lisa's kids. Her dad had been a little weird when she'd said she wanted to bring someone—after all, Emily and Mason were already coming to the actual wedding—but to her surprise, Lisa had jumped in. "Of course you can invite a friend, Meg," she'd said, tucking her hand into Meg's dad's and squeezing pointedly. "The more the merrier."

Now here Colby was, slipping into her real life with surprisingly little fanfare, pulling her chair out when they'd gotten to the restaurant and teaching Brent how to make a football out of the paper napkin ring. He called her dad *sir*, which Mason had never done and which Meg could tell her dad was totally liking. And, yeah, he had a vaguely bemused expression on his face the whole time, like he was an actor who'd wandered onto the wrong soundstage by mistake and was waiting for someone to notice, but overall it seemed like it was going okay.

They were just finishing their spaghetti when her dad stood up at the head of the table, looking shy and almost boyish in his jacket and tie—Meg thought he was dressing more like a prep school bro since he'd been with Lisa, though she couldn't tell if she was imagining it or not. "I wanted to propose a toast," he said, lifting his wineglass. "To my beautiful bride, Lisa, the most incredible woman I've ever known." He reached out and took her hand with his free one, gazing at her with a kind of adoration so personal and private Meg nearly looked away. "I've never in my entire life been this happy."

Meg froze with her fingers wrapped around her glass of ice water, feeling—stupidly, she told herself—like someone had tipped its contents directly down the front of her dress. She thought of the blizzard that had hit Pennsylvania the winter she was in seventh grade, when their house had lost power for two full days and they'd sat in the living room wrapped in blankets playing Scrabble in front of the fire and listening to the news on an ancient battery-powered radio her dad had dug out of the garage. She thought of the trip they'd all taken to France when she was ten, her mom and dad kissing goofily on the banks of the Seine while Meg played photographer with the first cell phone she'd ever had. She thought of the day she was born, which both her parents had always made a big show of saying was the most incredible thing that had ever happened to either one of them.

But here, in this restaurant with his new wife and his new family, was the happiest her dad had ever been.

Meg forced herself to wait until he was finished speaking, gamely clinking glasses with her uncle Jim and both of Lisa's kids. The last thing she wanted to do was make a scene. Once she was sure nobody would notice, she pushed out her chair and slipped away from the table, heading for the ladies' room before doubling back at an arrangement of flowers almost as tall as she was and escaping out onto the street in front of the restaurant.

It was humid out here, the air thick and clammy, like summer had already arrived. Graduation was in less than three weeks. She thought of her mom back at the house, probably watching TV with a wineglass on the end table beside her—God, how was Meg ever going to leave her all by herself in their falling-down house? She'd seen the horrified look on Colby's face this afternoon when he'd walked in, the dirt and clutter suddenly glaring. She'd spent the last few months—the last few years—trying so hard to convince everyone around her that everything was fine that she'd almost convinced herself in the process.

But it wasn't.

She was trying to pull herself together when the door to the restaurant opened behind her; there was Colby with his hands in the pockets of his too-big khakis, the sleeves of his dress shirt rolled halfway up his arms. "Waiting for the bus?" he asked with a smile, and that was when Meg started to cry.

Colby's eyes widened. "Shoot," he said, crossing the sidewalk in two big steps and wrapping his arms around her a little awkwardly, like he wasn't entirely sure of the protocol here. "Meg, hey, hey, hey. What's wrong?" Then, when she sobbed harder instead of answering: "Okay. Easy." He glanced back at the restaurant, seeming to intuit her wordless panic. "You want to walk?"

Meg nodded gratefully. Colby took her hand, and they set off down the busy sidewalk, turning once and then again until finally they found a quiet, tree-lined side street, all bumpy cobblestones and brightly painted brick apartment buildings with decorative iron stars the size of dinner plates affixed to their fronts. "Did you know those are actually holding the houses up?" Colby asked, apropos of nothing.

Meg sniffled. "Huh?" she managed to say.

"The stars," he explained, lifting his chin at a row of them. "People think they're just there to look nice, but back a million years ago, masons used to use lime mortar on buildings like this, which doesn't hold up in the long term. So eventually, the front of the building starts to pull away from the rest of it. The stars are actually just decorative bolts to keep the whole face of the thing from crumbling down on some unsuspecting pedestrian."

Meg shook her head, momentarily surprised out of her meltdown. "How do you know that?" she asked.

Colby smirked a little. "I know stuff."

"Clearly," she said. "What else do you know?"

"What, like, about construction?" He ducked his head and tucked his hands back into his pockets, suddenly shy. "I don't know. A reasonable amount, I guess."

"Tell me?"

Colby looked at her curiously, but in the end he nodded and did it, keeping up a running monologue as they walked along the darkened sidewalk—about peg-and-beam framing and how to properly organize a workshop and machines that could lift whole houses clear off the ground—until finally Meg lifted a hand to stop him.

"I'm sorry," she said, taking one last deep, shuddering breath and wiping her face with the back of one hand. She sat down on the steps of a tidy little brownstone, smoothing her dress down over her knees. "This is embarrassing."

Colby shook his head. "Hey, what are you apologizing to me for?" he asked, sitting down beside her and running a hand down her backbone.

"I don't know." Meg took a deep breath, exhaling in a shaky sigh. It was still unfamiliar for him to touch her this way. "I'm just sad, is all."

"You ever tell your dad that?"

Right away, Meg shook her head. "What am I supposed to

say?" she asked, pulling back to look at him. "*Congratulations on being happier than you've ever been in your life, Dad—sorry you had to throw the rest of us away to get here*?" The words were out before she'd even known she was thinking them; she felt her eyes widen and clapped a hand over her mouth. "Sorry," she said, between two fingers. "That's awful. I didn't mean that."

Colby shrugged. "You can mean it," he said, stretching his long legs out in front of him. "If that's what you mean."

Meg sighed, tilting her head back so her hair pooled on the step behind her, staring up at the dark canopy of new leaves overhead. "I think maybe it's what I mean, yeah."

"Then why not tell him?" Colby asked. "If somebody's pissing you off, you ought to let them know."

Meg laughed; she couldn't help it. The way he said it made it sound so easy, not at all like the horrifying, humiliating spectacle she knew it would be if she were actually to do it. "Is this how I sound to you when I tell you that you should get involved with the electoral process?" she asked.

"What, like I have no idea what I'm talking about and should probably mind my own business?" Colby grinned. "Maybe."

Meg's mouth dropped open. "Rude!"

"I'm kidding. Mostly." He leaned over a little, bumping their shoulders together. He smelled like Dial soap and medicated face wash and drugstore deodorant, boy smells. "Anyway, it feels like it's probably a little late for either one of us to be minding our own business, right?"

"Yeah," Meg agreed. "It probably is."

"Can I ask you a question?" Colby looked over at her in the darkness. "Say you did talk to your dad, right? Say you went back into that fancy restaurant right now and told him how you're feeling. Or say you told your friend Emily the whole, unvarnished truth. What's the worst that could happen?"

"I don't know," Meg said immediately, though in fact she knew exactly what the worst might look like. She gazed out at the empty street for a moment. Took a deep breath before she spoke again. "So, every year right before Christmas, my school does a potluck."

"Okay," Colby said, leaning back on his elbows. "I'm listening."

"It's this big thing. Everybody in the whole school comes and brings their families, from kindergarten all the way on up, and you all cook or bake something, and they set it up on these tables in the gym and the jazz band plays and there's all these games—and whatever, I know you probably think it sounds unbearably corny, but—"

"I don't think anything," Colby said. "Keep going."

Meg sighed. "So last year, winter of junior year, my parents were still together. And yeah, they fought a lot, I guess, but they've always fought a lot. Arguing was just, like, what they did for recreation. It didn't mean anything; it wasn't scary. At least, not to me, it wasn't." She shook her head. "Anyway, the three of us have been going to this potluck together every year since I was five, but this time my dad had to work late doing something for Hal, so the plan was for my mom and me to go, and he was going to meet us when he got done. And my mom was in this terrible mood about the whole thing. I didn't know this then, but she thought he was having an affair—which he was, I'm pretty sure, with Lisa—on top of which she's always hated having to socialize with other parents."

"I mean, fair," Colby joked with a gentle grin. "Other people's parents are awful."

"I mean, sure. Yes." Meg tucked her hair behind her ears. "So whatever, she and I are at the thing together, but mostly I was actually with my friends, and Mason and I had just started dating, and we were having fun, and I guess I just didn't notice how much she was drinking."

Just like that, Colby wasn't smiling anymore. "Uh-oh."

Meg nodded. "Yeah." She'd never told anyone this story before; it occurred to her all at once that she hadn't even *thought* about it in ages, had in fact kind of forced herself to forget it, and that telling Colby now was a kind of remembering she suddenly wasn't sure she wanted to do. Still, she made herself keep going. "Anyway, by the time I finally realized what was going on, she was totally off her ass. And I was trying to keep anybody from noticing, and trying to convince *her* that we should go home, when my dad showed up." She tugged at her bottom lip. "And I was super relieved to see him—one, because he's my dad, and two, because I thought he was going to handle it."

"But he didn't?"

Meg shook her head. "He and my mom wound up immediately getting into this giant screaming fight."

Colby grimaced. "About what?"

"Him being late, I guess? Her being drunk? Does it matter?"

"No," he said quietly. "I guess not."

"The two of them just lost it in front of everybody," Meg told him, shame spreading like a rash all over her body at the memory, hot and itchy. "Yelling, calling each other names, hurling these awful accusations back and forth. And I was begging them to be quiet, and all these little grade school kids were staring at them, and everybody else—my friends, my friends' parents, every teacher I've ever had—was trying to act like they didn't notice." She squeezed her eyes shut, opened them again. "Finally, the principal had to ask them to take it off school grounds."

"Woof." Colby rubbed a hand through his hair. "I'm sorry."

"Thanks."

"What did Emily say?"

"We never talked about it," Meg admitted.

"Wait, seriously?" Colby's eyes were two full moons. "Why not?"

"She never brought it up," she said with a shrug. "And, like, I definitely wasn't going to. And then my parents decided to split up over the holidays, and she was really great to me while that was happening." Meg blew a breath out. "But it was just, like . . . all of a sudden I realized how I must look to everybody else, you know? How my family must look. That what I thought was normal, all that fighting . . . wasn't."

She lifted her face to look at him. "I told myself that I was going to do everything I could never to be part of another scene like that." She heard the challenge in her own voice. "And so far I haven't been."

Colby raised his eyebrows. "Sounds exhausting."

"Sometimes." Meg smiled. "Lucky for me, I get to blow off steam arguing with you."

"You do, huh?"

"Uh-huh." She sighed again, then heaved herself up. They'd been gone too long already, and disappearing was almost as noticeable as causing a fuss. "I like Lisa, for the record," she clarified as they headed back around the corner, tucking her hair behind her ears and fanning her face a little bit so that nobody inside would be able to tell she'd been crying. "I mean, *like* is the wrong word, maybe. She's a huge nerd—"

"She's a *huge* nerd," Colby agreed with a grin.

Meg laughed. "But the point is, she's not a wicked witch or anything. So what's my problem?"

"She's not your actual mom," Colby said with a shrug, no hesitation at all. "And no matter how fine she is, it's not going to be the same as your family together and whole."

Meg stopped in the middle of the sidewalk, putting a hand up to her mouth. "I'm sorry," she said, the words tripping over one another in their rush to get out of her mouth. "God, I must sound so spoiled to you, complaining about all this stuff when both my parents are—" She broke off.

Colby shrugged. "It's not a contest," he said easily, though she thought he might have flinched.

You could talk to me about it, she wanted to tell him. *You could tell me the rest of the truth.* "I'm really glad you're here," she said instead.

Colby grinned at that. "I'm really glad I'm here, too."

She took his hand as they went back into the restaurant, the zing of the contact all the way up her arm and the skin of her back and stomach prickling inside her clothes. Having him here in person, his actual physical body beside her, was half-pleasurable and half-maddening, like the moment before a sneeze.

"There you are," her dad said, slinging an arm around her shoulders and squeezing. Meg only smiled in reply.

They were just finishing dessert when her phone dinged in her purse. *So??* Emily said. *Is he here???*

Meg took a deep breath and looked across the table at Colby. "Okay," she said, "you want to meet my friends?"

TWENTY-EIGHT

Meg

Em and Mason were hanging out with a bunch of their friends at Liberty Park, a big outdoor mall with a movie theater, a bowling alley, and a million shops and restaurants. "Listen," Meg said, taking Colby's hand as they strolled down a fake-cobblestone walkway hung with old-fashioned string lights and crowded with couples on dates and clusters of college kids already home for the summer, "just so you know, Em can be kind of a tough crowd."

Colby glanced at her sidelong, lips twisting. "You know," he said, "I kind of got that impression."

"I don't think she'll be a bitch to you or anything, but—" She broke off. That wasn't true, strictly; in fact, she thought there was at least a 50 percent chance Emily would be a bitch to him. "Maybe just don't take anything she says personally, that's all."

"Noted," Colby said. He squeezed her hand and bumped their shoulders together, easy, though she could tell from the tone of his voice he was a little bit tense. "It's fine, Meg." He grinned. "Anyway, I'm really tough."

"Oh, right." She smiled back at him, she couldn't help it, his eyes and his jawline and how *tangible* he was, here in her town, where she lived. "My mistake."

Her friends were sitting on the patio outside the fancy ice cream place, an indie situation with flavors like herbal chai and ginger molasses that Meg normally loved but that seemed faintly ridiculous to her with Colby by her side. "Hey!" she called, her voice just a little too loud.

Emily looked up from her waffle cone, her eyes widening faintly at the sight of them. Then she tilted her head to the side. "Hi!" she called, hopping up out of her chair and offering a megawatt smile. "You must be Colby."

Colby smiled back. "You must be Emily."

"My reputation precedes me, I see," Em said grandly, then motioned him over. "Come here so I can interrogate you at great length about your intentions, please and thanks."

Colby shot Meg a sort of helpless look, but he did what Em told him, sitting down in the empty chair beside her and gamely answering her string of cheerful questions. She was trying, Meg realized; both of them were trying, because both of them cared about her. She didn't actually think she could ask for anything more than that.

"Cones are on me," she announced, kicking gently at Colby's chair on her way into the ice cream shop. She grinned at Emily once before she went.

Half an hour later, Meg balanced on the patio railing, the warm night air ruffling her ponytail as she listened to Emily tell Colby the story of the time they'd accidentally locked themselves in the student council storage room at Overbrook without their cell phones. She couldn't believe how well this was going. She'd expected things to be awkward between Colby and her friends, hostile even, but instead it was like they'd all known each other for ages. Maybe she'd been worried for nothing after all.

Colby wandered back over in her direction once Emily was finished, his cheekbones even sharper than normal in the neon light from the shop. There was a half-moon scab the size of a dime beneath his eye that hadn't been there the last time she saw him; he'd gotten hit with a stack of boxes at work, he'd explained when she'd pointed it out. "So, what's your summer looking like?" he asked, leaning against the railing beside her.

Meg thought about that for a moment. "I'm going to work a few more hours at WeCount," she said. "Spend time with my mom, I guess. And also, you know . . ." She glanced at Emily, who was standing across the patio talking animatedly to Adrienne about the bedding she wanted to get for her dorm room. "Get ready for Cornell."

Colby followed her gaze, his eyes widening. "You still haven't told her?" he asked quietly. "I thought you said the interview with the Annie Hernandez people went well."

"Shh," Meg hissed. Then, barely above a whisper: "It did. Really well, actually. But that doesn't mean I'm a hundred percent going to get it. And even if I do . . ." She trailed off. "I don't know. What about you, huh? What are you up to this summer?"

Colby made a noncommittal sound, fussing with the napkin around the base of his cone instead of looking directly at her. "I think I'm going to take that job after all," he said finally. "With Doug."

"Seriously?" Meg grinned, hopping down off the railing and flinging her arms around his neck. "Colby! That's such good news!"

He shrugged, all broad, embarrassed shoulders. "I mean, we'll see. Don't get too excited yet. It might be a disaster."

"Oh, whatever, of course I'm excited. I'm proud of you, you know that?" Now it was her turn to be embarrassed, a little; still, it wasn't like it wasn't true. "Is that weird to say?"

Colby rolled his eyes, but he was smiling. "As long as you don't, like, ruffle my hair."

"I'm not going to ruffle your hair, asshole." Meg punched

him lightly in the side. She could tell he was proud of himself, too, the way he ducked his head and jammed his free hand into a pocket of his khakis; more than that, though, she could tell he was proud to be telling *her.* As soon as Meg had the thought, she was hit with wave of fondness so fierce she almost couldn't breathe for a second. It felt like when they'd gone to the beach in New Jersey when she was a kid, like getting caught in a riptide.

Just like that, she was done with her ice cream, tossing her cup into the trash and wiping her hands on her dress. "Um," she said, clearing her throat a little, "do you want to get out of here?"

Colby looked at her over his cone, surprised. "Now?"

"Yeah."

"Where do you want to go?" he asked, and Meg shrugged, lifting her chin to look him in the eye.

"I don't know," she said. "Anywhere."

All at once, he seemed to take her meaning. He swallowed, his Adam's apple moving inside his throat. "Um, sure," he said, finishing his ice cream in two giant bites and sliding his rough hand into hers. "Let's go."

They said good night to Emily and Mason and Javi and Adrienne, then took her car and drove around for a while. She showed him the WeCount office and her favorite bookstore and the park where she'd broken her wrist when she was little, hanging by her knees off the monkey bars. "It took my parents a full day to take me to the doctor," she confessed, remembering. "I was trying to be brave and act like everything was fine."

Colby smirked in the green glow of the dashboard. "That . . . is extremely on brand for you."

"Shut up." Meg reached over to nudge him in the shoulder; he caught her hand and kept it, linking it with his in his lap as she drove past the food co-op and the hipster salad place. "I'm sorry," she said finally; she was aware of trying to gather her courage, of anticipation hanging in the car between them like a physical thing. "Is this boring? This, like, extended Life and Times of Meg Warren tour I'm taking you on right now?"

Colby shrugged, leaning back in the passenger seat. "Why would it be boring?" he asked. "I want to know everything about you."

Meg's whole body got very warm all of a sudden. "Okay," she said, nodding. "One more place, then."

In the end she brought him to the senior parking lot behind Overbrook Day, turning the car off at the far end of the lot underneath the low branches of some evergreen trees. The lot was empty and quiet, just the orange glow of the safety lamps attached to the buildings and an owl hooting somewhere farther off. It gave Meg the same feeling as she'd had in the hotel room that night in Ohio, like if she didn't know better she'd think they were the only two people on Earth. She didn't know what it meant that it felt like she and Colby made the most sense in places like this: just the two of them separate from the rest of their lives and everyone else who knew them, an invisible signal carrying a pair of voices through the air.

Colby leaned across the gearshift and put a hand on the back of her head, his mouth warm and a little bit cautious. Meg tucked her fingers into the collar of his shirt. She didn't think she'd ever been as aware of her body as she was when Colby was kissing her—the obvious parts, sure, but also her hips and the backs of her knees and her eyelashes, all her systems humming some inaudible sound. Colby challenged her. He infuriated her. He made her feel like she could reach out and grab the world in both hands.

"Wait," she muttered finally, opening her eyes to look at him in the darkness. Her whole face felt swollen and smudged. She'd unbuttoned his shirt to the waist, rucked up his undershirt so she could feel the muscles jumping in his stomach. His skin was impossibly warm. "I just—let's go home, okay?"

Colby backed off right away, wiping his palms on his thighs and clearing his throat a little, wincing as he thunked the back of his head on the passenger-side window. "Sure," he said, nodding about a thousand times.

"No, I just, like—" Meg broke off, shook her head. Then she laughed. "Home, where my bedroom is."

"*Oh.*" Colby nodded once more—his whole body relaxing, then tensing again. "Oh." He laughed, too, the sound of it echoing all down her backbone. "Okay."

Meg grinned and put the car into drive.

TWENTY-NINE

Colby

Meg had to get her hair done for the wedding the following morning.

"You want to come with me?" she asked, knocking on the door of the guest room and handing Colby an iced coffee. He'd wanted to spend the night in her bed, and from the way her mom's door was shut tight, he thought they probably could have gotten away with it, but in the end she'd walked him back to the guest room, kissing him for a long time in the darkness before scampering down the hallway alone. "I mean, I can't imagine what would be more fun for you than sitting in a hair salon reading *Cosmo* for an hour."

"I like *Glamour* better, actually," Colby said, trying and mostly failing to keep the dumb smile off his face. It was weird, he thought, gazing across the room at her and feeling himself blush a little as he thought of the quiet, secret sounds she'd made last night: it wasn't that he felt any different now, exactly. He'd always thought that when this finally happened—*if* it ever finally happened; sometimes it had felt like there was a not-insignificant chance he'd be a virgin until he died—the first thing he'd want to do was brag about it to Jordan and Micah and anyone else who would listen. Now that it actually *had*, though, he didn't want that at all. He wanted to protect her or something. He wanted to protect whatever this was.

Now he took a sip of the iced coffee, which was extremely bitter and expensive-tasting. "I can tag along," he said. After all, it wasn't like he had anything to do around here without her. He certainly didn't want to spend the morning with her mom, who kept eyeing him as if possibly he was going to make off with her jewelry. What he *really* wanted to do was find someplace he and Meg could be alone again, where he could lay her out on her back and stare at her for the foreseeable future.

Well. Not *just* stare.

As if she could read his thoughts, Meg closed the door to the guest room behind her and climbed into the bed beside him, setting her own coffee cup on the nightstand. "Hi," she said, pulling the quilt up over them both. Her bare feet brushed his, smooth and cold.

Colby gulped, every single nerve ending in his body open and alert all of a sudden. "Hi yourself," he managed to say.

Then, as she slid one hand up under his T-shirt: "Is this okay? I mean, is your mom . . . ?"

"She's at the store," Meg promised, rubbing her sharp nose along his collarbone. "We have, like, twenty more minutes at least."

Colby grinned.

At the salon, he sat on a pink suede chair and flipped through a couple of wrinkly *Us Weekly*s while she went and got her hair done. He scrolled idly through apartment listings on his phone. The place on Cypress was still available, and he was imagining making Meg breakfast in the tiny galley kitchen when all at once it rang in his hand—*Doug*, said the caller ID, and Colby swallowed.

"I've gotta take this," he called to Meg, though he didn't think she could hear him over the sound of the hair dryers. He stepped outside into the busy weekend morning, early-summer sunlight prickling on his arms and legs.

"Colby," Doug said when he answered. "I got your message."

"Hey," Colby said. The salon was in the middle of a little shopping district, people pushing strollers and walking their chocolate labs and drinking lattes. He could see a farmer's market set up by the commuter rail station at the end of the block. "Yeah, I was just calling to see when you wanted me to start."

"Colby, I actually offered the job to someone else."

Colby blinked. "You did?"

"Yeah," Doug said. "When I didn't hear from you, I figured you weren't serious, and construction is supposed to start in a couple of weeks, so . . ."

"Oh," Colby said. Oh, *fuck*, he felt stupid. He could feel it growing inside him, expanding like an overfull water balloon, like his whole body was made of cheap plastic and couldn't accommodate the stretch. "Okay."

"Hey, I'm really sorry, Colby. But I called you twice—did you not get my messages?"

"Uh," he said, his whole body prickling with embarrassment. He thought of all the times Meg had asked him if he'd followed up yet. He thought of all the times he'd blown her off. The rush of regret was hot and shameful in the moment before it turned to anger: He'd been worried about the rug getting pulled out from under him, hadn't he? And sure the fuck enough, he'd been right. The guy hadn't said anything about a time limit, or about having somebody else lined up if Colby didn't move fast enough. Where the hell did he get off? "No, I got 'em."

"I wish you'd called me back, buddy."

Don't call me buddy, Colby barely managed to keep himself from saying. "Yeah, uh. Well. Thanks anyway."

"Colby—"

"Okay. Uh. Bye." Colby punched the screen to end the call.

For a moment, he just stood there, staring blindly out into the traffic. So that was the end of that, he guessed. This was why it was stupid to get your hopes up about stuff in the first place: because people were generally full of shit, and they inevitably let you down, and then—

He glanced down at the phone in his hand, his brain shorting out for a white-hot second as he caught sight of the date on his calendar app:

May twenty-fifth.

Holy shit, today was—

And he hadn't even—

And he wasn't—

"Hey," Meg said cheerfully, coming out of the salon behind him with her hair in a fancy updo, tucking her wallet back into her purse. "You ready?" Then her eyes narrowed for a moment. "Everything okay?" she asked. "Who was on the phone?"

Colby hesitated for a moment. There was no fucking way he could tell her—about Doug or his dad or the anniversary, any of it. He could not believe he had to go to her rich father's wedding right now. "Sure," he said finally, jamming his phone into his jeans pocket. "Let's go."

THIRTY

Meg

"Are you sure everything is okay?" Meg asked for what felt like the twentieth time since this morning, sitting rather miserably at a big, round table in a fancy seafood restaurant while her dad and Lisa swayed to a song by the Cure.

She could tell it felt like the twentieth time to Colby, too. "Everything is fine," he said, which was obviously a lie. He'd been in a terrible mood since he'd gone with her to get her hair done this morning, sullen and withdrawn and generally crabby. He'd sulked all the way through lunch at her favorite grilled cheese food truck in Montco, then taken forever to get changed back at her mom's house. She'd knocked on the door to the guest room five minutes after they were supposed to leave for the ceremony and found him sitting half-dressed on the mattress staring sulkily at a pair of paisley socks. She'd hoped he'd cheer up when they got to the actual wedding, but if anything he'd just gotten grouchier: he hadn't even danced when the DJ had played "Motown Philly," even though last night he'd made this big show of telling her what a secretly stellar dancer he was. "Seriously."

"Are you sure?"

"I'm sure, Meg." Colby reached across the table for his soda and didn't quite look her in the eye. "Can you stop picking at me?"

"I'm not picking at you," she said, aware that it wasn't entirely true. But it was like he'd gone somewhere she couldn't get to him, and she didn't know him well enough to know how to get him back. Sure, it had felt awkward between them in person before—they'd fought, even—but it had never felt like this. She had no idea what she'd done wrong. It occurred to her that her dad's wedding was kind of a stupidly high-stakes event to have brought him to, and for the first time she wondered if maybe that hadn't actually been the best idea.

Meg frowned and glanced around the restaurant, all white tablecloths and gleaming wood, waiters in white jackets bustling around with crumb scrapers in hand and enormous live lobsters scuttling around in a tank near the maître d' stand. They'd had the ceremony on the patio at sunset, Lisa's daughter,

Miley, reading a poem by e. e. cummings while a violinist Meg's mother would have utterly hated played softly in the background. She'd reached out and laced her fingers with Colby's, feeling wobbly and overwhelmed, but he'd pulled his hand away and scratched the back of his neck instead.

"Okay," she said finally, pushing her chair out and standing up. The DJ was playing a Jackson 5 song now, and her uncle Jim was waving her over from his post near the buffet. "Well, I'm going to go dance, then."

"Okay," Colby said with no affect at all. "Go ahead."

Meg sat down again. "Can you stop?" she asked, faintly aware of how shrill she sounded. Emily and Mason sat across the wide circular table, just far enough away that they could pretend not to notice. She lowered her voice anyway. "Why are you talking to me like I'm other people? It's just me."

Colby sighed, scrubbing a hand through his messy hair. "Look," he said, "I'm sorry. I'm not trying to be an asshole. I just don't know why you need to talk everything to death, is all."

"Really?" Meg's eyes widened. "I thought that was, like, kind of the entire point of our relationship, actually."

Colby frowned. "Yeah, I'm a dumping ground for your every thought and feeling, I know."

"I—*wow*." Meg blinked back sudden tears. All at once, everything about him being here seemed insane. "You're being kind of an embarrassing dick right now, do you know that?"

That was the wrong thing to say; Colby seemed to fold in on himself, like a video of a collapsing star. "I'm embarrassing you, huh?" he said, and his voice was so quiet. "Well. That was only a matter of time, I guess."

Meg's eyes narrowed. "What does *that* mean?"

"You know what it means."

"I don't, actually."

"It means I don't know what you were trying to prove bringing me here, Meg. And obviously you don't, either, so—"

"I invited you here because I wanted to spend *time* with you," Meg snapped, "although, honestly, right now I have no idea why."

"Yeah," Colby said, his features twisting meanly. "I'd say that sounds about right."

"Look," Meg said, her voice low and urgent, shooting a glance at her friends across the table. Emily and Mason's voices had risen slowly; she suspected they were purposely drowning her and Colby out. "Can we go and talk about this outside, please?"

"Fine," Colby said, shoving his chair back and stalking toward the exit.

"We'll be right back," Meg announced to Emily and Mason, who'd finally abandoned all pretense of their own conversation and were openly gawking across the table. She bit back her grimace, forcing a cheery, reassuring grin. Holy crap, she could not believe she was plastering on a smile about *Colby* of all people, the one person in her whole life who never made her feel like she had to be fake.

She followed him out into the parking lot, teetering a bit on her stupid heels. It was cooler than last night, the brackish breeze wafting in off the river. Her hair was coming loose from its bun. "I don't know why you're being like this," she said.

Colby leaned against the railing of a wheelchair ramp, like it was taking all his energy just to hold himself upright, and shook his head. "Forget it."

"No," Meg insisted, "tell me. I thought everything was going great until this morning. Like, are you sorry we had—" She broke off. "I mean, is that what it is?"

"No!" Just for a second, Colby looked horrified. "Jesus Christ, Meg, of course not."

"Then *what*?" she asked, relieved in spite of herself; still, it came out a lot more like begging than she meant for it to. "I don't get it. We were supposed to have this totally fun weekend, my friends really liked you last night, you've got this great new job—"

"I don't, actually."

That stopped her. "What?" she asked, not understanding. "Why not?"

Colby shook his head again, shoving his hands in his pockets.

"Because I fucked it up, okay? Does it matter how?"

"I mean, to me it does." Meg gazed at him, baffled. "I don't get how—"

"It's done, okay? That's all that matters. And I already texted Moira and told her I was leaving the warehouse, so—"

"But how can it just be done?" Meg couldn't help pressing. It seemed like an infinitely fixable problem to her, the kind of thing that could be solved with a carefully worded email or call. "I'm sure if you just call that guy back and ask—"

"Can you stop it?" Colby exploded. The anger in his eyes, in his *body*, seemed endless; it reminded her of the middle of the ocean. It reminded her of staring up into space. "I know you think everyone who doesn't agree with your way of handling a situation at any given moment is a dumbass who just hasn't thought the big thoughts like you have, but you might be surprised to learn that's not actually how it works."

"That's not what I think," Meg interrupted, even as she was dimly aware that it kind of had been; God, she didn't know which one of them annoyed her more. She hated this, standing out here fighting where anyone could see them. It was exactly what she'd spent the last year and a half trying to avoid. And he knew that! He *knew* that, and still . . . "You're being so enormously unfair right now. Like, what exactly is your problem with me all of a sudden?"

"My problem is you are so completely divorced from reality—"

"How am *I* the one divorced from reality?"

"You can't even tell your best fucking friend you don't want to go to Cornell!" he bellowed, throwing his arms out like he was daring the sky to open above him, and that was the moment Emily came through the front door of the restaurant.

"Wait, what?" Emily's eyes narrowed, her gaze darting back and forth between them. "Um. Meg? What's he talking about?"

"Nothing," Meg said, eyes blurring with tears as she kept her gaze trained on Colby; he'd dropped his arms now, a boxer with no one to fight. "I'll see you inside in a minute, okay?"

"Meg—"

"Everything's fine, Em. Really."

"I just—" Emily broke off. "Okay."

Once they were alone, Meg stared at him another minute. "Um," she said, and it came out like a whisper, "I think you should probably go."

Colby nodded once, just faintly, glancing around the parking lot like he was surveying for physical damage. Meg understood the impulse. It seemed like there should be broken glass around him, dishes smashed on the concrete. It seemed like it ought to be the end of the world.

"Yeah," he said. "I guess I should."

THIRTY-ONE

Colby

Colby did a quick mental inventory of everything he'd left at Meg's house, decided it was nothing he couldn't live without, then got in his car and headed straight for the highway, turning up the radio as loud as it would go. He wanted to forget her smile. He wanted to forget that he'd come here at all. Most of all, he wanted to forget the way she'd looked at him: like he was so fucking disappointing, like everything she'd worried was true about him actually was.

So? he thought, the city disappearing in the rearview. Let her be disappointed, then.

It started raining somewhere near Lancaster, only then it didn't stop, water sluicing across the windshield faster than his shitty wipers could take care of it. Colby gritted his teeth and kept driving, shoulders hunched and jaw clenched hard enough to ache. He hated weather like this; it was exactly how it had been the night his dad—

Stop it.

He pulled over at a service station outside Allentown to piss and buy a Snickers and use the rest of the cash in his wallet to fill his gas tank, which he hoped was enough to get him home. The clerk was a pale blond girl with a small, painful-looking mountain range of acne across her jaw. "Have a good night," she said, picking up the battered sci-fi novel she'd been reading. Colby thought this would be the loneliest job in the world.

By the time he got back on the highway, it was really pouring, his toes curling up inside his uncomfortable shoes like he could keep better traction on the road that way. The night was black as the inside of a grave. He turned the radio down so he could concentrate and flicked on his high beams . . .

Just in time to see the deer darting out into the middle of the road.

Colby swerved at the very last second, the car fishtailing all over the empty highway before skidding to a stop three inches from the guardrail. The deer scampered off into the woods. For a second, Colby just sat there, fingers white-knuckled around the steering wheel and the iron tang of his own heart in his mouth.

Then, before he knew exactly what he was doing, he wrenched off his seat belt and got out of the car.

The rain was apocalyptic. Colby's hair plastered against his forehead; his shirt soaked through right away like a second skin. The roar of it was incessant, deafening, just like it had been that afternoon last year when—

Cut it out, he ordered himself, but he already knew it was useless. He dropped his shoulders and let the memory come.

He'd been dicking around with Micah outside the office park, the two of them playing chicken with the nearing rolls of thunder; it was only once the sky had finally opened that they'd dashed into their cars and called it a day. Colby thought about that a lot, though he knew it was probably useless—that maybe if he'd been home a little earlier, if they'd just microwaved some mozzarella sticks and watched fucking *Beaches* on cable or whatever—

Anyway.

When he got home his dad's car was in the driveway instead of in the garage, where it usually was. Colby let himself in through the back just like always, found Tris losing her mind at the door. "Buddy, if you gotta go, you gotta go," Colby scolded mildly, nudging the dog out into the sodden yard and getting himself a glass of orange juice. Tris plastered her furry body against the slider and howled until Colby let her inside again. "What's up with the dog?" he called into the living room; when his dad didn't answer, he raised his eyebrows at Tris. "Where's Dad?"

The TV was dark in the empty living room, and the shower

wasn't running. He wasn't taking a nap in his bedroom, which he'd been doing more lately, though all of them seemed to have agreed to act like they didn't notice. Colby finished his orange juice, put his empty glass in the dishwasher.

That was when he opened the door to the garage.

Once, when Colby was in middle school, Tris had disemboweled a giant possum and brought it into the house as a present, and his mom had walked right past it on the living room floor. "I honestly didn't see it," she insisted later, even though everyone kept saying she must have. "I think my brain just protected me."

Which was to say: for a long fucking time, maybe a full minute, all Colby registered in the dank, mildew-smelling garage was the sound of the dog barking her head off and the single shoe that had fallen onto the concrete floor.

Now he wiped his face even though it was useless. He never let himself think about that night, and this was exactly why. He stood there for another long moment, the rain pooling in his ridiculous dress shoes as he remembered the rest of it: how he'd tripped over himself and scraped the palms of his hands in his scramble to find something to cut his dad down with, how he'd called 911 and done clumsy CPR.

How he'd tried so hard—holy shit, he had tried *so fucking hard*—and it hadn't meant anything at all.

Colby watched the place where the deer had disappeared. Then he got back in his car and headed home.

THIRTY-TWO

Meg

When the party was finally over, she helped her dad and Lisa load presents into Lisa's SUV, waving at the two of them as they pulled out of the parking lot and toward Lisa's house in Penn Wynne. She thought for sure Emily had left, too, but as Meg headed for her Prius, she caught sight of her sitting on a bench by the back door of the restaurant, a bottle of prosecco she'd filched from somewhere clutched in one manicured hand.

"Hey," Meg said—approaching carefully, no sudden movements. "You're not going to drive home, are you?"

Emily shook her head. "Of course not," she said, her eyes glittering in the dim light coming off the restaurant. "Mason didn't drink anything. He's getting the car now." Then, lifting her chin like a challenge: "Did he leave?"

Meg swallowed hard, not bothering to ask who she was talking about. "Yeah," she said. "He left."

Emily nodded. "Is it true, what he said? Are you not going to come to Cornell with me?"

Meg sighed. "Em, can we just—"

"Yes or no, Meg?"

Meg took a deep breath, and then she just said it. "Probably not," she admitted. "No."

Emily seemed to absorb that for a moment, taking a swig from the bottle of prosecco before setting it down on the pavement. "Don't text me, okay?" she said, getting unsteadily to her feet. Then almost to herself: "Yeah. Just, like . . . don't."

"Emily," Meg said, "come on," but Mason was already pulling up in the car by then, the slow crunch of tires on concrete. She could hear Bob Dylan playing on the stereo as Emily got clumsily inside.

"Tell your dad congratulations again," Mason called, waving through the passenger-side window. Meg watched the taillights until they disappeared down the street.

The house was dark when she got home, just the sound of the cicadas through the window and the hum of the refrigerator clicking on and off. Meg was grateful for the quiet—she wanted to get into bed and sleep for a hundred years without trying to spin tonight into something that a) wasn't a disaster and b) wouldn't somehow hurt her mom's feelings. She changed into leggings and a T-shirt and scrubbed her makeup off in the bathroom sink, pointedly avoiding looking at the guest room, but as she was creeping down the hallway, her mom's door opened.

"Is that you?" she asked, blinking a little, swaying the same as Emily had back in the parking lot and curling her hand around the door frame for balance. Her blond hair was mussed and her face was creased from the pillow, but she was still wearing the clothes Meg and Colby had left her in that afternoon. She must have passed out, Meg realized dully, though not for long enough to sleep off whatever it was she'd drunk in the first place.

"It's me," Meg said, pasting what she hoped was an even expression on her face and heading down the hallway in her mom's direction. "You okay?"

"I'm fine," her mom said, turning and shuffling back into the bedroom. If it occurred to her to ask where Colby was, she didn't let on. "How was your thing?"

Hearing her mom describe it that way made Meg want to cry more than anything else had all night, though she couldn't have explained why in any articulate way. "It was nice," she lied.

Her mom nodded, heading into the master bathroom and shutting the door behind her. Meg sat down on the edge of the rumpled bed. It smelled stale in here, though, so she got up again and opened the window above the hope chest that held her christening gown and baby pictures. She was doing the one near the TV when the bathroom door opened again. "Leave that," her mom said, though instead of getting back into bed, she fished a pair of Birkenstocks out of the overflowing closet. "It's too cold."

Meg frowned. "What do you need your shoes for?" she asked. "Where are you going?"

Her mom didn't look at her. "Errand to run."

"What?" Meg shook her head, already knowing what it was in the pit of her stomach; the gas station at the end of the street sold cheap, syrupy-looking wine. "Now? It's after eleven, Mom."

"Are you the parent now, Meg?" her mother snapped, raking her hands through her bedhead. Then, more gently: "It'll be quick."

"Mom," Meg said, following her down the narrow hallway. "Come on. What is it? I'll get it for you."

Her mom ignored her, trailing a hand along the wall for balance. Meg blew out a breath. What was she supposed to do? Her mother was a grown woman. She couldn't just tackle her to the ground. "What if I make you a sandwich?" she tried finally. "And then if you still want to go out after that—"

"*Enough*, Meg," her mom said. "I've had enough from you tonight, okay?"

"I haven't even been here tonight," Meg argued, stung by the unfairness of it. "And I'm just saying—"

"Yes, Meg, I know," her mom interrupted. "You've been

with your father and his blushing bride."

That stopped her. "Mom," she said. *"Really?"*

That was when her mom tripped on the runner at the top of the stairs.

It was a bad fall, loud and sloppy; Meg thought both of them screamed. She ran the few feet to the top of the staircase just in time to see her mom land crumpled at the bottom of it, her left leg twisted unnaturally underneath her. Blood seeped from a gash in her head. "Mom," Meg said, thundering down the stairs so fast she almost fell herself and had to grab the railing hard to keep from stumbling. "*Mommy.* Can you get up?"

Her mom was still screaming, the kind of cries Meg would have expected out of a child; adrenaline coursed like ice water through her veins. "You're okay," she forced herself to say, though her mother obviously wasn't. "I'm going to call 911, okay?"

The ride to the hospital was a blur. The EMT couldn't have been that much older than Meg, a skinny dark-haired kid who looked like Andrew, Emily's brother. It felt like years ago that they'd argued at the party; it felt like even longer since Colby had left. "Is she on anything?" the EMT asked as he slid the backboard underneath Meg's mom and lifted her onto the stretcher.

Meg hesitated. Her instinct was to lie—her instinct was always, always to lie—but when she opened her mouth to deny it, she found she'd run out of ways to make any of this all right.

She thought of Colby asking her, weeks and weeks ago, and how she'd known the truth then, even if she hadn't been able to utter it.

"She's drunk," Meg said now, taking a deep breath and climbing into the ambulance behind them. "She's an alcoholic."

"Okay," Meg said, sitting beside her mom's hospital bed a couple of hours later, squinting at the clipboard the nurse had handed her to fill out. "It says they need a full medical history."

Her mom made a face. "Because I fell?"

"I'm just telling you what it says, Mom."

"I know. I'm sorry." Her mom leaned back against the pillows. "Leave that," she said, closing her eyes briefly. "I'll do it in a little while."

Meg frowned. For some reason, it felt important to complete this task as quickly and efficiently as possible, but it wasn't like she was making any progress, so she set it down on the windowsill and tucked her chilly, clammy hands between her legs. Her mom had a broken ankle, a sprained wrist, and a bruise on her cheekbone that was already starting to blacken; they were watching her for signs of a concussion, though the doctor didn't think it was severe. The guy they'd seen had been kind of an asshole, brisk and dismissive; he'd barely even looked at her mom, and Meg had felt herself bristle. *This is my* mother, she'd wanted to say. She hated him. She hated her mom. She hated herself most of all. She should have prevented this somehow, should have taken more precautions. She should have done more to make sure everyone was fine.

"I'm sorry," her mom said now, opening her eyes again before reaching out and laying her good hand against Meg's face. "Tonight was a disaster. I never wanted you to see me like this."

I see you like this all the time, Meg thought reflexively. Tonight was just worse than usual. "I know" was all she said.

Her mom fell asleep not long after that, her breathing deep and even; Meg watched her for a while, wondering what on earth to do next. Every time she thought about what could have happened, her stomach turned over. She had no idea how to make sure it didn't happen again.

She was looking at her phone to see if Colby had somehow called without her noticing—he had not—when there was a quiet knock at the door. She looked up and there was Lillian in a thin gray hoodie and high-tops, Phillies cap perched rakishly on her head. "Hey," she said, holding up a Tupperware. "I got your text."

Meg bit her lip to stop it from trembling. "I'm sorry," she said, scrambling awkwardly to her feet. "I know it's the middle of the night. I just kind of didn't know who else to call."

"No worries," Lillian said, tucking the brim of her cap into the back pocket of her jeans. "Like I told you, I stay up late."

"How'd you get them to let you in?" Meg asked, pulling her bag off the second chair so that Lillian could sit down and taking the Tupperware—lemon bars, she saw—and reaching out to squeeze Lillian's hand. "It's gotta be past visiting hours, right?"

Lillian shrugged. "My mom is an RN at Mercy," she explained. "I speak nurse."

Meg smiled. "I'm really, really glad you came."

"Anytime." She looked over at Meg's mom, who was snoring quietly. The IV had already started to bruise her arm. She looked older than Meg thought of her as being, a line of silver showing at her roots where her hair dye had begun to grow out. "So what's the plan?" Lillian asked.

"I don't know," she said, blowing a breath out. "I thought I could just keep everything spinning if I worked hard enough, you know? Like if I just convinced everybody that life was normal and okay and, like . . . proceeding as planned, then it would be."

"You realize that's not how life actually works," Lillian pointed out.

"I mean sure, *now*," Meg said, gesturing around at the hospital room, although truthfully, she'd known it wasn't working for a long, long time now. After all, hadn't that been the miracle of Colby to begin with? That he was the one person in her life who didn't believe her sales pitch—and liked her anyway?

Well. At least for a little while.

"You gotta talk to your dad, Meg," Lillian told her. "And not, like, at some amorphous down-the-road future time. You guys were in the emergency room tonight, you know what I'm saying? That makes this an emergency."

Meg sighed again, reaching up to run her hands through her greasy, tangled hair. It was still sticky from all the hairspray they'd put in it at the salon, her fingertips catching on bobby pins. "It's his literal wedding night," she argued.

"And you're his literal daughter."

Meg leaned her head back for a moment, staring at the acoustic tile in the ceiling. Hadn't Colby been telling her pretty much the same thing this whole time? "Yeah," she said. "I guess you're right."

"I should go," Lillian said a little while later, getting to her feet and setting her baseball cap back on her head, artfully crooked. "Maja will be up in a couple of hours, and she needs the car to get to work. But text me if you need me, will you?"

"I will." Meg hugged Lillian goodbye and got herself a cup of coffee from the vending machine. She watched middle-of-the-night infomercials on mute. She tried, and mostly failed, not to think about Colby, who was probably all the way across Pennsylvania by now, successfully not thinking about her. Even though she knew better, she couldn't help picking up her phone and scrolling back in their texts: inside jokes and random pictures and *good mornings*, not to mention a surplus of emojis on her part that made her feel like a total dumbass now.

For what it's worth, he'd written almost back at the very beginning, in response to some inane worry she'd had about the piddly results of the sock drive she'd been running at school for a homeless shelter in South Philly, *I don't actually think it always has to be your sole responsibility to make sure everything goes perfectly all the time.*

Well.

Meg tugged at her bottom lip for a moment, imagining texting like he had that night after their fight in Ohio. Wondering if he'd made it back home. Then she glanced at her mom, sleeping openmouthed in the hospital bed, and knew there was another call she had to make first.

She got up and headed out into the hallway, clutching her phone hard enough to make her knuckles ache and sliding down the wall until she was sitting on the linoleum.

"Hey, Dad?" she said when he answered. "I need help."

THIRTY-THREE

Colby

"This is a bad idea," Jordan said two nights later, standing at the edge of the empty fountain and squinting at the instructions on the back of a box of fireworks in the orange glow of the parking lot's safety light. Micah had gone to visit his uncle in West Virginia over the holiday weekend and come back with a trunk full of them: snakes and poppers and parachutes, Black Cats and Lady Fingers and half a dozen roman candles that were probably going to take somebody's thumbs off before the end of the night.

Colby leaned back against the hood of his car and tipped his head up at the sky thick with fireflies, a bottle of Bud Light sweating not-unpleasantly in his hand. He thought it was his third, or maybe his fourth? He'd been trying to take it easy for a while there, but now, two days after he'd gotten back from Philly, it didn't seem like there was much of a point. He watched as Micah tossed a ground spinner into the fountain, the whistle and crack of it like tiny gunshots splitting the quiet night. This was worse than a bad idea, he thought idly; watch Keith show up and arrest them all, and Colby'd be right back where he started, sulking in a holding cell like the last two months hadn't happened at all.

He'd known it wasn't going to work with Meg from the very beginning, he reminded himself, repeating it like a mantra for the thousandth time: Even if this weekend hadn't been a total fucking calamity, what kind of future did they have? Him lying to all his friends and driving up to visit her on her yuppie college campus on his days off from whatever grunt job he managed to find for himself? Casually avoiding talking about anything real with her and her Patagonia-wearing classmates, both of them irritated and resentful and biting their tongues all the time? Eventually breaking up anyway, because they were just too different? It was better this way.

Even if it didn't feel like it.

He was thinking about digging another beer out of the cooler when his phone buzzed in his pocket. He looked down at the display screen, swearing softly under his breath even as his heart tripped over its shoelaces:

Meg.

Colby almost dropped the damn thing onto the concrete,

thumbing frantically at the button to silence it and jamming it back into his pocket. He wasn't going to answer. There was no fucking point.

"Shit," he said, louder this time, and headed for the grassy shoulder at the very edge of the lot.

"Hey!" Micah called after him, a box of sparklers in one hand; he had a plan to make a video of himself drawing shiny dicks in the air and upload it onto YouTube. "Where you going?"

"I gotta take this," Colby said, then kept going until he was far enough away that he was sure nobody could hear him. Both Jordan and Micah had made fun of him for an entire day after Meg had come to visit, then never asked about her again. He wasn't in any hurry to reopen that particular can of worms. He took a deep breath and swallowed his nerves down, staring out at the empty road. "Hey."

"Hey yourself," Meg replied, her voice clipped and distant. "How are you?"

"Uh. I'm good." Colby cleared his throat, setting his beer on the curb and sitting down beside it. It felt like a lot longer than just two days since he'd heard her voice. "I didn't think you'd call," he said, rubbing hard at the back of his neck.

"I knew *you* wouldn't," Meg countered immediately. Then: "What's that sound?"

Colby glanced over his shoulder at where Jordan and Micah

were launching firecrackers in the direction of the tree line, neon light streaking through the air. "What sound?" he asked, even as he reminded himself there was no reason to lie to her at this point. It didn't actually matter what she thought.

"That—" Meg broke off. "Forget it," she said. "Don't tell me." Then she sighed. "Anyway, I won't keep you. I just wanted to make sure you made it home."

She could have texted if that was what she wanted. Colby didn't know what it meant that she'd called. "I did."

"Okay."

Neither of them said anything for a minute. Colby flopped back into the scruffy, weedy grass. "Meg," he said, at the same time as she said, "Colby . . ."

Both of them exhaled, laughing a little bit. "You go first," she said.

Colby stared up at the sky for another moment, stalling. He didn't actually know what he wanted to say. He wanted to tell her he sort of wished they'd never met each other. He wanted to tell her everything had been easier before she came along. He wanted to tell her there was a not-insignificant chance he was in love with her, but when he opened his mouth to try and say it, "It was never going to work" is what came out.

Meg breathed in then, so quietly he almost didn't hear it, and for a moment Colby was sure to his particles he'd made a horrible mistake. "Okay," she said, before he could take it back.

"That's . . . about what I was going to say, too."

"It is?" Colby asked, sitting up so fast he got dizzy. He didn't know if he believed her or not.

"Yeah," Meg said, her voice bright and just this side of brittle. "Absolutely. I mean, we're just too different, right? It was always kind of a joke, you and me."

"Totally," Colby agreed, trying to ignore the weird stinging behind his rib cage, like he'd gulped a mouthful of soda down too fast. He thought of her shy, sleepy smile that morning in the artificial light of the hotel room. He thought of how warm her skin had been in her car the other night. "I mean, let's be real: it was a disaster every time we met in person."

"A total cluster."

"Seriously." Colby stood up, adrenaline zinging through his body like possibly he was going to have to run somewhere in the immediate future. He took a deep breath and glanced over his shoulder. Jordan and Micah were arguing about the best place to set off the roman candles, Jordan's beanie askew on his head even though it was close to eighty degrees. His regular life right here in front of his face, same as it ever was. "Okay," he said finally. "So . . ."

Meg made a sound at the back of her throat, noncommittal. "Yeah."

"I guess . . ."

"Yup." That sound again, almost like a hiccup. Almost, but not quite, like a sob. "Um," she said. "Bye, Colby."

Colby opened his mouth, shut it again. Kicked over his beer by mistake. *This is stupid*, he almost told her, looking down in quiet bewilderment as it foamed around his sneakers. *I'm sorry. I keep thinking about you. I really, really don't want to not talk to you every day.*

"Bye," he said.

Colby hung up and stared out at the empty road for a moment longer. Then he turned around and went back to his friends.

June seeped by in a hot, colorless blur. Colby slept a lot. He had no fucking job to speak of. Mostly, he drove around, but he wasn't going to be able to keep doing that much longer, either, since he had next to no money for gas. He spent a lot of time at Paradise, lying on the hood of the car and staring up at the light flickering through the leaves on the trees.

That was what he was doing one afternoon when he heard Matt's car pulling down the dusty path, the distinctive hum of his engine. Colby wondered how Matt had known he was here, then decided it didn't matter. Matt got out of his car and came over to Colby's, sitting next to him on the hood without bothering to ask if he could. "Where'd that come from?" he asked, motioning with his freshly shaven chin.

Colby looked at the Annie Hernandez yard sign he'd plunked into the weedy grass, then back at Matt. "Dunno," he lied, shrugging a little. Truthfully, it had cost ten bucks he didn't have. "Was here when I showed up."

Matt looked skeptical, but he didn't comment. "I brought lunch."

Why? Colby thought, but that felt unnecessary, and he was hungry besides. "Thanks," he mumbled, taking the Subway bag from his brother's outstretched hand.

Matt nodded. "How was your wedding?"

Colby busied himself unwrapping his sandwich; Matt had sprung for the meatball marinara, which was both of their favorite. "It sucked, actually."

"Too bad."

Colby shrugged. "It's fine," he said through a huge bite of meatball. "I barely knew her."

"Really?" Matt seemed surprised by that. "I would have thought you really liked her, if you could be fucked to drive all the way to Philly."

"Yeah, well," Colby said, hoping Matt would take the hint and move on. "Waste of gas."

Matt did, but only sort of: "What happened with Doug?" he asked instead, like possibly he'd made a list of annoying, invasive questions in his head on the drive over here and was determined to work his way through each and every one. "You start working for him yet or what?"

Colby shook his head. "Didn't work out."

Matt smirked over his sub. "Because he tried to date you?"

"Can you shut the fuck up?" Colby snapped, surprising himself a little. "I swear to God, Matt, you say shit like that and it makes *you* sound like a joke, not him."

Matt raised his eyebrows and Colby got ready to argue, but then Matt just sort of shrugged. "Fair enough," he said. "Sorry."

Huh. Colby tilted his head, surprised; that was a lot easier than he'd thought it would be, actually. He wanted to tell Meg, only then he remembered he and Meg weren't talking anymore. He put his sandwich down.

Neither one of them said anything for a minute. Colby could hear a pair of birds chattering away in the trees. The sun beat down on the back of his neck, insistent; probably he was going to get a burn. "I fucked it up," he said finally. "The job with Doug. Is that what you want to hear? I actually wanted it this time, and I blew it."

Matt raised his eyebrows. "That's not what I want to hear at all, actually," he said quietly. "That sucks."

"Uh-huh." Colby kicked at the bumper. "Sure it's not."

"I'm serious," Matt said. "Believe it or not, asshole, I actually want you to succeed."

Colby glanced at him sidelong, looking for the catch; still, he had to admit Matt sounded sincere. "Okay."

Matt sighed. "Look," he said, rattling the ice in his waxy paper cup of Coke, "I'm sorry about what happened at the house that day. No matter how pissed I was, I shouldn't have said—"

"Dude, I don't want to start . . ." Colby shook his head. "We were both idiots. It's fine."

"No, I know, but what I said about you and Dad—"

"Matt, really."

"Fuck, man, can you just let me say this?" Matt looked irritated. "Jesus. Dad was sick, and I don't blame him for what he did. For a long time I did, but not anymore."

Colby swallowed the last of his sandwich, the bread sticking in his throat a little. "Oh no?"

"No," Matt said. "But that shit runs in families, and I don't want . . ."

Colby felt his eyes widen. "I'm not going to kill myself, Matty." He blew a breath out, this strangled-sounding laugh. "Jesus."

"I know that," Matt said quickly. "Of course I know that, I just. . ." He scrubbed a hand through his hair. "It's not your fault you were the baby, okay? That's what I'm trying to tell you. I don't blame anybody for . . . anything. It is what it is, that's all."

Colby glanced over at him, squinting a little in the sunlight. He'd known it was true, he guessed, that there wasn't anything he could have done to change what happened; still, it was different to actually believe it. "It must have sucked for you," he allowed after a moment, which was the most generous thing he'd said to his brother possibly ever. "Having to know all that stuff while I was walking around with my thumb up my ass thinking everything was fine."

Matt shrugged. "It didn't tickle, no."

"No," Colby echoed. "I guess not."

"I used to be so fucking jealous of you," Matt continued, almost to himself. "Because you guys had this great relationship, you know? And it was like I had seen too much or knew too much for him to ever have that with me. But you still got to hero-worship him; you didn't know any better. So it was like when he was with you he still liked himself or something."

"I didn't hero-worship him," Colby said immediately, feeling himself bristle.

"Dude, it's not a knock on you," Matt said. "It doesn't make you an idiot to believe in your father, of all people. And just because he didn't turn out to be the perfect guy you thought, just because he had demons or whatever, doesn't mean it's stupid to believe in anything else ever again, either."

Colby dropped his head forward, rubbing at the too-hot back of his neck. "Yeah," he said, because it seemed pretty clear he had to say something. Already his brother's words were worming their way into his skull. "I hear you."

For a second, it seemed like Matt was going to press him about it, but in the end he just shook his head. "Look," he repeated, crumpling up his sandwich wrapper and tucking it into the plastic bag, "bottom line is, I think you're an idiot for wanting to work with that dude. But if you do, you should convince him."

"Oh yeah?" Now Colby smirked; he couldn't help it. His brother sounded—well, actually, he sounded like Meg. "Just go to his house, throw myself on his mercy, embarrass myself?"

"There are worse things in life than embarrassing yourself," Matt pointed out. "Besides, you already do that all the time."

"Fuck you," Colby said, but there was no heat behind it. Then, more quietly: "Maybe."

"Think about it, at least." Matt boosted himself up off the bumper. "I gotta get back to work."

Colby nodded. Once, back when they were real little kids, Matt had pulled a nail out of the bottom of Colby's foot in the woods behind their house without ever batting an eyelash. Colby didn't know why he was thinking about that right now. "Sure thing," he said, lifting the pop his brother had brought him in a makeshift salute. "See you."

Once Matt was gone, Colby lay back on the hood of the car, the metal uncomfortably hot through the fabric of his T-shirt and the sunlight prickling the bare skin on his arms. The logical part of him knew Matt had no clue what he was talking about, at least as far as things went with Doug; in terms of embarrassing displays that would solve exactly nothing, he might as well have suggested Colby get fully naked and do cartwheels across the football field at next year's Homecoming. Still, he could feel the idea lodged under his skin like an extremely stupid, ill-advised splinter.

For a second, he wished he could ask Meg what she thought about it, though it wasn't like he didn't already know exactly what she'd say. He remembered that night on the phone: *I just want you to be happy, actually.* He hadn't believed her at the time, and he thought he was probably right not to; still, he guessed that didn't mean she hadn't had a point.

Maybe it wasn't the *dumbest* idea in world to try again, he conceded grudgingly, the sound of her voice echoing deep inside his brain. Maybe it was only the second or third dumbest.

Colby dug the heels of his hands into his eyes and shook his head to clear it. Then he heaved himself up off the hood and got back in the car.

THIRTY-FOUR

Meg

She found Emily at her locker before their free period on Tuesday, tossing old worksheets into one of the big recycling bins that had appeared in the hallways so people could start cleaning out their clutter. Graduation was only a few weeks away. "Can we go somewhere and talk for a minute?" Meg asked, jamming her hands into her back jeans pockets. "Like. Please?"

Emily rolled her eyes, huffed a breath out. Then all at once her shoulders sagged. "Fine," she said, slamming her locker shut and heading for the senior entrance without looking back to see if Meg was following. "Hipster salads?"

Meg hesitated, just for a moment. "Why don't we do coffee instead?"

Outside, it was warm and rainy, that steamy smell coming

off the concrete in the mostly empty parking lot of Rise & Grind. "So," Meg began once they'd gotten their lattes, sitting down at a wobbly, slightly sticky table by the window, "I'm not coming to Cornell."

"Uh, yup," Emily said crisply. "So I gathered." She sighed and took a deep breath. "Like, I'll be honest: I feel like I don't even know you anymore."

Meg nodded. "I think maybe you kind of don't."

Emily's eyebrows shot up. "Seriously?" she asked, like she'd been expecting Meg to protest, and normally Meg would have. Even now she felt the urge to do it like a physical thing—to smooth everything over, to do what she could to make it okay. Instead, she took a deep breath and set her cup down on the table.

"My mom broke her ankle on Saturday night falling down the stairs because she's an alcoholic and she was drunk," she blurted, counting off on her fingers. "I'm, like, ninety-nine percent sure I'm in love with Colby, which probably doesn't even matter at this point because I don't think I'm ever going to see him again. And I don't actually like the hipster salad place."

Emily just stared at her for a second. Meg watched as she synthesized the new information, like a plant making food from the sun. "What's wrong with the hipster salad place?" she asked.

Meg barked a laugh. "Are you *kidding*?" she asked. "Everything I just said, and *that's* what you're choosing to focus on right now?"

"No, no, no," Emily said, holding her hands up. "I just meant—" But Meg shook her head.

"Look," she said, "I'm sorry I don't like the hipster salad place, okay? I'm sorry we're not exactly the same anymore. Maybe we're not actually brain twins, but that's no reason for you to be so mean and judgy and, like—and, like—"

"Meg!" Emily broke in. "I'm sorry, okay? I just—I didn't know any of that stuff. About your mom, or Colby, or—"

"You don't know those things because you made it so I couldn't tell you."

"Of course you could have told me!" Emily's eyes widened. "What did I do that made you think you couldn't tell me?"

"I—all of it!" Meg said. "The way you were about the first time I talked to him on the phone or, like, when you found out I went there—"

"Going there without telling anyone was not a good idea, Meg!"

"I *know* that," Meg protested. "Don't you think I know that? And I get why you reacted the way you did, but then you never even asked what happened once I got there, like you weren't even curious about it because it wasn't something you would have done yourself. And then you were so fixated on both of us being at Cornell—"

"I thought you wanted to go to Cornell!"

"I *did*, Emily!" The words came out like a reflex—but no, even that wasn't exactly true. Meg blew a breath out, tried again.

"Or at least, I didn't have a better plan. I was such a mess last year, and you were so into the idea that it just made sense. But then once I actually got in and started trying to picture myself there . . ." She gazed down at the table for a moment, trying to organize her thoughts into something more coherent. Lifted her face again. "So much of our friendship has always been about being the same, you know? And it just felt like maybe that was all going to fall apart if I didn't want the same stuff we had always wanted, or I liked someone who was different from the people we'd always liked, or I admitted I was mad about something you did, or—"

"Wait a second." Emily raised her eyebrows. "Mad about something I did?"

Meg sighed. "Come on," she said, embarrassed. "Seriously? Are you really going to make me—"

"What, me and Mason?" Emily looked surprised, then sad. "You said you were okay with me and Mason."

"Of course I wasn't *okay* with you and Mason!" Meg threw up her hands, nearly upending her coffee cup in the process. A mom with her toddler two tables over shot her a dirty look. Well, too bad! Meg thought wildly. Here I am, making a scene! "We had been broken up for like a week, Em! Who does that? What kind of best friend—"

"What kind of best friend starts dating him in the first place when you knew I liked him?" Emily demanded.

Meg blinked. "Wait," she said, thinking for a moment that

she'd misheard. Surely, Emily hadn't just said . . . "What?"

"I *liked* him, Meg!" It was almost a wail. "Before you guys ever—I *liked* him. And it was like you didn't even notice."

"I *didn't*," Meg said immediately. "I never would have—"

"Well, I did," Emily said. "I liked him so much at the beginning of junior year—or before that, even. Way back when he still had those bad glasses."

Meg shook her head, the whole story reshuffling itself in her head like a deck of cards. Emily couldn't have—of course she would have *known* if—

"Those were terrible glasses," she said absently.

Both of them were quiet for a moment, just the sound of an old Norah Jones song piping in over the speakers. Now that she stopped to actually think about it, it felt obvious: the way Emily had been the one to pull Mason into their friend group to begin with, the way she'd sat him at their table at her sweet sixteen and been so angry when he and Meg snuck off together. Meg wondered if she really hadn't registered those signs, or if she just hadn't wanted to. It was weird and kind of crummy to realize she'd been thinking of herself as totally in the right this whole time when possibly there was a whole other perspective she'd never stopped to consider. "I'm sorry," she said, looking across the table. "I didn't realize."

"I'm not saying you stole him or anything like that," Emily said, sitting back in her wobbly coffee shop chair. "I never actually came out and told you I liked him. And, like, I know nobody can steal a boy who doesn't want to be stolen. I'm not Taylor Swift from ten years ago."

Meg snorted. "I had literally that exact same thought about you," she admitted. "The Taylor Swift thing."

"Yeah, well." Emily smiled, just a little. "Brain twins, et cetera." For a long time, she didn't say anything, running her thumbnail back and forth along the edge of her plastic cup. Then she looked up. "I'm sorry," she said. "I know it was messed up, how we handled it. And even if we handled it perfectly, it probably still would have been messed up, and we can talk about it, or not talk about it if you don't want, but—"

"It's okay," Meg said. "I mean, it's not really, but it's not like I want you guys to break up, or I want him back or anything like that." She shrugged, thinking again of Colby and wishing she weren't.

"I'm sorry I was a bitch about Colby," Emily said, as if she were reading Meg's mind. "And I'm sorry I made you feel like you couldn't tell me the truth about things. I think maybe when everything was happening with your mom and dad, I got kind of used to being, like, the boss? I felt like I was doing the right thing—like that was what you needed from me. But I can see how eventually that would translate into just being overbearing and, like, hard to talk to."

"I *did* need a boss for a while," Meg admitted, remembering how effortlessly Emily had cruise-directed their lives back then, casually reminding her about student council meetings and curating their plans for the weekend and deflecting friends who asked too many nosy questions. She thought of how Mason had been back then, too—how he'd kept their routine going, but carefully. How he'd never pushed. He'd been trying his best, even if it hadn't ultimately been enough for either one of them. It occurred to her that possibly she owed him an actual conversation about that. "I get what you were doing, and I really appreciate it. But now . . ."

"Yeah," Emily said, nodding. "I get it, too. And I know it probably felt like I was putting all this pressure on you about Cornell. But I never wanted you to feel like you had to hide who you were or what was going on with you or how you felt about something just to keep being best friends with me." She stopped, and all at once Meg realized she was on the verge of tears. "And I really want to keep being your best friend."

Meg nodded, her own throat closing up a little. "I want that, too."

"That totally sucks about your mom," Emily continued—wiping her face with the back of her hand, businesslike. Meg hadn't seen her cry in years. "And I feel like crap that you thought I would give you a hard time about it or think less of you or something, because it must have been really miserable to have to handle it by yourself. God, Meg, I am so, so sorry."

"I wasn't totally by myself," Meg promised, thinking of Lillian in her baseball cap and Maja's lemon bars—thinking of Colby, even if he wasn't around anymore. "But I missed you."

"I'm here now, if you want to talk about it," Emily said, wrapping her fingers around her coffee cup. "I mean, I get if you still don't feel comfortable, or—" She broke off, waving her hand vaguely. "But I'm here."

Meg smiled at her across the table with relief and exhaustion and gratitude. "I'm here, too," she said.

"Why did you break up with me?" Meg asked, standing unannounced on Mason's front porch later that afternoon.

Mason blanched. He was barefoot in a pair of khaki shorts, a can of LaCroix in one hand and his glossy dark hair sticking up all over his head. "Meg—"

"Like, was it honestly just that you wanted to date Em instead?" she asked. "You can say if it was. I'm not here to give you a hard time about it. I'm just curious."

Mason looked totally gobsmacked, and Meg guessed she couldn't blame him—after all, it wasn't like she'd ever confronted him about anything before. "Sorry," she said, suddenly self-conscious. "I'm not trying to make a scene."

Mason smiled then, just faintly. "A scene in front of who?" he asked, gesturing out the front door at the empty cul-de-sac.

"Oh." Meg's cheeks colored. "Good point."

He came out onto the porch and shut the front door behind him, sitting down on the top step; after a moment Meg sat down beside him, the warm afternoon sunlight prickling her bare legs. Back when they first started dating they used to sit out here at night and wait for her dad to come pick her up.

"It wasn't because of Emily," he said finally. "I get why it seems like that, and I get it if you don't believe me. But it wasn't."

"Okay," Meg said slowly. "Then what?"

Mason shrugged. "You just kind of became a different person while we were together. Does that make sense?" he asked. "Like, when we first started hanging out, you were never afraid to say what you wanted, or what you thought about something, even if it meant making other people a little uncomfortable."

Meg blinked. "I wasn't?"

"Meg." Mason smiled. "You tried to fight me over Elon Musk sending his car to space the first time we went out."

"Oh." Meg frowned. She'd forgotten about that. "Well, Elon Musk is the actual worst."

"So you told me!" Mason laughed. "But then, when everything started happening with your mom and dad, it was like you just . . . went away, sort of."

Meg huffed, stung by the unfairness of it. "I mean, my parents were getting a divorce, Mason!"

"No, I know that," he amended quickly. "Come on, of course I know that. I *knew* that, which is why I never wanted to give you a hard time about it. But even once all the dust settled, it just kind of felt like you never really came back."

"Came back how?" she asked, although truthfully it wasn't

like she didn't already sort of know what he was getting at. Still, she wanted to hear it from him.

Mason shrugged. "You started agreeing with everything I said all the time, for one thing," he said, pulling some crabgrass out from between the flagstones. "Like about big stuff, but also just stupid shit like what we should do on the weekend or what movie you wanted to see. Like, I couldn't tell if you really didn't have an opinion all of a sudden or if maybe you just didn't care enough to argue." He twisted a blade of grass between two long fingers. "One of the things I liked about you to begin with was how much you cared about things, you know? How willing you were to fight about them. And after the divorce, it was like you just stopped."

Meg bristled, even as she knew Mason probably had a point: After all, hadn't she told basically the same story to Colby the night of her dad's rehearsal dinner? She'd never wanted to be a part of anything like the scene at the potluck ever again, and she'd done everything she could not to be. Still, it had never occurred to her that maybe her big opinions were one of the things that had attracted Mason to her to begin with. It hadn't occurred to her that maybe the two of them never arguing wasn't a thing Mason wanted, too.

"And, like, obviously, you eventually started caring about some stuff again," he said, drawing his knees up and resting his tawny forearms there, "like getting the solar panels on top of Overbrook and stuff like that. But it just seemed like you didn't really care about . . . me, I guess? Like, even when we broke up, it was like you didn't even give a crap."

"I gave a crap!" Meg protested, thinking back to how carefully she'd swallowed down her anger and her hurt that night in the parking lot outside Cavelli's, how she'd waited until his car was out of sight to let herself cry. She'd wanted to be agreeable, and it had come out like apathy: the thing she hated most of all. "You could have talked to me about it."

"I tried," he said with a shrug. "Like, even when we were broken up, I kept trying. But you always said everything was okay. Once I even tried picking an argument with you on purpose, just to see what would happen."

"At the party at Adrienne's?" she asked, and Mason nodded. "God, I thought you were being such a dick that night."

"So you did notice!"

"Of course I noticed," Meg said, laughing in spite of herself. "I just didn't want to—cause a problem, I guess. I'm sorry."

"It's not all your fault," Mason said. "I mean, I'm sorry I was an asshole who picked a fight just to see what would happen. And I'm sorry I wasn't the kind of person you could feel safe causing a problem in front of."

They were quiet for a moment, looking out at the cul-de-sac. An old man shuffled along the sidewalk alongside a scrappy little terrier; two little kids ran through the sprinkler across the street. "That dude Colby," Mason said finally, glancing at her sidelong. "Can you cause problems in front of each other?"

Meg snorted; she couldn't help it. "That's about the only thing we could do, actually." Still, she thought, it wasn't that simple. Her parents' arguments had turned them into the worst versions of themselves, mean and vindictive. But she kind of thought the arguments she and Colby had made them better. She hadn't known arguments could do that until she met him—or she had, maybe, but she'd forgotten, same as she'd forgotten how to be herself.

"Past tense, huh?" Mason asked. "So it's done?"

"Yeah," Meg said, clearing her throat a little; she kept waiting for it to hurt less, although so far it kind of didn't. "It's done."

"That's too bad," Mason said. "I mean, don't get me wrong, he seemed like kind of a douche at your dad's wedding. But from what Emily said, you really liked him."

"Yeah," Meg said again, tilting her head back. "I really did."

THIRTY-FIVE

Colby

The following morning, Colby got up early and drove to a neat-looking craftsman near the high school, with a wide front porch with a swing at one end of it and a row of tomato plants along the fence at the side. He climbed out of the car and rang the bell, then wiped his sweaty hands on his thighs and told himself to stop being such a loser. God, this whole thing was fucking dumb.

A guy he didn't recognize answered the door—pleasant-looking, with round glasses and a short-sleeved plaid shirt buttoned over a paunchy belly. A terrier danced manically around his feet. "Hi there," he said, looking at Colby curiously. "Can I help you?"

"Um," Colby said, his voice cracking. He cleared his throat. "Is Doug here?"

The guy nodded. "Sure thing," he said, then turned and called down the wide, paneled hallway. "Hey, love? There's a kid here to see you."

Doug appeared at the front door a moment later, wiping his hands on a dish towel. "Colby," he said, a brief twitch of his eyebrows the only outward sign he was surprised at the sight of Colby in a collar on his doorstep. "Good to see you."

"I messed up," Colby blurted, not bothering to say hello or show any manners whatsoever. His mother would have been ashamed. "By not calling you back in time. I think I was scared that the job would turn out to be a letdown, or, like, that *I* would be a letdown to *you* and you'd decide you were wrong to offer it to me, or just that, like, the rug would get pulled out somehow, you know? But, like—whatever, none of that is your problem. That's my problem, and I'm trying to fix it, but—" He broke off, realizing abruptly that he was rambling. He'd never admitted this stuff out loud before. He hadn't even really known he was *thinking* it. "Sorry." He cleared his throat. "I really want this job, is my point. And if I made you think I didn't, or that I didn't care one way or the other, then that was a fu—a mess-up on my part. So if you can give me another chance, I think you might figure out that I can add value to what you're doing here."

Doug looked at him for a long time, not saying anything. Then he bent down and picked up the dog. "Why don't you come in?" he said.

Colby nodded and followed them into the kitchen, eyes darting as he tried to take in all the details of the house without looking like he was casing it for a robbery. It was the closest thing he'd ever seen to what he'd imagined in his head when he thought about building something in Paradise: Built-in shelves with photos and books on them. A stained-glass window at the foot of the stairs. A kitchen with butcher-block counters and a breakfast nook with benches on either side, sun streaming in through a skylight above the island. Colby sat at the table and took the cup of coffee Doug put in front of him, waiting silently while he got half a crumb cake out of the fridge.

"Your dad used to talk about you all the time, you know that?" Doug asked, putting a slab of cake on a plate and sliding it in Colby's direction.

Colby shook his head, surprised. "No, sir," he said. It was funny to think of his dad out in the world talking about him. It was funny to think of his dad out in the world doing anything, really. At some point, Colby's memories of him had started to narrow to the very end part, but of course he'd been more than that: he'd been the star of an old-guy bowling team and an excellent remover of splinters and the person throwing Colby in the air as a kid in the picture that hung in the hallway back at home—over and over, up and up. "I didn't know that."

Doug nodded. "You and your brother," he said. "All the time." He took a sip of his coffee. "He left you the Paradise property, didn't he? What are you going to do with it?"

Colby frowned, caught off guard by the question. "I mean, nothing right now," he replied, picking the crumbs off the top of his cake. "I don't have any money."

"But when you do?"

He opened his mouth to say he hadn't thought about it, just like he'd told everyone else who'd asked since the day they'd read the will—just like he'd tried to tell Meg—but for some reason, all of a sudden, it felt like a cowardly thing to lie. "I want something like this," he confessed, looking around the kitchen. The dog had gotten bored and passed out on the rug in front of the sink. "Like what you've built here, I mean. I don't know how I'm gonna get it, or if I ever will, even. But, uh . . . That's what I want."

Doug nodded at that, taking a sip of his coffee. "Look," he said finally, "I've got another project starting in a couple of weeks, an addition on a place over in Castleton. We can try it, see how it goes."

"Really?" Colby asked, immediately cursing himself for sounding so fucking eager. Then again, maybe there were worse things than sounding eager every once in a while. "Um, I appreciate that," he said, unable to keep himself from grinning. "Thanks a lot."

Doug nodded. "I'll call you with more details when I've

got them," he said. "And pick up the damn phone this time, all right?"

"I will," Colby promised. "I will be sure to do that."

He finished his cake and waved goodbye before heading out across the driveway. The sun was warm on the back of his neck.

Later, he brought Joanna an iced coffee from Bixby's and they sat on the curb outside the hair salon, her feet in her flats narrow and officious-looking against the blacktop. It was a warm, steamy afternoon, the smell of trees and car exhaust thick and heavy in the air. "I owe you an apology," Colby said.

"Uh-oh." Joanna's lips twisted knowingly. "What'd you do?"

"I think it's, like, more what I didn't do?" Colby frowned, scrubbing a hand through his hair. It had felt important on the way over here to own up to what he'd done with Joanna, but now that they were face-to-face he didn't know exactly what to say. "I'm sorry. I'm not trying to be vague."

"Oh no?" Jo leaned over and nudged him with her shoulder, the vanilla-cupcake smell of her hitting his nose. "Don't worry about it, Colby. It's fine."

Colby blinked. "It is?"

"Sure," she said with a shrug, running a freshly painted thumbnail along the plastic lip of her cup. "We're friends, right? We've always been friends. And if the timing isn't good for you, or whatever . . . I don't know." She smiled. "Life is long."

"No, I know, but . . ." Colby broke off. He had the distinct impression he was getting off entirely too easily here. Shouldn't she be pissed at him? After all, he'd objectively been kind of a dick about the whole thing. "I just mean—"

"I'm a big girl, Colby." Jo smiled. "I knew what I was getting into with you. Like I said, we're good."

"I . . ." Colby searched her face for a moment, hunting for traces of insincerity and finding none. She meant it, he realized slowly. She was serious. She didn't think there was anything wrong with how he'd acted—or, if she did, she was willing to let him get away with it. She didn't expect anything else. It used to be he'd liked that about her—her willingness to meet him where he was at any given moment. Now, though, he wasn't so sure he did. "I'm sorry anyway," he said firmly. "I should have done a better job with you."

"Maybe one day you will," Jo said lightly, getting to her feet and brushing the seat of her skirt off. "In the meantime, Colby, you take care of yourself."

Colby lifted his hand to say goodbye to her, sitting on the curb as her figure receded and waiting for the inevitable pang of regret. He was surprised to find it never came—and that instead he found himself thinking of Meg's voice on the phone late at night, the way she drove him nuts and made him laugh and talked about the world like it was some old jewelry box she'd found at a curiosity shop, full of treasures just waiting for someone to blow the layer of dust off. He thought of what he'd said to Doug this morning: *I was scared that the job would turn out to be a letdown, or, like, that* I *would be a letdown . . . or just that, like, the rug would get pulled out.*

He dug his phone out of his pocket and gazed down at it for a moment. It felt heavy as a stone in his hand.

THIRTY-SIX

Meg

Meg borrowed a dress of her mom's for graduation, a silky pale peach situation with a cinched waist that she remembered from when Hal used to play gigs at fancy historic theaters. "You look beautiful," her mom said when she came down into the living room. "Actually, I take that back; you look *fierce*. Honestly, sweetheart, I am so, so proud of you."

"I'm proud of you, too," Meg said, and it was true. Her mom had gone from the hospital into a ten-day inpatient program in south Jersey; since she'd gotten back she'd been going to meetings every evening in the community room of a synagogue not far from their house. Two days ago, Meg had come home from school to find her standing at the kitchen island with a tube of cookie dough and a spoon. "It's my turn to bring snacks," she'd explained, looking a little sheepish.

"You want help?" Meg had asked, setting her backpack in the breakfast nook. She couldn't remember her mom baking anything since she was a little kid.

Her mom had nodded. "I should have just bought something," she'd said, digging an ancient cookie sheet out of a cupboard. "But I want them to like me. Is that pathetic?"

"I think it's human," Meg had said, and her mom had smiled in a way that made her look like a teenager, flicking the kitchen television to HGTV. In the end they'd eaten most of the cookie dough before they got it into the oven and had to run out to the store for another tube.

"Dad and Lisa are going to meet us at school so I can give them their tickets," Meg said now, tucking the envelope into the outside pocket of her tote bag. "You guys don't have to sit together, obviously, I just—" She broke off.

"It's fine," her mom said, squinting at the antique mirror hanging in the foyer and slicking on a coat of plummy lipstick. She looked different since she'd stopped drinking, Meg thought, even though it hadn't been that long yet: her eyes were clear, and her face was less swollen. She'd started shuffling around the block in her walking cast every morning before she went to work, listening to the true-crime podcasts Meg had shown her how to download onto her phone. "I'll behave, I promise."

Meg grimaced. "No, I know you'll *behave*. I'm not saying—"

"Meggie, sweetheart," her mom said, turning away from the

mirror before laying two gentle hands on Meg's shoulders and squeezing. "I'm teasing. Today is about you, okay? You've done so much—at school, yeah, but also around here. Try to enjoy it."

Meg nodded. She'd stayed at her dad and Lisa's while her mom was away, helping Lisa cook plant-based dinners from some mail-order meal kit and running errands with her dad on the weekend. It had reminded Meg of when she was a little kid, kind of—the two of them going to the hardware store and the dry cleaners and the nursery, stopping for a dozen doughnuts on the way back. After school during the week, though, she'd driven home to her mom's house and gotten to work: scooping her hair up into a messy knot and blasting Fleetwood Mac as loud as the sound system would go while she vacuumed the bedrooms and dusted the baseboards and scrubbed the inside of the refrigerator, opening all the windows to get the air moving around. She'd watched a YouTube video and figured out how to hang the art in the hallway; then, encouraged by her success, she'd gone ahead and painted the living room a fresh, clean white. She'd gone to the Philly farmers' market with Lillian and Maja. She'd taken Lisa's kids to an arcade.

She hadn't talked to Colby at all.

She missed his laugh and his bitten cuticles and his dry sense of humor; she missed him more than she'd ever missed anyone before. And the worst part was how she'd been kind of right that night in the hotel room; he *did* lift neatly out of her life, as far as everyone else in it was concerned. Like maybe he'd been her imaginary friend. She'd thought about texting, about getting in her car and driving all the way to Ohio, but in the end she knew it wasn't going to accomplish anything. It had been fun for a while, but now it was over.

It was never going to work.

Meg swallowed hard and straightened up, turning and slinging her purse over her shoulder. "Come on," she said, slipping her hand into her mom's and squeezing. When she'd gotten back from the rehab place, they'd cleaned out all the closets and cabinets one by one. Meg knew they had a long way to go—when she'd driven to New Jersey for the family therapy session, her mom's counselor had explained about the probability of relapse and maybe even more inpatient rehab, that addiction was a lifelong disease that could be managed but never cured. Still, in this house in this dress on this warm, sunny morning, it felt like they were making a start. "Let's go."

Two nights later, her coworkers threw her a little graduation party in the tiny conference room at WeCount, with paper cups of Trader Joe's lemonade and a fistful of Mylar balloons Lillian had picked up from Party City. Maja had made lavender sopapillas. Rico played the sunscreen song on his phone.

"To the newest member of the Annie Hernandez campaign," he said, offering a lemonade toast. "They're not going to know what hit 'em."

Meg grinned. It had been easier than she'd thought, telling her parents she was taking a year off from school to see what happened, that she'd rethink what she actually wanted and apply again. Meanwhile, in the days since she'd gotten the call about the internship, she'd found a roommate through the campaign and lined up interviews for some waitressing gigs to supplement her piddly stipend. She'd leave for Columbus at the end of the month. She didn't think she'd ever been this terrified—and for the first time since she could remember, she was kind of thrilled by the idea of what came next.

After the party, they all drifted over to their stations, Meg pulling up her call log on the computer—the software was working for once—and brushing some pastry crumbs off the front of her shirt. She'd just hung up with a single dad in Cincinnati when Lillian's round face appeared over the partition. "Hey, Meg?" she said. "There's a call for you."

Meg frowned. "*For* me?" she repeated, her heart doing something strange and complicated deep inside her chest. WeCount's number wasn't listed on their website. There was only one person she could ever imagine calling her here.

Lillian nodded. "I'll transfer it over."

Meg tugged at her bottom lip for a moment, reminding herself not to get her hopes up. It was true that in the weeks since her dad's wedding there had been a million things she'd wanted to tell him—about Emily and her mom and her internship, about all the ways knowing him had made her brave—but no matter how many times she came close to calling, she hadn't been able to make herself reach out. Probably she had been right: they *were* just too different.

But maybe that didn't mean what they had wasn't worth fighting for.

Now she took a deep breath and lifted the receiver. Imagined her own heartbeat echoing out across the line. "Hello?" she said, trying to keep her voice even. "This is Meg."

"This is Colby," he said, and she smiled.

THIRTY-SEVEN

Colby

The truck stop was right on the side of the highway, the neon sign glowing like Christmas in the blue-purple twilight; it came up so fast and sudden that even after waiting for it for four hours Colby nearly missed the turn. He pulled into the giant lot and shut the car off, sitting motionless in the driver's seat for a long, quiet minute. He shoved a piece of gum into his mouth, then decided he didn't want to be chewing gum when he saw her and spit it into a receipt he found on the floor of the passenger seat. Finally, he took a deep breath, wiped his sweaty palms—why were his palms sweaty? Fuck—on his jeans, and went inside.

She was already sitting in a booth in the brightly lit diner, her own hands folded primly in front of her like she was waiting for a job interview. Holy shit, Colby loved her so much. As soon as he had the thought, he knew it was true, and that there was nothing to be done about it. Her gaze, when she glanced up and saw him, was dark and steady and clear.

"Hi," Colby said, sliding into the seat across from her.

Meg smiled, a little uncertain. "Hi."

For a moment, neither one of them said anything, the silence stretching out like every mile they'd both traveled. It was even more awkward than it had been the first time they met. Colby thought again that they were probably too different; he thought of all the million reasons why this would never, ever work.

Still: she'd shown up here, in this place right in between them.

He had shown up here, too.

And maybe that was all either of them—maybe that was all *anybody*—could ask.

Colby took a deep breath then and looked across the table. He felt like his heart was sitting there on the Formica, bloody and raw. "So, um," he said, and his voice was an apology and a declaration and a gamble, "I was wondering if you could tell me again why I should register to vote."

For a moment, Meg only stared at him, wonder and disbelief playing across her expression. Colby was sure he'd blown it, that he'd come with too little too late.

Then, almost imperceptibly, she nodded.

"Sure," she said, and Colby heard her smile before he saw it. "I can probably help you with that."

ACKNOWLEDGMENTS

All I have ever wanted is to be able to write the next book and, as always, I owe an enormous debt of gratitude to the incredible team that keeps on making it happen: Josh Bank, Joelle Hobeika, Sara Shandler, and everyone at Alloy, for their big ideas and good humor and endless enthusiasm. My keen-eyed editor, Alessandra Balzer, for steering the ship, and everyone at HarperCollins, but especially Sabrina Abballe, Sam Benson, Donna Bray, Kathy Faber, Caitlin Garing, Caitlin Johnson, Nellie Kurtzman, Caitlin Lonning, Kerry Moynagh, and Andrea Pappenheimer. Thank you, Ana Hard and Jessie Gang, for putting together the most gorgeous cover I have ever seen in all my days on this earth. Dahlia Adler, Robin Benway, Brandy Colbert, Christa Desir, Corey Ann Haydu, Emery

Lord, Jennifer Matthieu, Julie Murphy, Elissa Sussman, and Sara Zarr, for long talks and quick questions and troubleshooting and general brilliance. All the booksellers and teachers and librarians and bloggers and Bookstagrammers who have been so good to me all this time, for your attention and kindness and all the often-uncompensated work you do behind the scenes. Lisa Burton O'Toole, Rachel Hutchinson, Jennie Palluzzi, Sierra Rooney, and Marissa Velie, for first reads and cheerleading and being my very faves. Jackie Cotugno for literally everything, always, but especially this year. Tom Colleran for being my home for almost two decades. Annie Colleran, I'll be yours for the rest of my life.

Also, not for nothing: hey, go vote! xo